Where Legends Lie

Where Legends Lie

Michael A. Black

Published by:
Genius Book Publishing
PO Box 250380
Milwaukee Wisconsin 53225 USA
GeniusBookPublishing.com

ISBN: 978-1-958727-32-4

240624 LH Digest

For all those of us who didn't make it back home

Acknowledgments

The author wishes to thank the following individuals, without whom this book would not have been possible.

Dave Case

Diane Piron-Gelman

Tiffany Schofield

"The world is grown so bad,

That wrens make prey where eagles dare not perch."

—William Shakespeare, *Richard III,* Act I, Scene 3

Prologue

Jolo, Sulu Archipelago
The Philippines
The Battle of Bud Bagsak
July 15, 1913

Day Four

It was like being wide awake and being caught in the middle of a nightmare.

How many hours had it been?

He wished he knew. It was as if time itself had stopped.

The sweat poured out of Jim Bishop so copiously that it felt like a steady stream of water being poured over his face. His eyes burned and he had to keep blinking to try and clear his vision, but it was no use. The cloying moisture clung to his eyelids. His lips tasted the constant saltiness. It was their third trip up the mountain that day, and once again, their advance stalled as the crater came alive once more. One moment it was all green bushes, thick shrubbery, and clusters of trees and temporal placidity, and the next instant it gave way to a surging wave of brown men dressed in red loincloths and accompanying red headbands, their veins bulging out in bas-relief along limbs bound tight by constricting ligatures and vines. The Moros, or the *pulajans* as the Filipino Scouts called them, seemed to rise up from behind every bush, every tree, virtually from the dark earth itself. The surge of humanity descended from the lip of the crater, brandishing their razor-sharp *talibongs*. The rhythmic chant, "*Tac-tac, tac-tac, tac-tac,*" sounded in unison like an advancing drumbeat.

Tac-tac, tac-tac, tac-tac—Tagalog for Cut-cut, cut-cut, cut-cut.

And that's what they did.

Jim stopped and raised the muzzle of his Winchester 1897 shotgun, racking the slide back and then forward to chamber a round.

The man next to him, a young lieutenant who'd just arrived in the country two weeks ago, turned and darted to his right toward the cover of a cluster of trees perhaps ten yards away. From the corner of his eye Jim saw the young officer's foot snare the elongated vine trigger.

"Sir," Jim yelled, taking his eye off the enemy for a split second. "Don't move!"

But his warning was a millisecond too late.

The vine trigger snapped and released a twisted branch in a horizontal arc, sending a row of sharpened spikes into the lieutenant's body with a sickening thump.

The officer cried out, but the sound was reduced to a pathetic gurgle as he went limp, bouncing off the branch and flopping down onto his back. A trio of gaping holes, already filling with blood, was stitched across the front of his brown uniform shirt. His legs convulsed, like he was still on his feet, still trying to move away, but with each movement more blood and slithering intestines seeped out of his wounds.

Jim ran to the man, but could tell he was dying.

He wanted to offer some comfort, some assurance that it would be all right, but he couldn't bring himself to lie. A few seconds later, he saw that it didn't matter anyway. Vacuous eyes, still wide open from the shock, stared directly upward, unflinching under the unbearably bright sun as it shone down.

Dead, Jim thought.

There was no time for sentiment or mendacious words

The ominous mantra continued unabated: "Tac-tac, tac-tac, tac-tac . . ."

The Moros were almost upon them. The sons of bitches were savages, fighting with bows and arrows and spears and traps. They had some guns, but not a lot, and those huge talibong knifes could chop you apart with one solid swing. They gave no quarter, nor did they expect any. Worst yet, they kept the families with them like human shields—old men, women, children. It was sickening.

Shots rang out to Jim's left.

From his kneeling position by the dead lieutenant, he raised the shotgun, aimed at the nearest advancing *pulajan*, and pulled the trigger. The double-aught buck load ripped into the Moro's side, tearing a large swath of skin and a hunk of meat away. The Moro stumbled for two steps as his mouth twisted into a scowl, the talibong still raised above his head.

Damn, these Moros are tough, Jim thought as he worked the slide and chambered another round. The oblong blade caught a glint of sunlight for a moment before descending in an oblique arc.

The shotgun discharged again and this time the pulagam went down, enveloped in a crimson mist.

Jim felt the flecks of blood and body tissue dapple his face as the world suddenly went silent for several seconds.

Another one came at him.

A shotgun boomed off to his left.

Larry Rush was next to Jim now, the trail of smoke trickling upward from his shotgun muzzle as the advancing Moro's head exploded like a muskmelon struck by an axe handle. The man did an awkward, headless pirouette as he went down. Rush chambered another round and moved next to Jim.

"The lieutenant dead?" Rush asked. He was shouting, but his voice still sounded far away.

Far away . . .

If only they could all be far away.

Jim grunted a response as he sighted in on another rushing Moro and fired.

Three more advanced from the left. Rush swiveled and blasted one, but the second one did a stutter-step, leaned back, and hurled a long bamboo spear. It sailed toward them. The next instant Rush dropped his weapon and grabbed his thigh as the pointed tip of the spear tore through the inner part of his pant leg. He toppled over, his eyes rolling back into his head.

Jim turned and fired. The rounds took down the assailant, but two more were closing in on them. He fired once more. One of the oncoming Moros took the hit in the side, but kept advancing, taking three slack steps before collapsing. Jim racked the slide back and then forward, chambering what he knew was his last remaining round, and fired again. The blast hit the closest man. He jerked forward, then curled into a fetal position as he fell to the ground.

No more ammo, Jim thought, gripping the Winchester's hot barrel and stock. Despite the overheated metal searing his skin, he managed to bring the rifle up just in time to block the descent of another Moro's two-foot-long talibong. The solid blade chunked into the wooden slide, splintering it. Jim twisted the rifle free and simultaneously rammed the base of the stock into the Filipino's face. The man's jaw jerked out of alignment and he paused just long enough for Jim to kick him in the groin as hard as he could. The Moro grimaced but drew back the large knife, ready to take another deadly swing.

A split-second burst of fire and smoke whipped between them, and the Moro's head snapped to the side as a shot rang out. Rush had managed to pull out his long-barreled Colt .45 revolver and fire it. Jim dropped the Winchester and drew his own revolver. Cocking back the hammer, he fired at the next group of advancing Moros. A burst of red blossomed on one man's upper torso, just under his clavicle, but that didn't stop him. A diagonal constricting loop of twine bisected the man's chest, limiting the bleeding and enabling him to keep moving. Jim adjusted his aim, lining up the rear, M-shaped sight on the revolver with the single bar of the tip of the barrel.

"Keep them damn sights flat across the top," his drill sergeant had yelled at him in basic training.

He squeezed the trigger. His next round pierced his adversary's right eye.

He fired four more times with undetermined results. The short, sweaty bodies kept coming, like a brown tidal wave capped with red. Jim turned to reach for Rush's gun but saw his was empty, too.

The lieutenant, Jim thought. He sidestepped to the right and knelt beside the fallen officer. His fingers scrambled to undo the dead man's flap holster before feeling a textured grip. He pulled the weapon out and saw it was one of those new 1911 semiautomatic pistols, something only a few of the officers had. They were supposedly sitting in crates in New York Harbor or someplace, their distribution to the troops in the Philippines delayed by yet another layer of bureaucratic inefficiency. It was rumored that a few, a very few, of the officers had managed to sneak a special shipment in, and that was apparently true. The magazine purportedly held seven rounds, but Jim had never fired one.

No time like the present to learn, he thought as he brought the pistol up, aimed, and squeezed the trigger.

Nothing.

In desperation he cocked back the hammer and tried again.

The next trio of Moros was almost on top of them.

The hammer clacked down and still the weapon didn't fire.

Was it a dud?

No, he thought. *It's just like a shotgun. There's no round in the chamber.*

Gripping the row of vertical lines on the rear of the slide, he racked it back, felt it catch, and then whip forward.

The Moro was raising his talibong over Rush's supine body when this time the Colt's round pierced the area just under the pulagam's left armpit. The Moro fell like a marionette whose strings had been abruptly severed. Jim adjusted his aim and fired two more rounds, putting one into each of the advancing would-be killers. He dropped to one knee and frantically searched the dead lieutenant's pouch for more magazines.

Suddenly the sound of distant thunder rumbled accompanied by a screaming sound. Another set of rumbles along with more whistles and a burst of explosions echoed further up the ridge, by the mouth of the crater.

Artillery, Jim thought. *Blackjack's got the 40th zeroed in on them.*

He felt a surge of hope as the area along the lip of the crater, where he knew the last Moro stronghold was, erupted in more roiling clouds of dust.

The Moro advance suddenly halted, their heads rotating back toward the spiraling dust clouds farther up the hill, their eyes widening in horror.

Jim knew their families, the women, the children, the elderly, were all up there in this last cotta. They had nowhere left to run. Orders were to wipe them all out.

A company of Filipino Scouts, their brown uniforms drenched with sweat, streamed forward from the right flank and the left, their rifles barking fire, their bayonets fixed. They'd taken the brunt of the Moros' attacks before and now they'd regrouped. From the look on their faces, no quarter would be given.

Nor none expected.

Thank God, he thought. *Maybe this nightmare is going to be over with now.*

☙

Historical Note

The final siege then started at seventeen-hundred-oh-five hours. Three hours later it was over.

Or was it?

Chapter 1

Three months later . . .

Southern Pacific Railroad Line
Somewhere in southern California

The Moro was rushing him once more, the talibong raised high over his head. Jim Bishop raised his pistol, a Colt .45 U.S. Army issue revolver, and squeezed the trigger. It was locked in place, refusing to move. He gripped the weapon with both hands and pulled. The trigger remained frozen as the Moro warrior's lips twisted from a fierce grimace to a malicious grin. The shiny metal flashed as the oblong blade eclipsed the sun, a sudden gleam darting from the pointed tip.

Jim knew what was coming next and tried to anneal himself against the inevitable penetration of the Moro's sweeping arc.

"No," he muttered. "No."

He snapped awake just before the talibong knife struck. The book he'd been reading dropped from his fingers and struck his lap, his breath coming in rapid gasps, his face and neck glistening with sweat.

Larry Rush's elbow nudged his side again.

"Jim, you all right?"

"Yeah." Jim raised his hand to his nose and pinched the bridge. "What time is it?"

Larry shrugged. "How should I know? I ain't got no watch."

Jim didn't either. He took in a deep breath and wiped some of the sweat off his forehead, but it did little good. His chest and armpits felt wet. They'd been on the southbound train since they left San Francisco the previous morning. How many hours had it been? It seemed like an eternity, like that long ship ride back. The hours, the days, melded into a blur. He looked around. The Pullman was about half full: half a dozen or so men, some with families, and an assortment of women and children. Jim turned his head to see if anyone was staring at him. A few of them were, especially the kids. He struggled to regulate his breathing. Two young boys whispered and pointed. One of them giggled.

"The dream again? The *pulajans*?" Larry said.

Jim nodded and swallowed hard. He reached down toward the rucksack on the floor between his feet and felt for the smooth hardness. It was there. Feeling better, he stood up with the fallen book in hand. "I'm gonna get some air."

"Here." Larry pulled his stiff left leg into the space between them and grabbed his cane. "Want to sit next to the window?"

"No, just some air."

Jim gripped the back of the seat in front of him and took in two deep breaths. The world came back into focus with its customary lucidity. He stepped into the central aisle and laid his book on his seat. "Don't let nobody steal that. I'm still reading it."

"You mean you *been* reading it." Larry grinned. "Since all the way back on the ship."

Jim didn't reply. As he turned, he noticed a distinguished-looking older gent eyeing him through a wispy cloud of smoke from his pipe. It made Jim hanker for a cigarette, but he had no tobacco.

"You got the makings?" he asked Larry, who patted his pockets and then shook his head.

Jim moved down the aisle toward the coach doors and pulled them open. As he stepped out onto the metal platform, he felt the rush of air cooling the perspiration on his face and neck. He took in a few more deep breaths.

The dreams never stopped, even though it had been three months and so much had happened: the massive burial detail, the long march back to the coast, word that he was being mustered out, visiting with Larry on the long sea voyage back to the States, being awarded the medals, his discharge, and now the prospect of being a civilian again and getting on with his life.

But to do what?

Through it all the only constant was the ghosts that visited him every night in his dreams. His constant companions . . .

Would they ever leave?

The question hung in his mind. Seeking distraction from it, he remembered Larry's proposal of a job.

"My sister and her husband are cooking for this motion picture studio place in California," Larry had said. "Told me they're hiring a bunch of workers, even somebody with a stiff leg like I got."

The tip of the Moro spear sticking out of Larry's pant leg flashed in his memory.

The door opened behind him and the older gentleman stepped out onto the platform. Jim caught a trace of the scent from the pipe and it made him hunger even more for a smoke. The old man arched an eyebrow and smiled as he reached inside his coat. He wore a fine-looking tweed suit, dusty gray, and had on a hat that matched. The perfect knot of a black string tie adorned his white collar and shirt. His face was tanned and adorned with deep creases fanning out from the corners of his eyes and bracketing his mouth. The bushy, mostly gray hair that was visible from under the hat appeared to have once been dark brown or black. His well-trimmed mustache was flecked with gray as well. The man nodded to Jim and pressed a calloused index finger into the bowl of his pipe, extinguishing it. After slipping the pipe into his inside breast pocket, he smiled as he withdrew a small cloth bag and several folds of rolling papers.

"Thought you could use these," he said, extending his hand with the makings toward Jim.

They stood frozen for a moment before Jim, stunned by the offer, accepted the items and thanked him. Despite the swaying of the railroad car and the metallic clippety-clopping of the wheels over the iron tracks, Jim managed to pour some tobacco onto one of the papers, rolled it, and then licked it closed.

"Much obliged," he said.

The old man produced a wooden match and flicked the primer with the thick nail of his thumb. He cupped his other hand around the match, shielding it from the wind, and held it toward Jim's cigarette. Jim leaned forward until the tip was engulfed in the flame and drew in the smoke. It burned his throat and he coughed slightly. Smoking wasn't something he enjoyed anymore and he wondered why he still craved it so.

Taking in the breath of hell, his mother used to say.

He took another pull on the cigarette, but this time just kept the smoke in his mouth instead of drawing it in deeper. The hot taste wasn't pleasant and he wondered if it was him or the tobacco. It tasted bitter.

"It's a Turkish blend," the old man said. "Got it in San Francisco."

"It's strong, that's for sure."

"Tobacco is the red man's ultimate revenge for us stealing his land."

"I thought you said it was Turkish?"

The old man's smile broadened. "That is correct. Touché."

He laughed, and Jim did too.

"Or perhaps," the old man said, "a little nip of this would be more to your liking?"

He waggled a silver flask that he'd removed from his inside breast pocket. As the lapel of his jacket slipped back into place, Jim glimpsed the butt of a revolver in a shoulder holster.

The old man held out the flask, but Jim made no move to take it.

"Oh, by the way." The old man pulled a gold watch from his vest pocket and flipped open the ornate lid. "It is now half past two."

Jim eyed the watch. It was a fine-looking mechanism. Expensive, no doubt. His grandfather had one like it.

The man waggled the flask again. "It's the finest bourbon west of New Orleans."

"Don't mind if I do," Jim said, accepting the flask. He carefully unscrewed the cap, held it between his fingers, and then took a quick sip. The whiskey felt like liquid fire sloshing over his tongue and then on down his esophagus, burning all the way. Jim coughed slightly as he handed the flask back. The old man brought it to his lips and downed several swallows before replacing the cap.

"Ambrose Bierce," he said, extending his hand.

"Jim Bishop."

They shook and something clicked in Jim's memory.

"Bierce?" he said. "The author?"

"Right again," Bierce said. "And I hope it wasn't my writing back there that gave you the nightmare."

Jim continued to pump the other man's hand.

"I really like your book, sir. *In the Midst of Life*. It's really good."

Bierce's gaze focused on him. "My preferred title was *Tales of Soldiers and Civilians*. I take it you could relate more to that?"

Jim was unsure what the author meant.

The other man's bushy eyebrows twitched.

"You have the look of one who's been there," he said.

Compressing his lips for a moment to suppress the unwelcome flow of bad memories, Jim then said, "Yeah. I just come back from the Philippines."

Bierce shook his head slightly. "Ah, another one of our shameful and infamous wars."

Jim felt like he'd been slapped. He said nothing.

A hint of a smile twitched Bierce's lips. "Fought by brave men such as yourself and your friend," he continued, "to do the bidding of those who say they know best, and claim to feel your pain. But no one knows war quite like the soldier, eh?"

Jim had never heard it summed up quite that way before, but it resonated with the empty feeling that had been his silent companion since they'd departed the Philippines. When they'd gotten on the ship, with news that they were going home, he'd been stunned that he felt no sense of satisfaction, no feeling of accomplishment. All he felt was a hollowness. Like it all had been for naught.

He took in a quick, substantial breath. "I picked up a copy of your book in the ship's library and liked it so much I kept it." He shrugged self-consciously. "Well, I guess technically I stole it. Unless I mail it back."

"I'm sure it won't be missed," Bierce said with a smirk. "You liked it?"

"Yes, sir. Especially that one about the soldier that sees the man on the horse."

"Ah, 'A Horseman in the Sky.' I rewrote that one several times."

"It sure is good," Jim said. "And that other one about the man getting hung."

A slight smile graced Bierce's face. " 'Occurrence at Owl Creek Bridge.' "

"Yes, sir. That's the one."

Bierce's right eyebrow twitched again. "And your nightmare . . . Some old ghosts coming back to visit?"

Old ghosts . . . Jim felt his face flush as he nodded.

"I take it you saw combat over there?" Bierce asked.

It took Jim a moment to respond and his voice failed him. He nodded again.

"The newspapers," Bierce said, "not that I believe any of them, stated that the war was officially over in oh-three."

Jim took one more light drag on the cigarette, keeping the smoke in his mouth rather than drawing it down into the discomforting area of his lungs, and snorted. "That's what the politicians claimed. But it was far from over down south. Not till we finally went after them and—"

He didn't finish the sentence. The image of the big mountain in the distance as they made that final approach, looming out of the greenish blue sea like the hump of a massive creature waiting to swallow them up. So lush, so green, so deadly. Jim found himself gazing at the passing scenery. It looked green too. The heat from the burning cigarette seared his fingers and he flinched, dropping the smoldering butt.

The circular ash glowed momentarily until Jim ground it out under the sole of his boot. Army boots. Same with the pants. The only piece of clothing that was new was his blue shirt, and it was pretty much soaked through with his sweat from the dream.

"I heard your friend say something," Bierce said. "Pulagam, was it?"

"Right. Pulagam. That was what we called them. Took it from the Filipino Scouts, the Philippine army. *Pula* means red in their language, and the Moros—Filipino Muslims—wore red bandanas. They lived on the southernmost islands. Refused to surrender even after the war supposedly ended in oh-three. Like I said, they fought on and on until we finally ended it a couple of months ago."

The unpleasant visions of Bud Bagsak came drifting back into his memory. He averted his eyes to the rapidly passing terrain.

"I take it that it wasn't very pretty?" Bierce asked. "But then, war seldom is."

Jim glanced up at him. His writing . . . The vividness . . .

"You've been there too, haven't you?"

Bierce's expression tightened and it was his turn to avert his eyes to the passing scenery.

"It was a couple of wars ago now," he said. "Back in sixty-one. I was nineteen and an idealistic young lad. I enlisted in the Union Army when the war started. My first taste of battle was at Philippi. That was the initial land battle of the war. Got commissioned as a first lieutenant after rescuing a comrade at the Battle of Rich Mountain. Then I was so full of myself, I applied to go to West Point. Actually thought about making the military my career. Then came Shiloh, Chickamauga . . ." He paused and shook his head. "I was disillusioned, but still an idealist. It all came crashing down at the Battle of Kennesaw Mountain. The reality of war all caught up to me there."

"Pretty bad, was it, sir?" Jim asked. His own army experience paled in comparison, but he felt they'd probably chewed on some of the same dirt, albeit in different lands.

Bierce smiled and removed his hat. Jim noticed a thick ridge of scar tissue about the size of a penny around a declivity on the other man's left temple.

"You were wounded?" Jim asked.

"A Rebel sniper caught me in his sights. The bullet entered here." Bierce placed his left index finger on his temple as he rotated his head slightly. His fingers traced back from the scar to the area behind his left ear. "The bullet lodged there. I felt like my skull exploded. Someone, I don't know who, picked me up and carried me to the rear. Of that, I remember nothing."

"God in heaven," Jim said.

"He's purported to have been there, but I sometimes wonder." Bierce's nostrils flared as he drew in a deep breath. "We both know He wasn't anywhere on the battlefields."

Jim wasn't sure how to take this man. He seemed friendly and outgoing, yet at the same time bitter and aloof. But they did share the commonality of a soldier's journey.

Bierce replaced the hat. "But that was a long time ago, and luckily, I've always had a hard head." Patting the right side of his coat, he smiled.

"Shall we take another nip before going back inside?" The silver flask was in his fingers again, his eyebrows arching.

The visions of the *pulajan* had almost entirely faded from Jim's memory and he accepted the flask.

"Don't mind if I do, Mr. Bierce."

"Please," the other man said. "Call me Ambrose."

"All right." Jim sipped whiskey and handed the flask back. "But tell me something. Those old ghosts, as you called them. They ever go away?"

Bierce took a long pull, thought for a moment, and then took another drink. He compressed his lips as he capped the flask and slipped it back into his pocket.

"I expect I'll leave mine at the graveyard gate," he said.

1880
Sheriff's Office
Contention City, Arizona

Sheriff Lon Dayton, clad in his long johns and barefoot, held the Colt Peacemaker in his right hand, the hammer back. He was conscious of being barefoot as he edged open the door and glanced up and down the main street of the town, first one way, and then the other.

Nothing seemed to be moving at this early hour. No sign of whomever it was that made the sounds of the running footfalls, but the musky and foul smell of sweat hung in the air.

At least whoever it was had his boots on, the sheriff thought with a grin. And his socks, too, hopefully. The wooden planks felt rough and cold against the soles of his feet and sent a quick chill up his legs.

It was just past dawn and two of the roosters behind Delmonico's Restaurant were in a crowing contest, but other than that, he neither heard nor saw anything. Except for the knife: a ten-inch blade driven perpendicularly into the front door, affixing a folded slip of paper to the wooden surface. That must have been the distinctive thump that had roused him, and then the sound of the running footsteps over the wooden boardwalk. Dayton considered himself a light sleeper, which was a necessity for the town's sheriff. Seeing nothing out of the ordinary, he concluded that the note, and the knife, had been jammed onto the outside of the wooden door of the sheriff's office as some sort of message to him.

But why hadn't they just slipped it underneath?

He holstered his weapon and grinned.

It was probably a good thing that no one was around to see him dressed in his underwear and wearing his gun belt. Wouldn't the church ladies be scandalized, and so would Miss April May Donovan, the new schoolmarm. An image of her pretty face flashed in his memory for a brief second.

Luckily, there's no April in this hot September day, he thought.

In another week it would be his birthday. Time was sailing by. He'd be thirty-five, with two hundred and twenty-eight dollars in the bank and the hope that Miss April would accept his proposal of marriage. But he hadn't asked her and there was no guarantee. Not for him. The town's sheriff . . . The September Gun.

It took considerable effort to pull the knife loose. The depth of the slice was about half an inch, judging from the amount of the blade that was jammed into the wood, and fixed at about shoulder height.

It must have been a quick overhand plunge.

Better the door than me, he thought as he stepped back into his sparse office. The rifle rack on the right wall still had all the weapons secured by lock and chain. On the opposite wall the big corkboard showed numerous gaps where the dwindling number of *Wanted* circulars were affixed. The proclamation was posted right beside them. Dayton had spent the last month and a half distributing them all over the county and beyond, as ordered.

Territorial Governor Frémont Issues Amnesty Proclamation.

Dayton wondered if he'd been wasting his time. The outlaws had been on the wane anyway. Too many well-armed towns, too many Pinkertons on the railroads, too many bounty hunters. The main one left was the Bascom gang. His gaze traced over the only *Wanted* poster with a photographic representation of a group of eight mostly hard-looking men, centered around the big, barrel-chested fellow in the center wearing a fancy suit and one of those derby hats. That one, he knew, was Wallace "Dutch" Bascom. It was part of Dutch's local mystique that he and the gang had been so bold as to pose for the photograph at the territorial governor's inaugural fair and then mail a copy of the photograph back to Frémont. It was considered to be the ultimate in audacity and had purportedly infuriated the governor. As a result, they now had a five-thousand-dollar reward, more than double the previous one, for their capture on their heads, courtesy of the railroad.

Wanted, dead or alive, and one of them looked to be no older than a boy.

Dayton shook his head.

Three wooden chairs and the big desk rounded out the rest of the furniture. Neat and sparse, just the way a sheriff's office should be.

Again, he was concerned that the thunk of the knife being driven home hadn't roused him sooner and given him enough time to see who the messenger was, but he had been sleeping in his room in the back. It had probably made no more noise than a single knock.

What the hell did it matter anyhow?

He reassured himself that he would have woken up had it been something more significant, such as whomever it was breaking down the door.

A solitary tumbleweed blew down the street, carried by the eastern wind.

Dayton closed the door and carried the knife and the note back to his big wooden desk. He examined the blade first. It was a bit thin and worn down, but clean and still shiny. He rubbed his thumb gingerly over the finely honed edge.

Sharp as a razor, he thought.

The hilt was hard wood, probably oak, and sported a finely carved totem of sorts that was worn smooth in spots. The lower side of it formed a crude representation of a man's face. Dayton wondered if it was Indian work, but then decided that was unlikely since the profile's chin sported a full beard. Dropping the knife on the desk, he unfolded the paper and looked at a crudely printed note in black ink, all capital letters. The page was smudged with dirt and whirling, line-like impressions that appeared to have been left by a man's dust-covered fingers. They were big fingers, too.

He read the note, which had several cross-outs:

> DEER SHARIF DAYTON
> I HEARED THAT THE ~~GUVENR~~
> GUVINERS DONE GON AND OFFHERD US
> ~~ANESTI~~ AMNESTY. IF THIS IS TROO IT'S A
> DAM GOOD ~~THING~~ THING. WE SEEN THE
> PAPR YOU SENT SAYING THIS IS TROO. I
> HEARED YOU GIVE YER WORD THAT IFN
> WE COME IN AND GIV UP OURSELFES
> YOU AND YER DEPUTEES AINT GON
> TO SHOOT US. I HAV NOWED YOU FER
> YERES AND YOU HAD ALWYS BEN ~~HONA~~
> HONERST AS FAR AS I KIN TELL SOS
> IF THIS IS THE ~~TRU TRUD~~ TRUTH ME
> AND THE BOYS WIL GIV USELVES UP
> HAV THE CHURH BELL RUNG 10 TIMS
> THIS MORNIN IFN YOU AGREE AND 10

MORE THE DAY AFTR ~~TAMR~~ TOMARA
IFN THE ~~GUVI~~ GUVENR AGREES. WE WIL
KNOW CAUSE IT AINT SONDAY ~~YIT YAT~~
YET. THEN WE WELL ~~BE~~ GIVE USELVES
UP WEN YOU SAY. YOU GIT WTH THA
~~GUVINR~~ GUVENR AND HAV THAM PAPRS
READY FER US—ALL 13 OF US AND WE
GIV USEVLS UP. UNDRSTAND? RING
THEM BELLS AND IFN YOU DO. WILL BE
IN TUTCH.
    NO TRIKS OR WILL BE SHOTING AR
WAY OUT. YOU ALWYS BEN HONERST SO I
TRUST YOU SO FAR BUT IFN THS IS A LIE
I WIL KIL YU. OF THS I SWEAR.
    YOURS TRULE
    DUTCH BASCOM
    PS—I WANT MY NIFE BACK

His knife.

Dayton picked it up and felt the texture of the handle again.

Bascom, one of the last of the outlaw breed.

Dayton heard the sudden new sound of a horse galloping. He let the handwritten note fall to the desktop as his right hand instinctively dropped to his gun belt and he gripped the handle of his Colt Peacemaker. Whirling, he went to the door and pulled it open, surveying the area once again while undoing the leather thong that was looped over the weapon's hammer, securing it in the holster.

No riders in sight.

The sound of the hooves grew fainter.

Somebody was riding out.

Could be a trap to lure me outside, he thought. *But I ain't getting paid for standing around in my long johns.*

After closing the door, he slipped on his shirt, pants, and boots and undid the lock on the rifle rack to free up one of the Winchesters. Dayton cocked the weapon and pressed another round into the magazine before stepping out onto the boardwalk and shutting the door behind him.

Nothing moved except for another pair of tumbleweeds drifting along in the languid breeze.

Then he heard it.

A chunking noise—repetitive, rhythmic.

Chunk, pause, chunk, pause . . .

Dayton moved toward the sound, holding the Winchester at the ready.

Chunk, pause, chunk, pause.

The sounds grew louder.

Another noise.

Heavy breathing interspersed between the chunking.

Dayton moved past two buildings, the barbershop and the undertakers. A space of about twenty feet separated them from the next structure, the Red Sunset Saloon. The noises were coming from the saloon's rear yard beyond the tall wooden fence that enclosed the area.

Dayton checked the gate.

Open.

He used the toe of his boot to push the gate open wider and peered in.

The origin of the chunking sound was readily evident. The town idiot, Simple Sam Timmons, was shirtless and panting as he jammed a shovel into the soft earth. His upper body was slick with perspiration and Dayton could smell the odor of heavy exertion. The hole Timmons was digging was about three feet wide and about the same depth. A pile of dirt sat next to the adjacent outhouse.

As he rose with another shovelful, Timmons saw Dayton and smiled.

"Howdy, Sheriff. You get that letter?"

Dayton glanced around but saw no one else.

"What letter?"

"The one I stuck on your door."

"You did that?"

"Well, yep, I did." Timmons's nose twitched, and he closed off one nostril and blew a load of snot out of the other one. "This fella give me a whole nickel for doing it."

"What fella?"

"Oh, he's gone now. Was on a horse down at the other end of town, watching me. After I done it, he paid me and he just rode off."

"Which way?"

Timmons shrugged.

"I dunno. I ain't too good with no directions." He raised his hand and pointed to the west. "That way."

Dayton assessed the information.

"Did I do something wrong, Sheriff?" Timmons asked. "I'm sorry, if'n I did."

"No, Sam. How do you know this guy?"

"I don't. I was here digging a new hole for the outhouse. Mr. Meyers is paying me a whole dollar if'n I can get a new pit dug by tonight." He patted the wooden planks on the side of the outhouse. "This one here's getting pretty full."

The unpleasant odor emanating from the base of the structure made that fact evident. Dayton nodded.

"Okay, Sam. Better get back to work before it gets too hot."

"Hot enough already," Timmons said. "Where you going now?"

Dayton leaned the barrel of the Winchester on his shoulder and hiked his hat back on his head.

"I'm gonna go ring some church bells," he said.

Chapter 2

September 13, 1913
Southern Pacific Railroad Line
Somewhere in southern California

The backs of the wicker braided seats were affixed to a metal pivot that could be pulled forward, allowing four passengers to sit facing each other. After Jim had done that, he asked Ambrose Bierce to join him and Larry. The older gentleman extracted his carpetbag from the floor of the place he'd been sitting and did so. As he sat down, Jim made the introductions. Larry's eyes widened when Jim held up the copy of Bierce's book and explained that their new companion had written it.

"You wrote that?"

"I did," Bierce said. "That one, and a slew of others, all destined for the bonfires of history."

Larry didn't seem to understand what the author meant and gave his head a little shake. Jim wasn't so sure himself. This man Bierce was a strange one. Older and hardened, that was for sure, but with an underlying compassion.

The fact that he followed me out on the platform shows something, Jim thought. *He uses his bitterness as a shield, but deep down there's something more there.*

"Jim was reading that book all the way back from the Philippines," Larry continued. "Shucks, I almost know it by heart. I was laid up in the infirmary for a time, due to my leg, and he'd come and read to me most every day."

"A war injury?" Bierce asked.

Larry grimaced and nodded.

"Took a bamboo spear through it." He gripped his knotted wooden cane and held it up. "Damn Moros. My leg ain't been the same since. Not worth a damn." His eyes drifted to the floor. "Guess you could say the same about me. Not worth a tinker's damn now."

Jim gave Larry a light slap on the arm.

"That ain't so, Larry," he said. "Hell, Mr. Bierce was wounded, too, and look at all he done."

Larry's chin jutted outward. "You was?"

"Indeed," Bierce said, the right side of his mouth twitching with something akin to a smile. "Long ago, and far away."

"You can't get much farther away than them Philippines," Larry said. "Why, it seemed like forever we was on that boat a-going over and coming back."

"The ocean is vast," Bierce said, "dwarfed only by life's sea of regrets."

"So where was you hit?" Larry asked.

Bierce didn't reply.

Jim was going to say, "In the head," but thought better of it. *Best to let the man speak for himself,* he thought.

Larry evidently sensed that his question had crossed a line it shouldn't have, and added, "Leastwise, you still got all the use of your limbs, huh?"

The author still did not reply.

Larry's lips worked, like he was searching for words. "I didn't mean nothing by it, sir. I guess I shouldn't have oughta asked about it."

Bierce's gaze went from Larry's corpulent face to his stiff leg, and then outward, to the window. The lush green scenery continued to pass by like one of those picture machines in the penny arcade, only in color.

After a deep breath, Bierce turned his head back toward Larry and said, "I was shot here." He brought his finger to his left temple.

"In the head?" Larry's eyes widened. "Gosh. You're real lucky to be alive. Sorry about your misfortune."

"Misfortune touches us all, in one way or another," Bierce said. "It's the only kind of fortune that never misses."

The three of them sat in silence for several seconds and then Jim handed the book across to Bierce.

"I'd be much obliged if you'd sign it for me, Mr. Bierce."

Bierce smirked and was about to say something when he went into a coughing jag. After it passed, he swallowed and shook his head.

"My lungs are ancient," he said. "And roasted black from a lifetime of smoking. You'd do well to give up tobacco completely, Jim. Take it from one who's been there."

Jim recalled the unpleasantness of his last smoke.

"I think I'll do just that, sir. Don't really enjoy it much anyway."

"Wise decision." Bierce accepted the book and reached into his carpetbag. He withdrew a pen and a bottle of ink, the latter of which he shook and then handed to Jim. "If you would be so kind as to hold this."

Jim grasped the round bottle and removed the lid.

Bierce opened the book to the title page, dipped the point of the pen into the ink, and then sat with the instrument poised in the air. The train car rocked with a steady but uneven motion, and the author's hand still hovered over the page. Just as he lowered the pen to the paper, the train lurched savagely and then began the steady, rocking motion once again. Bierce's mouth twisted into a scowl. He shook his head and slammed the book closed, handing it back to Jim.

"I'll have to wait for a more opportune time," Bierce said. "Otherwise, my signature will look like that of an infirm old man, which is one threshold I have not quite yet passed. At least as far as the infirmity."

"Sure thing." Jim set the book down by his leg and sealed the cap over the ink bottle.

"How long did it take you to write that?" Larry asked.

"A lifetime," Bierce said. "One of the many steps in a long journey of regrets."

"For a rich and successful man," Larry said, "you sound kind of bitter."

Bierce emitted a harsh, guttural laugh.

"Very perceptive, young man," the author answered. "That's why they call me Bitter Bierce."

☙

The late afternoon drifted into evening and the whistle sounded as the train slowed to a halt just outside of Santa Clarita. The conductor came through advising everyone that the train would be stationary for a period of approximately thirty minutes, allowing the engineer and fireman and the rest of the crew to rest as the train was being resupplied.

"The dining car is also temporarily closed for restocking, but it should be open directly once we're underway again. For any of you who aren't in a mind to wait, there's an emporium of sorts just across the way, but be warned. Once the water supply has been replenished, we'll be ready to get underway again. We do have a schedule to keep. Five minutes before departure, the engineer will blow the whistle three times, which will be the signal for everyone who's departed to return immediately to the train. He will wait for two minutes and blow the whistle thrice again, after which, the train will depart. You may avail yourselves of something offered there, or partake in some liquid refreshments, at your own risk, of course." The conductor paused and flashed a knowing grin. After clearing his throat, he added, "Your possessions will be safe on board until your return. You may also send a telegram in the ticket office if you wish."

He stopped and leaned down, whispering something to two male passengers. Whatever it was he said, he punctuated it with a laugh as he straightened. The two men exchanged glances and then immediately got up and began striding down the center aisle like a pair of roosters, their faces showing expressions of delicious anticipation.

Jim glanced out the window and saw a cluster of sturdy-looking wooden buildings, a cistern, and a funnel-shaped waterspout. Next to it was a patch of ground, barren except for sporadic clusters of wildflowers.

An unmarked graveyard?

Jim was beginning to get a wary feeling.

Bierce waved the conductor over. The man had a mustache the size of a shaving brush and a massive belly that hung over the front of his pants.

"What type of establishment is that?" Bierce asked.

The conductor grinned and shot them a quick wink. "Let me just say that a man can get just about anything he wants there. Why, we've had passengers have so much fun, they damn near missed the departure completely." Another wink. "If one likes to partake in a bit of gambling and maybe some . . . feminine companionship."

Bierce canted his head to the side. "My good man, if I didn't know better, I'd say you were describing a house of ill repute."

The conductor's grin widened under his mustache and he barked out a laugh.

"Well, things are what you make them, ain't they?" His smirk was lascivious.

"You said we'll be here for thirty minutes," Larry said.

The conductor shrugged. "Give or take a minute or two." The tip of his tongue flicked out, going over both sides of the errant hairs with a licking motion. "Enough time to allow a man to go for a quick one. Just listen for the whistle."

He walked away.

Larry's face was flushed with excitement.

"What are we waiting for?" he said. "Let's go."

Jim shook his head. "I don't know, Larry. Could be more than we bargained for. Besides, I'm not looking to get laid."

"Well, I sure am." Larry gripped the seat with one hand and his cane with the other and rose from his seat. "I'm going."

He began walking down the aisle.

Bierce glanced at Jim. "Shall we venture over there and see if we can get a drink?"

Larry grinned as he pushed by the other two men.

"That sure sounds good," Larry said. "Don't it, Jim?"

Jim heaved a sigh. He grabbed his rucksack and the book and stood, recalling how he'd slapped the tourniquet around Larry's leg back at Bud Bagsak and then literally carried him to the rear to get medical treatment. He'd gotten used to looking out for his injudicious combat companion.

The conductor raised his eyebrows and pointed to Jim.

"You can leave that stuff here if you want, young fella," he said.

"I appreciate your offer, sir," Jim said. "But I'd just as soon take it with me."

The conductor gave a curt nod.

The restaurant was populated only by the two other men from the train. A pair of glasses sat on the table between them. Bierce pointed to a place by the front window. A heavyset woman in a dirty apron waddled over to them and asked, "What's your pleasure, gents? And just so you know, we already got two reservations and only one girl working right now."

Bierce looked at Jim and then at Larry.

"Three whiskeys, my dear," he said.

"You gotta pay first," the woman said. "That's the rules."

Jim frowned and leaned over to pull out his wallet, but Bierce placed a hand on Jim's arm.

"This one's on me," he said, removing a finely crafted leather wallet.

Larry grinned and looked at Jim.

The author handed a coin to the woman and told her to keep the change.

She looked down her nose at it. "There ain't none."

Bierce's eyebrows rose as he smiled at her. "Well then, my dear, you may keep it anyway."

Jim was amused by the author's felicitousness.

The woman's lips curled into a scowl as she pulled open the upper part of her blouse and jammed the coin into a dirty-looking undergarment. A door at the rear of the establishment opened and a masculine hand came out and waved to her. She nodded and waddled over to the two other male passengers who'd beat them there. Leaning over their table, she whispered something to them, and they got up quickly and followed her to that rear door. Both of their faces bore eager grins.

Bierce chuckled and shot a wink at Jim and Larry.

"Looks like our hippopotamus has lured two fish into the fray," he said.

"Hippopotamus?" Larry said. "I ain't never seen one of them."

"You have now," Bierce said, and laughed.

Jim laughed too.

"Looks like," he said, starting not to like this place. He'd seen way too many of them during his army days, and knew they usually meant trouble of one sort or another.

"Damn," Larry said. "If she's what they got here, I don't want no part of it no way. She sure is ugly. Maybe this wasn't such a good idea, coming here."

Jim rolled his eyes.

"Nonsense," Bierce said. "How does one gain experience in life if one does not occasionally venture forth into the breach? And I've already paid for our drinks."

"You didn't need to do that, sir," Jim said. "We can pay our own way."

"Let's just consider it a gift," Bierce answered. "From one old soldier to two younger ones."

"Mr. Bierce," Larry said. "We ain't in the army no more. In fact, we're on the way down to San Diego for a job."

"What type of work?" Bierce asked.

The right side of Larry's mouth jerked into a half-smile. "Should be a real sweet one. Me and Jim are gonna do some work on one of them moving picture things."

"Moving pictures?" Bierce leaned back in his chair. "Edison's debasement of the literate."

"Huh?" Larry's brow wrinkled.

Bierce dismissed the question with a wave of his hand. "Never mind. You were saying?"

"Yeah," Larry said. "My sister and her husband's down there now. She got us the job."

"As actors?"

Jim snorted. "Not hardly."

Larry quickly offered a further explanation: "I guess they're looking for men who know how to ride. My sister, Donna, and her husband got hired on as cooks. She's a wizard in the kitchen, and he helps, but not all that much seeing as how he's only got one arm."

"Another veteran?" Bierce asked.

Larry shook his head. "Nah, he lost it in a farming accident. He's an all right fella, though. Name's Richard Phipps."

"What will you be doing there?" Bierce looked up and smiled. The heavyset waitress was bringing the bottle and three glasses toward them. He held up an index finger and motioned for her to stop at the table. As she did, he removed a dollar bill from the wallet and handed it to her. Her eyes stayed glued upon the wallet.

"You looking for some action?" she asked.

"No, no, madam," Bierce said as he tucked his wallet back inside his coat. "Consider it an apologia for my rude and boorish behavior before, regarding your tip."

Her mouth worked as she eyed him. "Huh?"

Bierce smiled. "Please forgive an old curmudgeon's weak attempt at humor. A gentleman should never seek to make light of a working woman's plight, and always show a lady the proper respect. Especially one as pretty as you."

The waitress's face twisted from an expression of disbelief to one of abject flattery as her lips parted in a smile that exposed a gap-toothed row of uneven dentition. She set a glass in front of each of them and poured a generous portion in each glass.

As she walked away, Larry said, "Shucks, Mr. Bierce. You could most likely charm the horns off'n a buffalo."

The author smiled.

"I think I just did," he said as the woman disappeared into the back room.

Both Jim and Larry laughed.

"She did seem flattered," Jim said.

The right side of Bierce's mouth twitched.

"Flattered? Perhaps, perhaps not. I sense that she is more the spider than the fly."

Larry picked up his glass and swirled the contents. It had a strange odor to it.

Bierce motioned for Jim to pick up his glass and when he did, Bierce held his up and said, "*Salud*."

He downed a substantial amount of the amber liquid in one gulp, then started coughing and choking.

Larry did the same, but Jim only sipped his with caution. Larry immediately began coughing as well, and turned his body away from them, leaning over and dribbling a stream of spittle onto the wooden planks of the floor.

The bitter taste brought tears to Jim's eyes. It tasted like licorice and embalming fluid. Or maybe wood alcohol. Instead of swallowing it, he spat the liquid back into the glass, then set it down and frowned.

Bierce was grimacing now and began a hacking cough.

"I think whatever that was," he said, shoving the glass away, "came out of the wrong end of that particular hippo."

Jim used his foot to snare a nearby spittoon and poured the remainder of the liquid into it.

"No offense, Mr. Bierce," he said. "But I don't think my stomach can handle that stuff."

"Wise decision," Bierce said. The corners of his mouth were still turned down. "I venture to say that we've come within a hair's breadth of being foully poisoned."

Larry reached down and pulled the spittoon over. His cheeks bulged and he puked into it.

After he'd finished, it was the author's turn, although he didn't bother aiming for the spittoon. He just voided onto the floor.

Three sharp blasts of the train whistle sounded outside.

Had it been twenty-five minutes already?

"I believe they're playing our song," Bierce said. They started to turn to leave.

"Hey." The hefty woman came running back into the room swearing a blue streak and holding a rolling pin. A man followed behind her, brandishing a cudgel in one hand and a butcher knife in the other. "You made a damn mess on my floor."

Bierce heaved an expansive breath. "If anything, we have done a medicinal service. That pernicious liquid you served us will surely eliminate any vestiges of harmful bacteria."

"Pay up for cleaning or do it yourselves," the man said. "A sawbuck from each of ya."

"The old one's the one with the money," she said.

Jim straightened up and assessed them.

"Let's get outta here," he said.

"You ain't going nowhere till you pay what you owe," the woman said.

"Fifteen bucks, you old goat," the man said, his voice a growl. "Otherwise you're all three going outta here in a box. And not till y'all clean that up."

Reaching into his rucksack, Jim closed his fingers around the solid assurance of the grip of his Colt 1911.

Bierce rose on shaky legs, holding up his left palm in a placating gesture, and reached inside his coat with his right. Jim thought the author was reaching for his wallet, but instead he pulled out a shiny, nickel-plated revolver and pointed it at the advancing man.

"I think not," he muttered. "Now drop those weapons or I'll put one right between your eyes."

The two advancing adversaries halted immediately.

Bierce made a slight jiggling motion with the revolver.

The cords in the shop owner's neck visibly tightened and he let the cudgel and the knife fall to the floor. The woman muttered some profanity and Bierce rotated his arm slightly to point the weapon at her.

"That goes for you too, my dear."

She sneered at him and then dropped the rolling pin.

"Make sure you wash that before your next dough rolling," Bierce said, holding his non-gun hand out, palm upward. "And now, my dollar, if you please. Or even if you don't."

"Huh?" the woman said. She repeated the profanity. "I ain't gonna give you—"

Bierce cocked back the hammer, the sound seeming to echo in the confines of the large room. The woman didn't finish her sentence.

"Now see what you done?" the male proprietor said. "Damn you."

"Suffice it to say," Bierce said, "that your establishment will not be getting a five-star review."

"Go on." The proprietor's nostrils flared and his eyes shot to the chest-high counter upon which the cash register sat. "Give him back the damn money."

The woman's face scrunched up as she dipped her fingers into the exposed upper portion of her dirty brassiere, wiggled her digits around some, and came up with the aforementioned partially crumpled dollar bill. She tossed it toward Bierce. It rotated three times in the air before pausing for a split second and then resuming a side-to-side float to the floor a few feet away.

"There. Take your damn money." She made a hocking sound and spat, the moist gobbet landing on top of the currency with uncanny accuracy.

Bierce raised an eyebrow, exhaled, and then shook his head fractionally.

"I am not accustomed to paying to imbibe poison," he said. "Much less collecting a dollar bill now contaminated with the spoor of a termagant, which is no doubt as noxious as that of a Gila monster."

Lowering the gun, he squeezed off a round that pierced the center of the greenback. A wisp of smoke rose from the end of the barrel.

The sound of the shot had been like a too close clap of thunder, and Jim's ears were ringing. The heavyset woman screamed. Three more men rushed through the door from the back room, one holding a long-barreled pistol. Bierce aimed the revolver at him.

"May I suggest you drop that gun, sir," he said. "If you want to live, that is."

The man's eyes shifted from Bierce to the proprietor. He grunted something and the man let the weapon fall to the floor.

"Now be so kind as to kick it over here," Bierce said.

Again the man hesitated and Bierce repeated the command in a more forceful tone. The man kicked the pistol. It skidded across the floor.

"Would you be so kind as to use your cane to retrieve that?" Bierce said to Larry.

Larry dragged the pistol over with the hooked end and then picked it up.

"As I said before, madam," Bierce said. "You may now keep the change."

The door at the back of the room burst open yet again. Jim's grip tightened on his Colt, but then he saw the newcomers were the two other men from the train, both in states of semi-undress, their faces ashen with terror. After glancing around, the one looked at Bierce.

"Is it all right if we leave, mister?" he said.

Bierce nodded. "By all means. The bell has tolled, and as Falstaff said, 'we have heard the chimes of midnight.'"

They both scampered toward the door. As they ran, a hard-looking woman's face appeared in the doorway.

"Git back in there, Gracie," the heavyset woman yelled.

"But they still got their—"

"I said *git*," the proprietor bellowed.

Gracie frowned, shook her head, and ducked out of sight, slamming the door shut.

Jim wondered about the whore's unfinished sentence. What did they still have? Their money? Their wallets? Or maybe their lives. He thought about the wildflowers he'd seen in the adjacent field. Folks said those grew over unmarked graves.

"Think y'all's the only one 'round here with a gun now?" the proprietor yelled. His lips curled back to show a gapped row of a few yellowed teeth, each laced with a brocade of black streaks. "Got me a scattergun in t'other room. And I'm a-fixing to go fetch it once y'all's out the door. You ain't a-gonna even make it back to that train. 'Specially him with that gimpy leg. And there's a whole lot more of us'n than there is of you."

Jim stood and whipped his hand out of the rucksack, pointing the big forty-five semiautomatic at the proprietor. Knowing there was no bullet in the chamber, he let the sack fall to the floor, reached up with his left hand and racked the slide back, and then let it slam forward with an ominous clunking sound.

He saw the proprietor stiffen. The heavyset woman's eyes widened and she looked as if she were ready to dissolve into a pile of horse feces. Jim was pretty sure neither of them had ever seen a weapon like his. The slide whipping forward made a sound like chambering a round on a shotgun.

"We'll be leaving now," he said. "And once we get outside, I'll be watching and waiting. One of you so much as peeps your head out that damn door, I'll blow it off."

All of their eyes were on the gun.

Larry struggled to his feet, bent and picked up the rucksack, and started ambling toward the door with the assistance of his cane. Bierce still had his gun down by his thigh. He turned slightly and made side steps toward the door. Jim followed. Once outside, they faced the twenty-five-yard trek to the train just as three more blasts of the whistle cut through the air.

Time to reboard.

Bierce and Jim lowered their guns, but didn't conceal them. They hurried to the train and Larry used his good leg to stick his left foot into the metal stirrup. He grabbed hold of the adjacent railing and pulled himself up, swinging his stiff leg up after. Jim, still keeping his eyes on the wooden shack across the way, let Bierce go up next. The author snorted a laugh and replaced his revolver in the shoulder holster.

"I doubt those rummies will dare peek out after seeing that cannon you showed them," Bierce said. "What kind is it?"

"A Colt forty-five, nineteen eleven," Jim said. "Courtesy of the U.S. Army."

He didn't add that he'd taken it off of the dead officer he'd tried to save.

"How many rounds does it hold?" Bierce asked.

"Eight usually," Jim said. "If I would've had one in the chamber. I didn't, so it's only got seven."

Bierce clucked in approval. "More than sufficient to take care of that riffraff. You've got to let me see that once we're underway."

"I will." Jim motioned for the other man to ascend the three stairs, his eyes still watching across the way. When Bierce got on the platform, he slipped his gun out again and flattened against the back of the Pullman, training his sights on the establishment.

"Come on up, Jim," Bierce said. "I'll cover you."

Jim turned slightly and was up the steps in a matter of about three seconds. He clapped Bierce on the back. All three of them were laughing as Bierce and Larry went inside the train car. Jim remained where he was, his Colt down against his thigh, and gave one more glance toward the other building. There was no sign of movement at the door of the emporium. He remained on the outside platform as the engine huffed and strained and the train started moving once again. Finally, as the odious establishment receded into the landscape, Jim allowed himself to go into the car. After snapping on the safety, he stuck the Colt back in the rucksack.

Cocked and locked, he thought. *And I'm going to keep it that way.*

He heaved a sigh of relief, glad to be out of harm's way.

Chapter 3

1880
Delmonico's Restaurant
Contention City, Arizona

Sheriff Lon Dayton was dipping a fragment of toast into the remaining yolk of a fried egg when the restaurant door burst open, leaving the rotund figure of the mayor, Hizzoner Clyde Webber, practically filling the gap. Webber's face was unshaven and it appeared that he'd just thrown on a jacket over his union suit and slipped on a pair of voluminous pants. Both the pants and the underwear looked soiled and dirty. The place was somewhat crowded with the usual morning patrons. Dayton had claimed his usual seat by the door to the kitchen, his back to the wall so he had a clear view of anyone entering.

Webber looked around, his porcine features seeming almost too small for his expansive face, and his gaze settled on the sheriff. He strode over with a purposeful gait, pulled out a chair on the other side of Dayton's table, and plopped his enormous body down onto it. Dayton grimaced and hastened his eating. He was well aware that he was perhaps past the time for his own weekly bath, but Webber's body odor was almost overpowering in its distinct and distasteful pungency. Hizzoner's ripeness had long ago reached status of being legendary in Contention City.

"Lon," Webber said, his nostrils flaring. "What the hell was going on 'round here this morning?"

Dayton had just bitten off a piece of the toast, so he shifted it to his cheek.

"What do you mean, Mayor?"

Sally Grimes, the proprietor's young daughter and sometimes waitress, came over, set a cup down in front of Webber, and poured some coffee from the metal pot.

"Your usual, Mr. Webber?" she asked.

Webber glanced up at her and nodded, his jowly face twitching with something akin to a quick smile. She topped off Dayton's cup as well, wrinkling her nose and shifting her eyes toward the mayor.

Hizzoner took a long sip and then smacked his lips as he watched her walk away. Rumor had it that on his periodic trips to Phoenix to confer with the railroad barons and Territorial Governor Frémont, Hizzoner liked to frequent whorehouses that specialized in young girls. Very young. While Dayton didn't approve of that, there wasn't a whole helluva lot he could do about it. Phoenix was way out of Dayton's jurisdiction, and he also knew that he served as sheriff at Webber's discretion. Webber had appointed Dayton as town sheriff, and could also dismiss him in a heartbeat.

And I can't blame him for looking at Sally, Dayton thought. Even though she was only thirteen, she had the makings of a very pretty shape to her.

And as long as looking is the only thing he does here in Contention City. . . Dayton thought, leaving the mental statement unfinished.

The overwhelming knowledge that Webber held the upper hand, no matter what, was like having a case of saddle sores on a long ride.

Webber spoke again. "I was trying to get some sleep this morning when some idiot started ringing them Goddamn church bells."

Dayton suppressed a smile, continued chewing.

"It woke you up, did it?" He silently chuckled as he sipped his coffee.

"You're Goddamn right it did." Webber took another long sip and set the cup down hard on the table. Some of the dark liquid splashed onto the tablecloth. "Me and Fred Dyer and Martin Lipton were over at the Brass Cupcake last night playing poker. Till late. That damn reporter friend of Lipton's was there too. What's his name? You know, the one they hired to write them articles about how great the governor is?"

Dayton shook his head. "Can't recall."

He'd been introduced to the reporter when the fellow had arrived in town, but they'd had little contact after that. Dayton knew Territorial Governor Frémont had hired some fancy newspaperman to write up a series of favorable articles in the hope that it would pave the way for eventual statehood for the territory.

Dyer was a railroad man and Lipton worked directly for the governor. It sounded like an interesting match-up for a poker game. All of them, Webber included, had a lot of experience manipulating the facts to make themselves, or whomever they were working for, look good. *Good luck with that*, he thought as he sopped up some more of the yolk with another piece of toast.

"Poker, huh?" Dayton said. "You win?"

Webber blew out a derisive breath before gulping more coffee. His exhalation was almost as foul as his body odor.

"I wish. I wonder if that damn Lipton is a card sharp, or something."

Martin Lipton was overseeing the development of this area as well as the newest branch of tracks that passed through Contention City. The rails had already been completed in the town and were now continuing west toward the eventual destination of Barstow in California.

Progress, Dayton thought. Pretty soon the railroad would completely replace the stage line, which now seemed almost like an anachronism.

"He was probably taught by the best," Dayton said. "Isn't he supposed to be Frémont's right-hand man around these parts?"

Webber didn't reply. Instead, his tongue flicked out and snared a few errant drops from the thick red hairs on his upper lip. His hair was almost all gray, but the mustache was solid auburn. He brought the coffee cup to his lips once more and drank. They sat in silence until Sally brought a fresh plate of scrambled eggs, bacon, and several biscuits out from the kitchen and set it down in front of Webber.

He winked at her and grabbed the fork from the side of Dayton's plate.

"You done with this, ain't ya?"

Without waiting for an answer, Webber leaned forward and began shoveling the eggs into his mouth, chewing with it open, and continuously shoving the sticks of bacon in. Bits of yellow egg and grease coated his red mustache.

"Cox," he said. "That's it."

"Eh?"

"Cox," Webber repeated. "William Bradford Cox." He spewed out bits of food as he spoke. "That damn newspaperman outta Phoenix. He's supposed to have written a book or two as well."

"Impressive." Dayton dipped the toast into the last egg yolk.

Webber ran his tongue over his teeth, then crammed in more eggs and bacon.

"Who knows," he said between hurried efforts at mastication. "Maybe it'll put Contention City here on the map."

"Maybe."

"And then them damn bells woke me up," Webber said with a groan. "Shit. It must've been that stupid fool, Timmons." He gulped coffee and set the cup down. "Simple Sam. I seen him hanging around by the Red Sunset when I walked over here this morning." He frowned. "Can you believe it? The dumb son of a bitch was dunking his head in the damn horse trough."

Dayton popped the last bit of toast into his mouth and began chewing.

"He was probably just trying to cool off," Dayton said after swallowing. "He's digging a new pit for one of the outhouses."

Webber's frown deepened as if the thought disgusted him. He worked his tongue over his teeth again.

"Just the same, we oughta do something about that crazy son of a bitch. He's a damn menace, waking people up in the early morning hours. Can't you arrest him?"

"For what?" Dayton risked a half-smile. "Washing up in a horse trough?"

Webber was using the biscuits now to scoop up the remainder of the eggs and bacon.

"I dunno," he said. "You're the damn sheriff, ain't ya? Maybe for being a public nuisance, ringing them bells so early."

"Well, don't be too hard on him," Dayton said. "He's just trying to make an honest living, and besides, I know for a fact that it wasn't him who rang those bells."

Webber's brow furrowed. "It wasn't? How the hell you know that?"

Dayton took a sip of his coffee before answering.

" 'Cause it was me."

"You?"

Dayton nodded and took another sip. The coffee tasted pretty good.

Two men at an adjacent table had apparently been eavesdropping and started to shake, as if trying to suppress their laughter. This wasn't wasted on Webber, who regarded them with a sideways glance.

"What the hell you want to go and do something like that for?" he asked.

"Because," Dayton said, "it was a signal."

"Huh? A signal?"

"That's right."

"To who?"

Dayton set his cup down, reached into his shirt pocket, and pulled out the folded letter that had earlier been fastened to his office door. After unfolding it, he gave it to the mayor.

"Here," he said. "Take a look at this."

Webber shoved his empty plate aside, wiped his greasy fingers on his shirt, and squinted as he studied the letter. His lips moved over each word and he seemed transfixed. After he'd apparently finished, he blew out a long breath and then leaned back with a look of utter amazement.

"Is this thing real?"

"I suspect it is," Dayton said. "I can't see anybody going to all the trouble of delivering it like they did, much less paying Simple Sam to stick it on my office door at sunup."

The mayor looked deep in thought, his tongue flicking over his mustache like a snake exploring the high grass.

Dayton took the letter from the other man's hand and refolded it. Several greasy smudges now highlighted the paper.

"Damn," Webber said.

He leaned over to the side, his face contorting, and let loose a long and mellifluous burst of flatulence. Seconds later an extremely foul odor began wafting about. The two men at the adjacent table, their noses wrinkling, emitted grunts and coughs, but said nothing.

Dayton suppressed a smirk as he too caught a whiff of the foul stench.

"Is that your comment on the state of things?" he asked.

Webber didn't answer, his expression stoic, as if he were deep in thought.

Sally came through the door from the kitchen carrying two plates of eggs and bacon, and her face contorted as she walked by.

Webber leaned over again and grunted, farting a second time.

Dayton shoved himself back from the table.

"If you're going to keep that up, Mr. Mayor," he said, "you're going to clear this place out in a hurry. Maybe you should go see if Simple Sam's got that new outhouse pit dug yet."

"Yeah, yeah, whatever," Webber said. He hunched forward, leaning over the tabletop. "You think Bascom'll really show?"

At the mention of the outlaw's name, several of the restaurant patrons glanced up from their plates. Dutch Bascom had become a legend around these parts, both feared and respected by most everybody.

Dayton had hoped the mayor would have been more circumspect and not mentioned the outlaw. No reason to get folks nervous. At least not at this point. He considered his answer. He'd been debating that same question since he'd rung the church bells.

"I don't know," he said. "But I suspect he might. Times are changing and with these new, heavily fortified vaults in most all the banks, and the railroads hiring them Pinkerton agents to ride the trains, the outlawing ways are getting mighty hard these days. They're the last of a vanishing breed. Plus, old Dutch and the gang's got a pretty heavy bounty on their heads. It's reduced the field down to only a few. Dutch ain't dumb. Despite the fact that he can't spell so good, he's got to know his days are numbered. This amnesty proposal's probably the last chance for him and his boys."

The odor was starting to dissipate now and Dayton got up, aiming to leave before Hizzoner dropped another one.

Webber ponderously rose too.

"You notify the governor yet?" he asked.

Dayton shook his head. "I'm fixing to do that now. The telegraph office don't open till eight."

Webber's eyebrows twitched and he leaned over again. Dayton was afraid the man was going to break wind one more time, but he didn't. Instead, his fingers worked inside his pants pocket and he pulled out a gold pocket watch. He flipped the ornate lid open and his eyes narrowed.

"About ten to, now," he said.

"Time for us to finish this last cup of coffee then," Dayton said. He felt no urgency to notify Phoenix. He doubted the territorial governor would even be rolling over in bed at this hour.

Webber replaced the watch in his pocket, placed his palms on the table, and laboriously got to his feet. The table rocked under the strain of his bulk. When he'd straightened up, he emitted another resounding fart. The patron at the adjacent table jumped up since he was in the blast zone.

"Take care of that, will ya?" Webber gestured at the plate. "I gotta go do something."

I'll say, Dayton thought, as the two other patrons nearby began waving their hands.

Webber chuckled as he headed for the door with a ponderous wobble. Just as he got there, he let loose with a third, equally smelly fart that had the patrons at the closest tables groaning audibly in outrage and disapproval.

As soon as Hizzoner was out the door someone shouted, "Pee-yew."

Another added, "Good riddance."

"Now is that any way to talk about the leader of our community?" Dayton said with a sly grin. He asked Sally how much he and the mayor owed, and she told him. He reached into his pocket, removed his wallet, and paid her.

She smiled and thanked him, shooting a nasty glance at the door while waving her open palm in front of her face.

Dayton took out some additional coins, and dropped them on the table.

Sally saw that and smiled wider. "Thanks, Sheriff," she said.

The sheriff picked up his hat and placed it on his head, flicking his index finger along the brim in reply as he headed for the door. The residual odor still lingered and he was glad to be getting out of there.

Webber better take a bath and clean up his act if he wants to run for reelection, Dayton thought. *But I suspect he's got bigger things on his mind right now.*

༜

1913
Southern Pacific Railroad Line
Approaching Los Angeles, California

As the train lumbered along through the darkness the three of them sat in the still crowded dining car with, at Bierce's insistence, after-dinner glasses of sherry. The author held up his second glass of the yellowish liquid and frowned.

"Not the best of the vintage," he said. "But definitely a step above the noxious poison that termagant witch tried to ply us with at the whorehouse."

A couple of women in a group seated at the table next to them apparently overheard and glanced over with looks of officious disapproval. Bierce caught a glimpse of their reproachful expressions and turned, extending his hand with the glass in their direction.

"To your good health, ladies," he said, and downed the wine with one long gulp.

Jim took a sip of his, but found the taste too bitter. Still, Bierce was right. The pungent substance back there had soured his taste buds.

Larry downed his drink, slammed the glass down on the table, and grinned.

"You really think them sons of bitches back there was trying to poison us, Mr. Bierce?"

Bierce had removed his pipe and tobacco pouch earlier. He now picked up the pipe and began packing the bowl. It looked to be made out of ivory and was carved in the shape of a bearded man wearing a turban.

"Most assuredly. You'll notice, for instance, the conspicuous absence of those other two impetuous fools who ventured in there before us." He paused, placed the pipe stem between his teeth, and struck a match. The yellow flame flared momentarily with a hiss, and then settled into a steady burning as he held it over the well-packed pipe bowl. "What does their absence suggest to you?"

Larry thought for a moment and then shrugged. "I don't know. What?"

Bierce puffed on the pipe, expelling wispy gray clouds. His eyes went to Jim, who smiled.

"That they got relieved of their money," he said.

Bierce laughed and exhaled an expansive amount of smoke.

"Precisely," Bierce said. "It's the oldest game in the world, and a fitting accompaniment to the world's oldest profession."

Larry compressed his lips. "I guess that woulda been me, too. Had you two not stopped me."

Bierce winked at him and grinned through the haze of smoke.

"A good lesson learned," he said. "Never take your pants off in the presence of a lady you don't know, especially in a house of ill repute, or you'll leave a bit lighter in more ways than one."

Larry snorted and started to bring the empty glass toward his mouth, but stopped as he realized there was nothing in it.

Jim pushed his across the table. He'd barely taken a sip and wasn't feeling the urge. He had the rucksack on the floor next to his right leg, and could feel the weight of the Colt 1911 pressing against the inner portion of his shin.

Cocked and locked. No time for imbibing.

"Here, take mine."

"Thanks, Jim." Larry picked up the glass. His lips curled around the edge and he slurped up half of it. "I don't think this stuff is half bad, Mr. Bierce. Thanks."

Bierce had once again insisted on paying for all three of their meals and the after-dinner drinks.

"Sherry wine originated in Spain," Bierce said. "Once one has tasted the vintage in Europe, your palate is forevermore spoiled. No other substitute will do."

"You been to Europe, have you?" Larry asked.

"I have." Bierce blew out some more smoke and leaned back. Jim thought the man was a bit intoxicated, but he seemed to be handling it well enough.

"In England I was mistaken for Mark Twain on several occasions."

"Mark Twain?" Larry said. "Ain't he dead now?"

Bierce removed the pipe and arched his eyebrows, his head making a slight rocking motion.

"Alas, yes. The greatest writer of my generation, present company excepted, of course." He chuckled as he patted his own chest. "One almost as talented as he was cynical. And in that, he and I share a common bond. The damned human race, he would often say, and all who know me well call me Bitter Bierce."

Jim had read several of Twain's books on the trips over and back from the Philippines and said so. "In addition to yours, Mr. Bierce," he added.

Bierce chuckled. "You flatter me, young man, but the sweetest words to an author's ear are that his work has been appreciated."

"They sure are," Larry said. "Which one of your stories is your favorite?"

Again the author puffed on the pipe in contemplation.

"That's like asking me which of my children I liked the best."

Larry downed the rest of the sherry and got a lopsided grin on his face. "You got lots of kids?"

Bierce sighed.

"I had three," he said. "My one boy was killed, trying too hard to be like me. My second son . . . took his own life." The author paused for several seconds. "And my only daughter will no longer talk to me. My closest and only caring relative now is my niece, which reminds me, I must draft a letter to her."

He resumed smoking and said nothing more. The three of them sat in silence, jostling with the swaying motion of the train car.

Presently, the conductor came walking down the aisle. When he reached their table, he stopped.

"Been looking for you three," he said. "What the hell happened back there at the rest stop?"

"Why do you ask?" Jim said.

The conductor tilted his head to the side and squinted down at them. "Them two gents that got off with you been sitting there shaking and damn near crying since you all came back. Plus, I thought I heard some gunshots."

Jim didn't like being looked down upon and bristled.

"Why don't you ask them?" he said.

"I did," the conductor said. "They wouldn't say. So I'm asking you."

Jim started to rise but Bierce placed a hand on his shoulder and kept it there.

"Let us just say," the author said, "that the old adage that a fool and his money are soon separated is most applicable in this case. They were lucky to escape with their skins intact, as were we."

The conductor's expression hardened.

"What about them gunshots?"

Jim was about to answer when he felt the gentle squeeze of the author's fingers.

"I suggest," Bierce said, directing a hard stare at the conductor, "that you inquire about that with your cohorts at the establishment on the return trip. And do give them our regards."

The conductor pursed his lips but said nothing. The scowl never left his face as he turned and strode away with brisk, purposeful steps.

When he'd gone Larry leaned forward. "You think he was in on it, Mr. Bierce?"

"Most definitely. You'll recall that he was most selective in his recommendations regarding our stopover, singling out only those male passengers who were without the encumbrance of family or female companionship." Bierce paused and licked his lips. "A stopping place such as that, not far off, pardon the irony, the beaten track, does not spring up out of serendipity."

Twin vertical lines appeared between Larry's eyebrows. "Serendipity?"

"He gets a cut," Jim said. "A pimp on a train, steering potential clientele over to that little shack to get waylaid." He turned to Bierce. "You happen to notice that area next to that place back there?"

Bierce nodded solemnly, removed the pipe, and said, "Wildflowers aplenty. The traditional symbol of an unmarked grave. I would venture to guess that more than one poor unfortunate traveler has met his end at that point, to be seen no more."

"You mean you think they was gonna kill us?" Larry said.

"Rob us, most likely," Jim said. "Then kick our asses and send us limping back to the train."

Larry blew out a breath. "Damn. I guess I'm damned lucky, then."

"We're *all* damned lucky, my boy," Bierce said. "But not because of that little foray back there. We've all faced death and debauchery and emerged unscathed, for the most part. That is good cause to celebrate. Shall we have another sip of that awful sherry?"

"None for me," Jim said.

Larry started to say something, then looked at Jim, whose expression said it all.

"No, I guess not," Larry said. "I'm glad we'll be getting on another train soon."

"That's right," Bierce said. "You mentioned you were bound for San Diego, didn't you?"

"Right," Jim said. "We're switching to the Atchison, Topeka and Santa Fe line in Los Angeles."

"As am I," Bierce said. "The three who rode together continues."

"You're going to San Diego too?" Larry asked.

Bierce puffed on the pipe a few times. The red ashes glowed brightly on the top of the carved man's turban.

"I've been on a long trek," he said. "It began in Washington, D.C., where I rid myself of some vestiges of the past, then I revisited some old haunts of my youthful misadventures in those battlefields of yore, and then decided I needed to travel to San Francisco to tie up some loose ends and also to see the ocean one more time."

"And where you going now, sir?" Larry asked.

"I'm heading to Mexico."

"Mexico?" Jim said. "Supposed to be a lot going on down there, and none of it good. A revolution. Lots of killing."

"And possibly a last hurrah for an old warrior," Bierce said. "A chance to revisit the misplaced glory of the past."

Sounds like he's searching for something, Jim thought. *Or maybe he's like me, running from those old ghosts that still come visiting in his dreams.*

❧

1880
Telegraph Office
Contention City, Arizona

When Dayton entered the telegraph office about five minutes later, his nose twitched. He thought he detected Mayor Webber's oppressive and foul stench and wondered how it could possibly have followed him all the way down here from the restaurant. The telegraph clerk, Ed Macy, sat hunched behind the counter with a dispirited expression on his face. Macy was whip thin and bald on top, with a longish, unkempt fringe of dark brown hair going around above each ear. He wore a little green visor on his forehead.

"Leave that door open, would ya?" he said.

Dayton paused and left it ajar.

"Gladly," he said. "You been having gut trouble or something?"

Macy's dejected look deepened.

"Not hardly," he said. "That was compliments of our beloved mayor. He was just in here sending a telegram."

That piqued Dayton's interest.

"Oh? To who?"

"Well . . ." Macy paused and pursed his lips. "He told me not to tell nobody. Dammit, I shouldn't a said nothing to ya."

Dayton grinned. "I'm the sheriff."

"Yeah, but he's the mayor."

Waving his hand in front of his face, Dayton said, "Yeah, that's true. No mistaking he was here, either."

Macy's nose wrinkled as he got up from behind the desk and ambled to the counter.

"That big, fat son of a bitch. Waddling in here and shouting orders at me to hurry my ass up and send this telegram, stinking and farting and ordering me around like I was some nobody. Why, I learned to read Morse code in the army."

Dayton was still curious about the mayor's telegram and saw his chance. "I know. We sure would miss a lot if you weren't around here, Ed. And don't think a lot of folks hereabouts don't appreciate it."

Macy's lower lip engulfed his upper and he nodded.

"You're damn right, Lon. And I appreciate you saying so. Now, you say you got a telegram you want to send?"

Dayton nodded and motioned for the pad so he could write out his telegram.

Macy grabbed the pad and a pencil, started to hand them across the counter, and then stopped. Instead, he hastily scribbled some words and shoved the pad toward Dayton.

The sheriff rotated it slowly and read the message.

Norman Burnside Pinkerton Detective Agency Continental Building San Francisco, California.

Dayton raised his eyes to Macy, who was grinning. "Like I told ya, he said not to *tell* anybody. Didn't say nothing about writing."

Macy winked at Dayton, who grinned back.

The message surprised him.

The Pinkertons?

Dayton had dealt with them a time or two, and didn't like Burnside much. He was an arrogant, cocky little bastard who strutted around, acting like he was Wyatt Earp or Bat Masterson.

"What else did his message say, Ed?"

The telegram operator reached up and scratched his temple, then wiped his palm over the smooth expanse of scalp.

"Ed?" Dayton said.

Macy took in a deep breath, then let it out with a rush of words: "It just said for him to come here and bring a bunch of men."

It was about what Dayton had expected, but the mayor's reasoning perplexed him.

If the mayor felt I needed help, Dayton thought, *why the hell didn't he just say so back at the restaurant? Was he worried the gang would tear apart the town? That I couldn't handle it?*

The idea of deputizing a few men had already occurred to Dayton, but the notion of having to deal with a bunch of Pinkertons was off-putting. They were fairly competent, but their allegiance was to their employer, and not about upholding the law. Hired mercenaries, usually working for the railroads or the group of rich elitists who ran things. And they'd skedaddle once the gunplay was done, leaving the townsfolk, and Dayton, to clean up the resulting mess.

Maybe Hizzoner was interested in something else . . . The reward. Five thousand dollars was a substantial temptation. For a moment Dayton entertained the fancy for himself. With that kind of money, he could buy a nice spread, maybe ask Miss April to marry him.

He sighed and knew he would have to talk to the mayor about this matter, but first things first. Dayton knew he had to confirm the territorial governor was on board with making good his offer of granting amnesty to the Bascom gang, and then figure out the details of how to make it come off as peaceably as possible. The last thing Dayton wanted was something to go wrong and a lot of shooting to start. With the Pinkertons here, it diminished his overall control of the situation.

"Sheriff?" Macy's voice was timid, inquisitive.

Dayton looked up.

"You ain't gonna say nothing about that," Macy said. "Are ya?"

"About what?" Dayton tore the sheet from the pad and crumpled it into a ball.

Macy's lips worked into a smile, but he looked more nervous than gratified.

Dayton thought about how to word his message, and wrote out a short note regarding the possibility of the Bascom gang applying for amnesty. After he finished writing, he looked up at Macy.

"Ed, I'm trusting you." Dayton kept his voice low and even. "This has to stay between us for the time being. Understand?"

Macy's eyes widened as he read the printing.

"So that's why he wants them Pinkertons here?"

It was starting to spiral out of control already.

Dayton tapped his extended index finger on the paper.

"Send it and forget you saw it," he said. "And come get me when the reply comes. Understand?"

Macy swallowed hard, the smile passing from his face. He nodded, went to the telegraph, and started tapping.

Nothing to do now but wait, Dayton thought.

And he hated waiting.

Chapter 4

1913
Railroad Station
Atchison, Topeka, & Santa Fe Line
San Diego, California

The sound of the air brakes as the train did its slow skid into the San Diego station, the end of the line, made Jim think of the squeal of a bunch of pigs about to be led to the slaughterhouse. He hoped that he and Larry would meet a better fate. The dreams of Bud Bagsak and the volcanic crater on the mountain had revisited him once more as he attempted to sleep on the final leg of their train ride. He'd awoken again in a cold sweat with Bierce, who was seated right across from him, staring at him like some all-knowing soothsayer and slowly nodding his head.

Had the same dreams haunted Bierce before?

Jim wanted to ask him, but didn't. There was no sense to it. And anyway, it was his problem, nobody else's.

Would they ever go away?

Maybe Bierce knew. He seemed to know a lot and was an intelligent man . . . a famous writer. Surely he had the answers Jim sought. But now they'd arrived and it looked as though there would be no time to ask him.

The train slowed some more and then jerked to a full stop. People rose and began collecting their belongings. As Jim stood up, his hand squeezed his rucksack to make sure the Colt was still there.

It was, and this gave him a feeling of reassurance.

Larry was laboriously rising to his feet. Bierce was still sitting, digging in his carpetbag.

"Here," the author said. "I've been meaning to give you this."

He held out a worn-looking magazine with a battered cover and yellowed pages. Jim accepted it and looked at the faded cover. It was soiled and torn, but he was able to discern the title. *Town Topics: The Journal of Society.* The full publication information could not be read, save for the date: 1893.

Twenty years old, Jim thought. *He's carried this for a long time.*

"What is this, Mr. Bierce?" he asked.

The author's face flickered into a grin.

"Ambrose," he said. "We've been through enough that you can call me that. And Mr. Bierce sounds way too formal for brothers of the same struggle."

What struggle?

Was he talking about the dreams?

They must haunt him too, Jim thought.

Perhaps it would be that way for both of them . . . For the rest of their lives.

Jim was distressed by that possibility, but the author's gift touched him. He smiled. In the short time they'd known each other, he'd felt a strange kinship with this man.

Brothers of the same struggle.

"Turn to the table of contents," Bierce said. "It's been a while and this old, addled brain can't recall on which page my story lies. It's called, 'The Damned Thing,' which in this case is most appropriate."

Jim carefully opened the cover and ran his finger down the listings.

There it was: *"The Damned Thing" by Ambrose Bierce.*

"What is the Damned Thing?" Jim asked.

The author's grin was sly.

"Read it and see. I don't want to color your judgment by saying too much about it."

"All right, I will. Thanks. I'll get this back to you."

Bierce held up his open hands and gave his head a slight shake.

"No matter. I've no use for it."

"But you wrote it."

"More words to be scattered by the winds of time. Inconsequential in the grander scheme of things."

Jim didn't know what to say to that.

The three of them shuffled down the aisle letting Larry lead the way, ambling along with his stiff leg and cane. This Pullman car appeared to be a bit older and less elegant than the previous one on the Southern Pacific. It was less crowded as well. When they emerged onto the platform, the afternoon sun was just starting to fade from the effulgence of midday.

"Larry," a feminine voice called out. They turned and saw a heavyset woman trotting toward them, followed by a one-armed man. The expression on the woman's face reflected pure delight.

"It's my sister and her husband." Larry dropped his rucksack onto the thick wooden planks of the platform and steadied himself. He was nearly bowled over as the woman collided with him and wrapped her arms around him. Jim reflexively reached out and grabbed Larry's shoulder, keeping him from toppling.

"Easy, sis, easy," Larry said. "I ain't got no balance much anymore."

The one-armed man stood behind them with a wide grin spread over his face.

Finally, the woman released Larry. He stumbled back and caught himself. The one-armed man extended his right arm. The sleeve under his left shoulder hung down a few inches and then terminated in a thick knot.

"Welcome home, Larry," he said.

Larry shook the man's hand and then turned to make the introductions.

"This is my sister, Donna, and her husband, Richard Phipps." Larry indicated Jim. "This is Jim Bishop, the man who saved my life for sure."

Phipps extended his good arm once again.

"Pleasure to meet you," he said. "We owe you a lot for saving Larry."

"I didn't do that much," Jim said.

"Like hell," Larry said. "Why, he—"

Jim held up his hands and shook his head. "They don't need to hear all that."

Larry's jaw jutted out, his mouth gaping.

"Hell, Jim, without you, I'da been a goner." He turned back to his sister and brother-in-law. "Why, you should see the dandy medal he won. Go on, show it to 'em, Jim. It's a real beaut."

Jim shook his head.

Larry frowned, in puzzlement and a little in dismay. "Well, all right then. But it's real swell, believe me. He's a hero. Saved my sorry ass. I'da been dead if he wouldn't have saved me."

Jim was beginning to feel uncomfortable.

"And this fella," Larry continued, "is the famous author, Mr. Ambrose Bierce."

Both of the Phippses smiled, but it looked doubtful that either of them knew who Bierce was. Richard Phipps extended his good arm again.

"Pleased to meet you, sir."

"The pleasure is all mine." Bierce shook the other man's hand.

"I wonder what time it is now," Phipps said, glancing around. "Sure wish there was a clock around here."

Bierce pulled back the lapel of his jacket and removed the gold watch from his vest pocket. "It's one-forty-five."

Phipps eyed the gold lid as Bierce snapped the watch shut and replaced it in his vest.

"Well," Phipps said. "If we hurry back, we can give you something to eat. Teresa and her father are probably just cleaning up from lunch."

"That sure sounds good," Larry said, slapping his belly. "I ain't had nothing but a pair of stale biscuits since Mr. Bierce bought us dinner last night."

Phipps raised his eyebrows.

"Shucks, Mr. Bierce. You're welcome to come, too."

"We got room in the wagon for all of y'all," Donna Phipps added.

Jim turned to watch Bierce's reaction, hoping the author would in fact come along.

"Do you run a restaurant?" Bierce asked.

"Shucks, no," Phipps said. "We're cooks for this motion picture company. Thunderhead Motion Pictures Studio. Owned and run by a Mr. Franklin Creighton. He's a real tycoon. They're down here making moving pictures and me and Donna help fix all the food."

"We're hoping to get Larry and Jim jobs with us," Donna Phipps said.

Hoping?

Jim now wondered just how solid the job offer was. Larry had told him it was all but assured.

"Don't mind if I do," Bierce said. "It might be interesting to see firsthand how Mr. Edison's new invention is being promulgated."

"Proma what?" Phipps asked.

Bierce laughed and clapped Phipps on the shoulder, above the stump on his left arm.

"Come along," he said. "The mess tent awaits, and as some of us know too well, an army travels on its stomach."

The three of them followed the Phipps couple off the platform and past the wooden station house. As they came to the front of the building, Jim saw a small crowd had gathered around a long metallic wagon with no attachment for a horse.

"It's a Ford truck," Phipps said. "We use it for hauling people and supplies. Works real good, so long as you got gasoline."

The truck looked sort of like a traditional wagon with small wheels, but the whole thing was a little bit longer. The cab portion of the thing had two seats, separated by a long metal rod running perpendicular to the base frame. A small wheel on another rod rose up from the floorboards at an acute angle, and three pedals were on the floor portion. A solid horizontal shelf had a framed pane of glass encased in a metal frame perched upon the angular abutment Phipps called the hood. A crank was centered on the very front end. The rear portion had a metal shelf that extended back from the cab with wooden planks forming a pen of some sort. The four wheels had thick metal spokes molded into metallic rims that were encased in rubber tires.

"Gosh," Larry said. "We riding in that?"

"Sure are," Phipps said. "Mr. Creighton—he's the boss, let me borrow it. We use it for hauling stuff around to the different places."

"Excellent," Bierce said. "A comfortable and expeditious ride, without the inconvenience of those unavoidable and periodic odiferous and pernicious excretions of the horse."

Jim snorted a laugh. This would be a first for him, riding in a horseless carriage, but he had, after all, just come off of a train. The world was expanding and changing. There was no doubt about that. Glancing over the top of the roofed cab, Jim saw Phipps bending over in front of the vehicle and rotating the crank to the twelve o'clock position.

"Got to start the engine this way," he said, and gave the crank a few more quick rotations.

After a couple of turns a sputtering sound emanated from under the hood. The noise ceased abruptly and Phipps gave the crank another fast turn. The engine came to life again, belching a dark plume of smoke from a pipe sticking out of the rear of the vehicle, punctuated by a loud crack that sounded like a gunshot.

Jim automatically assumed a crouching position. Larry and Bierce did as well. A horse towing a wagon that had been coming up alongside them suddenly lurched and whinnied. The horse tried sidestepping away and the wagon jerked, jarring the driver.

"Damn infernal things," the wagon driver shouted, his expression a glare of anger.

"What the hell was that?" Jim asked.

Phipps was locking the crank back in place.

" 'Twas just a backfire," he said. "Happens sometimes, especially when you're starting it. Go ahead and hop up in back."

Now the engine noise had changed to a constant, rhythmic purring with only an occasional popping sound. Jim knew the truck ran on gasoline and oil. After a few moments the sputtering leveled out.

Climbing into the bed of the truck proved a bit too difficult for Larry with his stiff leg, so his sister insisted he ride in the front passenger seat with her husband. She went back and stepped on the metal rung about two feet off the ground that was affixed to the frame of the vehicle. Jim helped her up and then he and Bierce ascended as well. Jim was surprised to see a wooden bench lined both sides of the raised truck bed. Donna Phipps plopped herself down on the right-side bench and gestured for them to be seated on the left.

Phipps pushed one of the pedals down and manipulated the shift lever to a forward position. The truck lurched forward with a jerk and they began a relatively quick pace down the street. Phipps kept yelling for pedestrians and people in horse-drawn wagons to get out of the way. He occasionally reached over and squeezed a large rubber ball that omitted a strange blaring sound. As they got clear of the other traffic, the truck accelerated to a pace that surprised Jim and reminded him of the train.

The farther they went, the bumpier it got. The wind resistance increased, too. Both Jim and Bierce removed their hats so the wind merely ruffled their hair, but after a sudden gust Donna Phipps's bonnet blew off and was gone in an instant. Her face twisted into a sour expression as the garment tumbled along the roadway. The ride itself was a lot bumpier than riding a horse, and for Jim a lot more unpleasant. His butt hit hard against the wooden seat each time they rolled over a substantial rut, and he didn't think this relatively new invention would ever catch on.

Jim leaned back, trying to stretch a bit, and caught a glimpse of what looked like some kind of settlement up ahead. A large tent, some wooden buildings, horses, and people. Quite a few people, all milling about. A big sign on the left read in bold black letters: *THUNDERHEAD MOTION PICTURES STUDIO*. There was a profile of an Indian wearing a full feathered headdress below the lettering.

Looks like we're here, Jim thought.

1880
Sheriff's Office
Contention City, Arizona

Dayton didn't have to wait long for the territorial governor's reply. Approximately two hours after he'd sent the telegram, he was seated behind his desk with his gun unloaded, running a cleaning rod through the barrel, when Mayor Webber, Martin Lipton, Fred Dyer, and that reporter, William Bradford Cox, came marching into his office. Hizzoner hadn't bothered to put on a shirt or change out of his dirty undershirt. The grayish stubble of the morning still resided on his hefty cheeks. Lipton wore a black jacket over a white shirt and his chin was in need of a shave as well. The man had dark hair and mutton-chop sideburns that covered both cheeks and met up with a thick mustache. Dyer was not clean-shaven either and wore no jacket. His blue shirt had three concentric white rings of dried perspiration decorating each armpit. Dayton wondered if the man had slept in his clothes. The only one of the quartet who'd managed to get a shave in was the reporter, Cox. He alone looked rather fresh and dapper in a brown suit and derby hat.

Lipton glared down at the unloaded pistol and the six rounds sitting on the desk, then thrust a paper, obviously written on the tablet from the telegraph office, across to Dayton.

"Here, Sheriff," he said. "This is from the governor."

Dayton set his Colt Peacemaker down and took a look at the telegram. The first thing he noticed was that it was addressed to Lipton rather than to him.

> *INSTRUCT SHERIFF THAT*
> *AMNESTY PACKETS ARE APPROVED*
> *AND FORTHCOMING STOP MAKE*
> *OTHER ADJUSTMENTS AS PREVIOUSLY*
> *DISCUSSED STOP*
> *JCF*

Dayton wondered about the wording of that last statement. *Make other adjustments as previously discussed.*

He handed the paper back to Lipton and resumed the task of cleaning his weapon.

"Good to know," he said, glancing toward Webber. "We'll have to start making some special preparations for this, won't we?"

Webber's face flushed.

"I sent a telegram to the governor myself this morning," Dayton said. "Any idea why he didn't respond directly back to me?"

Lipton's eyes flashed toward the mayor and then back to Dayton. He smiled.

"Not to worry, Sheriff. I'm sure he assumed we'd be working together on this. I am the governor's liaison man, after all."

"What are the other adjustments he's referring to?"

"Well . . ." Lipton's tongue flicked out and darted over his lips. "As you know, the governor was appointed by President Hayes, and we're well on the way to applying for statehood, once the territory becomes completely civilized. When we originally discussed our progressive plan, amnesty wasn't on the table. But now that we've hopefully gotten that heathen, Geronimo, under control, we felt it would be prudent to clean up the remaining outlaw bands as expediently as possible. Thus, the offer of amnesty came up."

"Lord knows they've been a bane on the railroads," Dyer added.

"Not to mention the banks," said Webber.

Dayton wanted to ask him if that was why he'd contacted the Pinkertons, but didn't want to betray Macy's confidence. He was still seated and didn't like being in a subservient position to this quartet.

"I'm still waiting to hear about those other adjustments." He held the Colt at an angle so he could inspect the barrel.

Webber's eyes shot toward Lipton, who said, "Safety precautions, of course. While we can assume that Bascom and his gang intend to surrender themselves, we can't be caught off guard, can we?" His mouth twisted into a sly grin.

"For instance, it doesn't pay to let your guard down. One must be vigilant at all times. As a lawman, you'd do well to remember that." He smirked, then reached inside his coat and started to withdraw a pistol. "Just like this."

Dayton's hand shot down to his belt and he brought up his second gun, a dandy little double-action Colt Lightning revolver, before Lipton's gun had cleared its shoulder holster. The government man froze, his mouth tightening.

"I was just trying to demonstrate a point, Sheriff." Lipton's Adam's apple shifted up and down like a child's yo-yo. "No sense getting upset about it. Didn't mean to provoke you."

"You didn't," Dayton said. "But you'd do well to remember never to pull a gun on a man unless you have cause and intent to use it."

"Where did that other gun come from?" Dyer said, his eyes wide open in amazement. "I thought yours was on the desk there?"

Dayton said nothing. His gaze was still focused on Lipton.

"I was just trying to make a point," the government man repeated. He gently pressed his own weapon back into its resting place. "Please, it might go off."

"Lon," Webber muttered. "For Christ's sake."

"Another good rule to follow," Dayton said, standing and then slipping the Lightning back into his belt holster, "is never to clean your gun without having another one close by."

His gaze went to each of the quartet's faces and it gave him a sense of gratification that he was taller than all of them. He picked up the cleaning rod, affixed a small piece of material over the end, and rammed it down the barrel of the Peacemaker. After withdrawing it and inspecting the material, he set the rod down and started loading the weapon.

"Impressive, Sheriff," Lipton said. "And we're certain that you're capable of handling this matter, but we still think some additional preparations would be prudent."

After he'd loaded the last of the six cartridges into the Peacemaker, Dayton placed it in his holster without affixing the leather thumb strap that secured the weapon.

"Funny you should say that," Dayton said. "I was mulling over who I was going to deputize for this big event."

"Deputize?" Webber frowned. "Now look, Lon, you've done a fabulous job of cleaning up this town and the area around it. And we appreciate it. But most of them young guns you hired back in the day to help moseyed away once things got quiet. I know you still have Elmer Abbey to help out, but he's mostly busy running his blacksmith shop."

A smile crept over Dayton's lips.

"You suggesting bringing in some outside help, then?" he asked. He'd almost added "The Pinkertons."

Webber's mouth gaped as he struggled for a response.

"That's exactly what we mean," Lipton said. "We're thinking of hiring some help. A group of professionals. To augment your forces, so to speak."

Dayton pretended to consider this, tilting his head to the side.

"Got anybody in particular in mind?"

"Pinkertons," Dyer said. "We use them on the railroad all the time and they're very professional. I can vouch for them. There's a man named Norman Burnside I can highly recommend."

"Is that so?" Dayton cast a sideways glance at the mayor.

"We have to be sure we can trust these outlaws," Lipton said.

"Or that they'll even show up," Dyer added.

"Good point," Hizzoner said. "How do we know they even mean to show?"

"Well," Dayton said, "I'll have to verify that."

"How?" Webber said.

Oh," Dayton slowly rotated his head a little. "I got a hunch I'll be hearing something from them, one way or another, before too much longer."

❧

1913
Thunderhead Motion Pictures Lot
Near San Diego, California

Jim took a look around as he jumped down from the bed of the truck. The large tent was close to the entrance and the Thunderhead sign. Beyond that a ramshackle town extended down the dusty street. People were meandering away from the tent, which was open on the sides and perhaps thirty feet square and had numerous picnic tables and chairs under its awning. The side flaps were rolled up, allowing a free flow of air, and at the moment it was sparsely populated. Perhaps half a dozen people sat at the head table at the far region next to what appeared to be the chow line. Big metal bowls were lined up on two tables fitted end to end. A large metallic urn that Jim figured contained coffee sat on the one nearest to where they stood. He considered how good a cup of java would taste right now.

A collection of dishes, cups, and silverware littered the tops of the empty tables. Two people, a man and a woman, went from table to table picking up the items. The man was middle-aged and dressed in stained cook whites. The woman was younger, with long black hair braided and stuck up onto the back of her head. Her skin was a darker shade than the man's.

Mexican, probably, Jim thought as he admired her hourglass figure.

He started to extend his hand upward to assist Donna Phipps in her descent from the truck, but Bierce had already beaten him to it. The author shot him a quick wink. Donna's broad face held a big smile, but when she was on the ground she passed a hand over her scalp, smoothing out her hair as best she could.

"Lord, I must look a fright," she said. "If only I had my bonnet."

Jim felt a twinge of guilt that he hadn't jumped off the truck and retrieved it.

"It was given to me by my mother," Donna said. Her face had a forlorn, almost wistful expression now.

"Perhaps we can go back and look for it," Jim said. "It can't have blown too far."

Donna compressed her lips and then shook her head.

"It don't matter none," she said. "We got more pressing things to be concerned with. Let's go talk to Mr. Tucker about getting you and Larry hired on here."

Jim thought he detected a hint of anxiety lingering around her eyes. Again, he wondered if Larry's emphatic promise that the jobs were theirs for the taking might be a bit overblown.

Nothing's a sure thing, he thought. *I'd best remember that.*

He'd already made up his mind that if there was only a position for one of them, he'd back out and give it to Larry.

Richard Phipps had gotten out of the truck, as had Larry, and Phipps headed straight for the huge tent.

Bierce touched Jim's arm.

"I'd best stay here," he said. "Lest someone think I'm amongst those seeking employment."

Jim gave a quick nod.

Donna quickly went to the tables and started assisting the man and the woman in clearing the dishes, cups, and silverware. Jim and Larry trailed behind her husband as he walked up to the only table that was still occupied. As they went past, Jim stole another quick glance at the Mexican girl clearing the tables, catching a glimpse of her profile. He liked what he saw. Her features had something of a European cast to them. She was kind of pretty, with skin the color of light cinnamon, which made him figure that she wasn't full-blooded Mexican, but possibly mixed.

"Howdy, Mr. Creighton," Phipps said, a grin plastered over his face. "I sure appreciate the use of the truck, sir."

An older man wearing a white starched shirt spotted with dust and a tan Panama hat stopped talking and looked up. A pair of dark glasses obscured his eyes and his face was craggy, with a long, aquiline nose jutting outward like the beak of a hawk. He held a silver cigarette case that was partially open.

"What's that?" His voice had a high, nasally whine to it.

Phipps removed his hat.

"The delivery truck, sir," he said. "I already told Mr. Tucker. Me and the missus had to go into town to pick up her brother and his friend." He used his good arm to indicate Jim and Larry.

Creighton gave an irritated little bob of his head and went back to his conversation with one of the men on his left, a sallow, waspish guy with his thinning hair slicked straight back on his head. He wore a gray tweed double-breasted suit that hung loosely on his sparse frame. A cigarette smoldered between his fingers.

As they stood waiting, Jim did a quick assessment of the others seated there. To Creighton's right was a big guy with a handsome face. His broad shoulders stretched the fabric of his light blue shirt, which had a row of circular brass buttons up each side and along the top. He was leaning back, smoking a long cigar, and seemed not to be paying much attention to the conversation. Next to him was one of the most beautiful girls Jim had ever seen. Blond ringlets hung next to an angelic face, and he felt transfixed. She glanced at him briefly and then heaved a sigh, her heavily made-up eyelids hooding her eyes like a resting falcon. Her expression was one of utter boredom. On the other side of the table, next to the waspish fellow, a heavyset man was wiping his flushed face with a handkerchief. This one had beefy jowls and a corpulent body to match.

The final figure at the table wasn't seated at all. He was standing, and he cast an oblique glance at Jim and Larry. A trail of dark stubble tracked over his cheeks from a pair of long sideburns and extended over his chin, which had a cleft in the center. His long, drooping mustache was ebony and his outfit, trimmed with silver decorations suspended by black leather thongs, all combined to say one thing: *vaquero*. He also wore leather chaps and had long spurs on his boots. An unlit hand-rolled cigarette dangled between his lips.

"We've got to get this next scene shot," Creighton was saying. "We'll be running out of daylight before too much longer."

"Frank," the waspish man said, "there's still plenty of light left. If we're going to finish on schedule . . ." He had a short-brimmed black hat on and a pencil-thin mustache. His dark eyes darted around like a weasel's.

"Like hell." Creighton's head shook infinitesimally. He brought the cigarette to his lips and began patting his pockets.

The waspish man brought out a box of matches from his own pocket, opened it, and struck the primer on the scratch pad. The flame hissed slightly and he held it toward Creighton.

The other man leaned forward and stuck the end of his cigarette into the flame.

"Well, maybe," Creighton relented. "But we've got to keep on schedule. It's important that we have this whole thing wrapped up and delivered by the end of the month. And at the rate that idiot Monroe is going on producing those new pages—"

"He's an artist," the jowly, heavyset man said. "He's working on them now. He even skipped lunch, for the love of Christ."

"Aw, shut up, Howard," Creighton said. "You don't know the pressure I'm under. With that son of a bitch Klayman riding me every chance he gets."

The heavyset man's mouth twisted into a frown, but he remained silent.

"Take it easy, Frank," the waspish man said. "We both know Monroe's got the right stuff. He can make anything work. And Howard here's the best cameraman in the business."

"Speaking of which . . ." The heavyset man laboriously got to his feet. "If we're going to shoot that next scene, you, little lady, need to get to makeup."

"Faith looks good without any touchups," the broad-shouldered guy in the fancy shirt said. He blew a plume of smoke toward her face. She puffed a breath and waved her hand.

"Those things are disgusting," she said.

"Miss Faith Stewart," the heavyset man said, beaming. "The most fetching face in all of motion pictures. Makes Mary Pickford look like your cousin's sister."

The beautiful girl looked up at him and smiled.

Jim definitely agreed. She was *the* most beautiful girl he'd ever seen.

She stood and slapped the big, broad-shouldered guy seated next to her. "Ready, Artie?"

Her voice was mellifluous too. She was wearing a white satin blouse, the pockets embroidered with red arrows. And brown pants, tucked into the tops of a pair of tall leather riding boots. Jim couldn't help but admire her gorgeous figure, which was accentuated by the snug-fitting clothes.

Man, he thought. *She's something.*

Art took another puff on his cigar and stood up.

Jim noticed that the guy was tall. About as tall as he was, or maybe just a little taller.

"I'm raring to go," Art said.

His voice had a distinctive accent, but Jim couldn't quite place it. He'd heard a lot of different accents from troops over in the Philippines. He'd served with men from all over the United States, most of them Southern boys. This one definitely wasn't one of those, nor was it of the Midwestern variety such as his own.

Everyone else stood too. The vaquero adjusted a long wooden match in his fingers and flicked a heavy thumbnail over the end of it, erupting it into flame. He held it to the tip of his cigarette.

"Lobo," the waspish man said, "make sure the mount's saddled for Miss Stewart, will you?"

"*Es* no problem," the Mexican said. "I already *haf* Gordo seeing to it."

"Well, check anyway," Creighton said. "I don't like the idea of her riding that thing, even if it's only for a short distance."

"Oh, Frank," the beautiful girl said. "Will you relax. I've done plenty of riding before. And besides, at least it's not one of those silly sidesaddles."

"Remember," Creighton said with a sly smile. "You're playing a cowgirl schoolmarm here. Don't forget that."

"How can I?" Several of the blond curls fell over her shoulder as she canted her head and strolled away, her arm hooked under the tall guy's forearm. "You keep reminding me at every shoot."

All of the male eyes watched her departure, and then the men started to depart as well. As the Mexican they'd called Lobo walked by, Jim noticed a distinctive, sweet-smelling odor coming from his cigarette. It didn't smell like tobacco.

"Ah, Mr. Tucker," Phipps said. He'd been standing almost motionless. "Could I talk to you a minute, sir?"

The waspish man turned and put his hat on his head.

"Yeah, what is it?" His tone was rapid and harsh.

Jim wasn't getting a good feeling about this.

"Well, sir," Phipps said. "It was like I was telling you, my brother-in-law here and his friend just come back from fighting over in the Philippines and they ain't in the army no more so they was hoping to get a job and we sure could use some help in the kitchen here. So I was thinking—"

"Nah, nah, nah, nah," Tucker said in a rapid-fire burst, waving his hand dismissively. "This is a motion picture set, not a charity enterprise."

He started walking in the direction the others had gone.

"But, sir," Phipps said. "We really do need the help. Why, it'd give Mr. Delacroix more time to do the cooking. And they're swell at washing dishes. They were cooks in the army and all."

Cooks in the army?

Where did that come from?

Jim was about to laugh, if the situation hadn't been so humorless. He looked at Larry, and then at his brother-in-law, who had an equally pained expression on his face.

"Rich," Jim said. "It's all right. We'll find something."

Phipps looked on the verge of tears. "But—"

"Ex-soldiers, huh?" Tucker said over his shoulder. "Give 'em something to eat and send them on their way."

Phipps took a step forward to follow him but Larry grabbed his brother-in-law's arm.

"Let it go," he muttered. "But we'll take that grub."

Phipps lowered his eyes to the ground and nodded.

"Let me go get Mr. Bierce," Jim said. "We promised him a meal anyway."

As he walked away from the tent the grimness of the situation began to settle over him. He and Larry had used up just about all of their funds buying the tickets for the trip here and they were flat broke.

No money, no prospects. What the hell were they going to do now?

Chapter 5

1880
Main Street
Contention City, Arizona

Dayton had almost finished making his late evening rounds and was appreciating the fact that things seemed pretty quiet tonight. Most of the town was dark and even the Brass Cupcake was practically empty. No poker game for the mayor and his cronies this night. Only a few of the hard-core drinkers like Ike Lords and Terry Talley had bellied up to the bar, and both of them seemed intent on nursing half a bottle between them. Even the bar gals sat at the empty tables looking bored, with no prospects for anyone buying them a drink or maybe taking a trip upstairs.

Suits me fine, Dayton thought. *Now if only the Red Sunset is just as quiet, I could be looking to put my feet up on my desk and relax a bit.*

If relaxation was in the cards at all.

The fire in the circular stone pit adjacent to the Red Sunset saloon had a low flame burning, and the light coming from the inside candles on the chandelier looked weak as well.

If that place was as dead as the Cupcake, it could signal an early night for everybody.

But the somewhat troubling recollection of the day's earlier events still rankled him. The mayor's surreptitious telegram and the subsequent conversation with Hizzoner and his poker buddy cohorts niggled in the back of Dayton's mind like an irritating blister on his heel. He trusted Mayor Webber about as far as he could throw him, and the railroad man, Dyer, and the governor's lackey, Lipton, even less. He'd been thinking about looking into getting some deputies himself, but without a blessing from the mayor, who controlled the purse strings, that could prove problematic. He could hardly expect Elmer Abbey to step up for no or very little pay with the possibility of the Bascom gang riding in to get their amnesty, but also maybe having mayhem on their minds. Elmer had a business to run and had just gotten married the year before. He and his wife were expecting. And with this Pinkerton character, Burnside, coming in, it almost had the feel of a gunfight in the making. One thing for sure, if Dutch and his boys did ride in and trouble started, they wouldn't be going down easy.

Dayton drew in a deep breath of the night air. It had a certain coolness to it, after the oppressive heat of the day. That was the desert this time of year for you—hotter than hell during daylight, and suddenly cool after the sun went down. Lots of contradictions.

Speaking of contradictions, he told himself, trying to think about more positive things. Those wildflowers he'd noticed this morning behind the Red Sunset were in full bloom. The pretty little yellow things were a far cry from red roses, but they'd make a nice bouquet that he could take down to the school and give to Miss April May Donovan. Maybe even ask her to go on a picnic with him come the weekend. He wasn't getting any younger and if he ever wanted to marry and start a family, the time was getting close.

Close, hell, he thought. *The September Gun . . . That's me.*

He quickened his steps and listened to the echo of his boots on the wooden boardwalk in front of the array of shops—the general store, Doc Weems's place, the newspaper office, attorney-at-law Carson Tidwell's office, and the sheriff's office. He paused and looked in the big front window of the general store. A nice polka-dot bonnet sat prominently on a wooden display, a matching parasol lying in front of it.

Did a schoolmarm need a bonnet?

What about a parasol?

And how much were they?

The thinness of his wallet was always a factor, and would either or both of any such gifts impress the lady?

He contemplated how little he knew about the female persuasion as he turned and resumed his walk toward the other saloon. Everything seemed quiet down the street. No sign of any rowdies.

Just as he came abreast of the juncture separating the general store from the adjacent building, a voice emanated from the narrow opening.

"Don't move, and don't go for your gun," the voice said. "I ain't a mind to shoot you, but I will if'n I have to."

There was a youthful quality to the voice. A nervous one, too. It had the sound of someone who didn't want to be there.

"I appreciate that, partner," Dayton said, edging his body sideways to present a narrower target. His right hand dropped down and his thumb flicked off the leather thong that kept his Colt Peacemaker secured in its holster.

"Don't go for your gun, Sheriff," the voice said. "Please. Like I told ya, I'll shoot if'n I have to."

The statement was punctuated by the four distinctive clicks of a Colt pistol's hammer being cocked back.

Dayton figured he had little chance to pull off a clean draw and a quick shot if his adversary already had a gun out and a bead on him. Depending on where exactly in the shadows the man was, Dayton's options were limited even further. Trying to jump off to the side, out of the line of fire, was risky too.

But if he wanted to kill me, Dayton thought, *he could've done it already.*

"I'd prefer you didn't," Dayton said, keeping his voice low and even. "Now why don't you tell me what you want?"

"I—" The hidden voice faltered for a moment, then resumed. "I come to see you for something."

Silence reigned for several seconds.

Finally Dayton took the bait.

"What's that?"

"Dutch's knife," the voice replied.

Dayton felt a slight surge of relief. He'd been expecting that Bascom would be contacting him in some fashion to check on the amnesty deal. This was it. Bascom's emissary.

"Well, I'll be glad to give it to you, but why don't you lower whatever it is you're holding in there and let that hammer down real nice and easy."

"How do I know you won't draw and kill me if'n I do?"

Nothing like facing a nervous man with a gun, Dayton thought.

He could feel the sweat trickle down from his armpit.

"Then," he said, trying to figure out something to say. "Dutch wouldn't get his knife back, would he?"

He managed a smile to show his sincerity, but doubted the other man could discern it in the darkness. Perhaps he would be able to catch a glint of the moonlight off of Dayton's teeth.

More silence, and then the mechanical sound of the hammer's slow release.

"That's better," Dayton said. "You want to come over to my office, I'll give you the knife."

"Huh-uh" the voice said. "They say you're a mighty fast man with a gun. If'n I step out there, how do I know you won't shoot me where I stand?"

"If I had a mind to shoot you, you'd be dead already. I'm assuming Dutch wants to know about the governor's proclamation. Correct?"

"Procal what?"

The word had apparently stymied him.

"The amnesty," Dayton said.

"Yeah."

"You can tell Dutch that everything's been approved. The packets are on their way here."

"And so all we have to do is come in here and give ourselves up and we'll be free?"

"Yep."

Dayton could hear the other man breathing. Some more reassurance was probably needed.

"You got my word on it," he said.

The loud breathing continued, and then the other man said, "How do we know we can trust you? How do we know you ain't gonna shoot us in the back?"

"I ain't never shot a man in the back in my life. You tell that to Dutch. He'll have to trust me on that."

"You got to tell him yourself. He said he wants to look in your eyes."

It was Dayton's turn to fall silent. Bascom was shrewd and smart. He obviously had some sort of plan in mind. The question was, what was it?

"I'm listening," Dayton said.

He heard the other man swallow. He was so close, Dayton could almost discern the outline of his body. The guy wasn't very big at all. Probably the most expendable of the gang.

"I got a couple of horses tied out behind this building," the other man said. "All saddled up."

"And?"

"And, we ride out a ways and meet Dutch. You two talk, then you can ride back. We'll go the other way."

It sounded less than ideal to Dayton. Dangerous and risky, but what other choice did he have. And if they'd meant to kill him, he'd be a dead man already.

"All right," Dayton said. "Let's get moving."

"One thing. Can you go get his knife first?"

"His knife?"

"Yeah. It's sorta like his good luck charm. He wants it back."

Dayton mulled over this latest development. It could be a trap, but like he'd figured it, if they'd wanted him dead, he'd already be so. It was time to show some trust. Besides, Bascom lived by a code, albeit an outlaw's code, but a code nonetheless. And he wouldn't trust a lawman who was afraid to show his face.

Nobody would.

Dayton glanced down the street and saw the barkeep extinguishing the fire in front of the Red Sunset Saloon. A couple of drunks staggered out through the swinging doors. It looked like the town was bedding down for the night.

"The knife's in my desk in my office," he said. "I'll go get it and be right back."

He heard a grunt of approval from the shadows.

It was time to meet Dutch Bascom face to face.

❦

1913
Thunderhead Motion Pictures Lot
Near San Diego, California

Jim mulled over their predicament as he looked for Bierce. They'd come down here on the assumption that they had jobs waiting for them, and now all they had was the probability of a hot meal. At least he hoped it would be hot. He was finding out quickly that guarantees around here were few and far between. He wondered if between him and Larry, they had enough money for a room for the night. But they'd just come from sleeping in tents and out in the jungle, so they could no doubt do the same thing here. And at least here there would be no creeping Moros and their talibongs to worry about.

He searched for Bierce and caught a glimpse of the author's tall figure, lean and ramrod straight, strolling about twenty yards ahead of him toward what appeared to be a collection of wooden buildings along a street that was full of people and a few horses. There were also platforms at various points along the street with several cameras supported on tripods. Men stood looking through them and conversing. As Jim drew closer, he saw that many of the buildings were only halfway completed. The fronts were detailed with signs overhead, windows and doors, making them look like real places, but there were long wooden struts holding them up on the non-street side. Only a few of them appeared to be actual full-frame structures.

It was all some kind of elaborate charade. He wondered how real it would look to the people sitting in those nickelodeons watching it unfold on screen.

Then Jim saw something else that piqued his interest even more. A heavyset Mexican man stood holding the reins of a brown and white horse a bit farther down the street in front of one of the buildings. It looked to be a mare, and next to the horse was the pretty actress he'd seen before at the lunch tent. She was laughing as she tucked her blond ringlets underneath the crown of a wide-brimmed black hat. Jim watched and fantasized momentarily about being there next to her. But hell, he wouldn't even know what to say to a woman like that.

She wouldn't give me the time of day, he thought.

The Mexican vaquero, Lobo, leaned against an old-style hitching post, smoking. Lobo eyed Jim as he walked by, and the distinctive sweet odor from the Mexican's cigarette hung in the air. It didn't smell like tobacco and the Mexican's eyes looked glassy.

Jim took it for marijuana. He'd smelled it a few times over in the Philippines. Some of the Filipinos smoked it. He quickened his pace walking by the vaquero and called out to Bierce. The author paused and half-turned.

"Just gamboling about the town here," Bierce said. "If one could call it that. Fascinating sights, though. A land of make-believe."

"Larry's sister's fixing us a good meal," Jim said. "Thought you might like to get something to eat after that long train ride."

Bierce smiled. "Now that does sound like a tempting offer." He squinted slightly with his right eye. "So I take it you and Larry got the jobs?"

Jim shook his head and took a deep breath.

"No, sir. Looks like this meal's all we're going to get."

"But I thought you said it was all set?"

"That's what we were told, but it looks like that's not the case."

Bierce heaved a sigh. "Promises made and promises broken. A sad testament to the nature of man. I'm sorry to hear that."

"Yeah," Jim said. "Me too."

A Mexican walking another horse brushed by. This one was a big, golden stallion, fully saddled.

Nice-looking horse, Jim thought.

For a moment he entertained the thought of what it would be like to ride such an animal, but then his attention turned back to the beautiful maiden. He glanced down the way again to catch another fleeting glimpse of Faith Stewart, figuring it would be his last.

She was having some difficulty placing her foot in the stirrup of the saddle on the dappled mare. The horse kept sidestepping away from her. The heavyset Mexican bore down on the bridle and the horse stopped.

"Still smitten by Aphrodite, I see," Bierce said.

"I beg your pardon?"

Bierce smiled. "How was it Shakespeare put it? Frailty, thou name is woman."

Jim smiled self-consciously. "He sure was right, but she don't even know I exist."

The author smiled.

"But," Jim said, "I can dream, can't I?"

"Ah, perchance to dream." Bierce placed a hand on Jim's shoulder. "Take heart, my boy. You're young, strong, and have the rest of your life ahead of you. And you've—"

A horse's sudden snort and a woman's scream cut the sentence short. Both Jim and Bierce turned to see Faith Stewart leaning over the saddle on top of the spotted mare, which was bounding down the dirt street in fits and starts, the reins flowing down by the animal's shoulders. The actress clung with both hands on the saddle's pommel in obvious desperation. Her black hat flipped off and spiraled, end over end, as the mare began racing down the street, people dodging out of the frenzied horse's path.

Glancing toward the Mexican walking the big golden stallion, Jim took three long, running steps and then braced both his palms on the animal's flank as he leaped upward. In another second, he was in the saddle. He deftly ripped the reins from the hand of the Mexican attendant and kicked his heels into the horse's side. The beast took off down the street, sending Jim's hat tumbling from his head.

Jim adjusted his legs to match the big stallion's synchronous gait. He transferred the reins to his left hand and reached out with his right, giving the horse's massively thick neck a reassuring rub. The beast appeared to sense that his rider was no threat and the two seemed to bond together in a common purpose, almost as if the animal and man had become one.

Ahead, the painted mare continued its awkward, semi-halting stride, periodically rearing up and then driving its front legs heavily downward with a shake of its body. Faith Stewart screamed again, still gripping the pommel.

With two more long strides, Jim's stallion was next to the paint. He reached out with his right arm and yelled for Faith to let go of the saddle.

Her beautiful face was only inches from his, her blue eyes wide and terror-filled. With his arm around her back and his hand flat against the front of her body, Jim yanked her off the paint and onto his mount. The mare, suddenly relieved of its rider, ceased its awkward thrashing movements and took off at a run. As Jim helped the actress get adjusted behind him on the horse, another animal came dashing up next to them. The rider was a powerfully built black man.

"Miss Faith, you all right?" the man asked.

Jim waited for Faith to reply. He caught a glimpse of her nodding. "I'm fine, Henry," she said. "Thanks to him."

The black man looked Jim up and down and grunted something inaudible, then kicked his horse's flank and rode off after the errant paint with the aplomb of an expert rider.

He'll catch that runaway for sure, Jim thought.

As he was trying to figure what to say to the most beautiful woman he'd ever seen, he became cognizant of her soft breasts pressing against his back and felt an erotic thrill. Her breathing was still elevated and each panting breath heaved against him, renewing his ecstasy.

Another pair of riders shot past them. Two vaqueros, the heavyset one who'd been holding the paint's bridle, and the other one, Lobo. They looked like they knew how to ride pretty well, too.

Jim turned his head toward Faith. "I hope I didn't hurt you none, ma'am."

"What?"

"I mean, pulling you off the horse like that. I had to do it kind of fast."

She leaned her face against the back of his neck.

"Of course not," she said. "You saved my life. Thank you."

Unable to think of any appropriate reply, he merely said, "You're welcome."

A moment later he realized how dumb he must have sounded. He tugged on the reins and steered the horse back toward the main street and a gaggle of men running toward them. As he got amongst them, he saw that the group included the big shots who'd been sitting at the lunch table discussing things. The man with the dark glasses and the hawk-like nose, the one they'd called Creighton, spoke first.

"Faith, darling, honey, sweetheart, are you all right?"

Jim felt her breath along the side of his face as she replied. "Yes. Thanks to him."

Her arms tightened around his chest.

Creighton grinned and nodded at Jim, then reached up and slapped his thigh.

"Good work," he said. "No, make that *excellent* work. Don't go away."

Creighton then turned to one of the others, the big guy he'd called Howard. "Please tell me your cameramen got all that," Creighton said.

Howard was breathing hard, like he'd run all the way, but he smiled and gave a curt nod.

"Good, good," Creighton said. "You make damn sure Monroe inserts that scene into the script."

"Well, I'll talk to him—" Howard scratched his expansive belly.

Creighton shook his head emphatically. "I don't care how he does it, just do it. Understand?"

"Will do, boss," Howard said. More personnel had approached, including the tall, broad-shouldered guy in the fancy shirt and white hat who'd been with them at the luncheon table. He stared up at Faith.

Creighton grunted, swiveled his body, and jammed an extended index finger against the chest of the smaller, waspish man with the pencil-thin mustache.

"Hire this guy, Tucker," Creighton said, flipping his hand back in Jim's direction. "I want him on set from here on out."

"Ah, in what capacity?" the other man asked as he shot a glance up at Jim.

"Do I look like a give a damn?" Creighton said. "His quick actions saved Faith, and with her, the entire motion picture, and my studio as well."

"But—" Tucker started to say.

"No buts, dammit. I want him on set from here on out."

Tucker was shaking his head. "We don't need another cowboy. And we've got Lobo and his boys."

Creighton held up his palm in the other man's face and scrutinized Jim. "He's about the same size as Art. And he can ride, too. Give him a white hat and a decent shirt . . . And if we shoot him at a distance nobody will be able to tell the damn difference."

"Sounds good to me," the tall guy in the fancy shirt said, grinning. "The less time I have to spend on those filthy beasts, the better."

Creighton laughed. "Exactly. Besides, he's my good luck charm."

"Mine too," Faith said, planting a kiss on Jim's cheek and giving his body another luscious squeeze. Jim thought this one had the promise of something more. While it sent a thrill up and down his spine, this whole thing was spinning out of control. He knew what he had to do.

"Excuse me," he said. "Mr. Creighton, sir."

The director looked up at him.

Jim didn't like it that the dark lenses obscured the man's eyes. It made him nervous that he couldn't see them, but he knew what he had to say.

"I appreciate your offer, sir, but my friend Larry is the one that really needs the job. He was wounded over in the Philippines."

Creighton's brow furrowed. "The Philippines?"

"Yes, sir. We were both over there in the war and he got hurt. Real bad."

The motion picture man's face twitched. "But I thought that damn thing was over with a couple of years ago?"

"Not hardly," Jim said. "But it is now."

A smile spread over Creighton's lower face and he chuckled. "I'm glad of that. Otherwise you wouldn't be here." Turning back to Tucker, Creighton said, "Hire his friend, too."

"What? Frank, come on—"

"You heard me. He can help Whitey and Henry with the horses."

"But I told you, payroll's already at capacity. And we got Lobo and his boys—"

"Do it," Creighton said.

Tucker gazed skyward, raised his hands slightly, and then slapped them against his thighs.

Faith squealed in delight and pressed herself against Jim again, planting another kiss on his cheek. The Mexican who'd been smoking the marijuana cigarette came sauntering up, the heavyset guy by his side looking somewhat distressed, as they stopped at the periphery of the crowd.

"Besides," Creighton continued. "We've got more pressing issues. We've already got two reels with Faith's damn horse on film. Where are we going to find another horse with that pattern of distinctive coloring?"

"We ain't gonna have to do that, Mr. Creighton," a deep voice said. "I got something to show y'all."

Jim turned his head and saw the black man riding up to them with the painted mare in tow. The horse was now calm and placid, with no trace of the hysterical movements he'd seen before.

The man knows his horses, he admitted to himself, then felt the delightful sensation of Faith's body constricting against his once more.

I could get real used to this, he thought.

❧

1880
Just outside Contention City, Arizona

As they rode side by side on the trail, the light from the full moon illuminated things well enough that the going wasn't too treacherous. The light also allowed Dayton to discern the youthfulness of the other rider. He was no more than a boy, really. The contours of his face had a vague familiarity as well, and Dayton recalled the photograph of the Bascom gang he'd seen on the *Wanted* poster. The one standing off to the side, trying to muster a hard look on his youthful countenance—it was him.

"What's your name?" Dayton asked.

"Why?"

Dayton could sense the youth's wariness, and he didn't blame him. Bascom had no doubt sent his most expendable man on this mission. He thought about his next words carefully. This was all about building trust.

"Just like to know who I'm dealing with," he said. "So what should I call you?"

The other rider didn't reply at first. Their horses trotted several more steps and then he said, "I guess you're gonna find that out soon enough, ain't ya? It's Hedlund. Bruce Hedlund."

"Bruce?"

"Yep, but they all call me Whitey on account of my hair. Got these white streaks along the front and sides. Was born that way."

The kid's hat obscured any such demarcation at the moment. It had in the photograph as well.

"How old are you, boy?" Dayton asked.

Again, Hedlund didn't answer.

"I asked you—"

"I'm seventeen, dammit. Satisfied?"

That seemed about right. Maybe a bit enhanced.

"How long you been riding with Dutch?"

The young man worked his lips.

"A while, I reckon."

Dayton wondered how many robberies this young guy had participated in and if he'd killed anybody in the process. Dutch Bascom had. Plenty of times, if the legend was to be believed. He was supposed to be a fast gun as well.

"You ever shot anybody?" Dayton asked.

The youth's head swiveled toward him.

"What you asking me that for?"

"Just making conversation. You seem pretty young."

Dayton heard the young man huff.

"But then again," Dayton continued, "they say William H. Bonney killed his first man at age fourteen."

"Who?"

"Billy the Kid."

Whitey's lips curled back in a slight smile, as if flattered that Dayton was comparing him to the infamous outlaw-killer.

This kid's enamored by the legends, he thought. *I hope this amnesty comes through, for him at least, and gives him a chance to straighten out.*

Or maybe he was beyond that.

Time would tell.

They rode on in silence until they came to an outcropping of boulders that preceded a small series of hills leading up to the mountain. Dayton saw a flicker of movement up ahead on top of the big rock to the left and he stiffened, slowing his horse.

Was it an ambush?

He thought about reaching down and undoing the leather thong that secured his Peacemaker, but didn't.

If they'd wanted him dead, they could have accomplished that back in town. No, this wasn't a trap, per se. It was more of a test.

A chance to build some trust, he thought.

As they came abreast of the outcropping a voice came out of the semidarkness.

"That's far enough. Keep your hands high, Sheriff. We got you covered."

Dayton did so. He heard a scuffling sound.

More than one?

Another darkened form, larger than the first, moved on the big rock above them. There were at least two of them.

"Whitey, anybody follow y'all?" This voice was different. Lower than the first one, and much deeper as well.

"No, Dutch."

"Good," the second voice said. "Get his gun."

"Huh-uh" Dayton said. "I don't give up my gun to no man."

"Don't look like you got much of a choice," the second voice said. "Do it?"

Dayton's mind raced, evaluating his chances. He could drop down to the side of his horse and ride hard ahead, all the while undoing his Peacemaker and getting ready to return fire.

Or not.

Where would that get him?

And as he'd surmised before, if they'd wanted him dead, he'd already be so.

But this was all about building trust, wasn't it?

"Now give it up," the voice said. The sentence was punctuated by what sounded like a rifle being cocked.

Dayton struggled to keep his reply even and steady. "You can't expect me to do that, can you, Dutch? You gonna give up yours?"

No one spoke for what seemed like an interminable time, and then Dayton heard a low chuckle.

"This is all about trusting each other," Dayton said. "Correct?"

"I find it a bit hard to trust a lawman. Especially with that big old five-thousand-dollar *re-ward* on my head."

"Look," Dayton said, his voice still strong and steady. "I came out here to meet you in good faith. I'd be a fool to try something when you got the drop on me. But I still got my pride. I ain't going down without a fight. If I have to."

More silence and then Dayton heard the other man's heavy, exaggerated sigh.

"All right, then, dammit," he said. "You can keep your damn gun. Ride on ahead. Camp's up there, but keep in mind me and my boys got a Winchester trained on ya the whole way."

"Ain't likely I'll be forgetting," Dayton called back.

He and Whitey rode through the space. About twenty-five yards ahead Dayton saw a small fire burning with several figures standing around it.

Dayton counted five of them. With Whitey and the two on the rock, that made eight—the entire Bascom gang. He wished he'd had the foresight to bring along his Colt Lightning, but he'd left it locked up in his office. He did have Bascom's fancy knife housed in a leather sheath and stuck into the front of his gun belt, but that would do little in a gunfight. Besides, with the odds stacked against him like they were, if trouble broke out he probably wouldn't get much of a chance to use it.

It's all about developing trust, he told himself again.

He shot a quick sideways glance at Whitey, who was still riding beside him.

"He ain't gonna shoot you in the back," the young man said in a low voice. "Dutch is a man of honor."

Dayton didn't dispute that, although from what he'd heard, Bascom was as ruthless and self-serving as they came. He'd been an outlaw for the past fifteen years when he emerged out of Missouri after the Civil War, riding with the likes of Wild Bill Anderson, the Youngers, and the James boys. All of them were either dead or in prison now and Bascom's gang, along with the Butch Cassidy bunch, were the last remnants of a vanishing breed. Soon they'd be as scarce as the buffalo. It wasn't surprising that Dutch was ready to jump at this amnesty.

Dayton and Whitey stopped their horses about ten feet from the campfire and dismounted. The five men standing by the fire all wore low-slung holsters and had wary expressions on their faces. Like they'd just as soon draw and fire at him.

Dayton figured the only thing to do was to show no fear.

He nodded and said, "Evening, gents."

It got no visible reaction that he could detect.

"I'll hold your horse, Sheriff," Whitey said, holding his hand out for the reins. As Dayton handed them to him, he took closer note of the young man's face, hoping to see it again down the road.

Hell, he thought. *He don't look old enough to shave every day.*

He heard the scuffling of feet behind him and turned. Two more men approached, one holding a rifle. The other man was a huge fellow with a barrel-like physique, and Dayton assumed this one was Bascom. As they drew closer the big man's features became more discernible in the lambent firelight and Dayton recognized his face. It was him, all right.

He strode up to Dayton and stopped a few feet from him. His rotund face had the same wide grin as the one in the photograph on the *Wanted* poster. This close, Dayton noticed the other man had a half-circle keloid scar on his left cheekbone. A knife wound, from the look of it. Bascom's lips were peeled back from a set of large teeth that were as crooked and gapped as a rickety picket fence. He pointed to two small rocks on the far side of the fire.

"Go ahead and sit," Bascom said, then added, "Curly, fetch me my bottle."

One of the five men by the fire turned and departed. The others slowly drifted into the background.

Dayton took his time walking around the fire. Bascom went by the other side to the far rock and lowered himself laboriously onto it. Dayton sat as well.

The one called Curly returned and handed a half-full bottle to Bascom, who accepted it and told the man to go keep a lookout. The other man departed at a quick trot.

They sat in silence eyeing each other for several seconds.

Finally, Dayton said, "Ain't nobody else coming, unless you invited them."

Bascom's head rocked up and down ever so slightly.

"That's good," he said. "For your sake."

Dayton smirked.

"Come on, Dutch. You didn't invite me out here to threaten me, did you?"

Bascom's tongue worked over his front teeth, and then he, too, smiled.

He pulled the cork out of the top of the bottle, brought it up, and took a swig. Then he handed the bottle to Dayton. Cognizant that the other man was scrutinizing his every move and knowing this was most likely part of some test, Dayton put the bottle to his mouth without wiping the rim and took a small sip.

The resonant chuckle began again and Bascom's smile widened.

"Now we got that out of the way," he said, "we might as well get down to brass tacks."

"Suits me fine." Dayton handed the bottle back to Bascom, who squinted.

"So you contact the governor like I told ya?"

"I did," Dayton said. He noticed a slight twitch of the other man's eye.

"Well, what'd he say?"

"Everything's in motion, Dutch. The amnesty papers are being sent by special messenger. Should be here by next Monday, or thereabouts, ready and waiting for you."

Bascom worked his tongue over his teeth once more and took another swig from the bottle. He extended it back toward Dayton, but the sheriff shook his head. "No more for me."

The big man shrugged, started to imbibe again, then paused.

"Damn shit's tastin' more and more like rotgut," he muttered.

Dayton couldn't argue with that. The tiny amount he'd tasted still lingered unpleasantly in his mouth.

Bascom spat into the fire. It made a hissing sound.

"Monday, huh?"

"That's right."

After emitting a substantial belch, Bascom snorted and then stared at Dayton. "All this on the up-and-up, Sheriff?"

"It is."

After a few copious breaths, Bascom spat again.

Dayton wondered if he was trying to extinguish the blaze.

"How do I know that for sure?"

"You got my word," Dayton said.

"Yer word?" Bascom snorted again and shot Dayton a half-smile. "That worth anything?"

Dayton knew the other man was trying to bait him. "It is to me, just like yours is."

Bascom stared back at him, saying nothing.

"I wouldn't have rode out here tonight unless I valued your word," Dayton said. "And I wouldn't have brought this."

He leaned back and using slow, deliberate movements, withdrew the knife from its sheath and jammed the blade into the soft earth between them.

Bascom's eyebrows tweaked upward and he grinned.

"Glad you brung it, like I told ya," he said. He reached down and pulled the knife from the ground, then held it up. "My granddaddy give me this one when I was thirteen. Did all the carving on the handle hisself." The tongue swept over his lips again. "Stuck me a man with it when I was fifteen. Kilt him deader than dirt, too."

After a few more moments of rotating the blade in the firelight, he grunted a thanks.

Dayton handed him the sheath. It was of finely tooled leather with a long thong to secure the hilt.

"Here," he said. "Fits pretty good."

Bascom's eyebrows danced upward again and he said, "This is real swell. Much obliged."

After he'd sheathed and pocketed the knife, the big man turned his head toward Dayton once again. "So how's this gonna work?"

"You give me the names of you and all your men—"

"Hey, wait just a Goddamn minute." Bascom's tone was gruff. "What you need them names for?"

"To have them put on the amnesty proclamations," Dayton shot back.

The big outlaw sat pensively for a moment, exhaled loudly, and then said, "Yeah, that makes sense. What else?"

"Not much else at all," Dayton said. "You and your boys ride into town and turn yourselves in, request the amnesty, take an oath that you'll no longer be committing any crimes or unlawful acts, pledge that you'll be upstanding citizens and obey the law, and we give you the papers, and you're free to do whatever you please."

"Who's 'we'?"

"Me and the territorial governor, John C. Frémont."

"He gonna be there?"

Dayton shrugged. "Maybe, maybe not. But his representative will be. In fact, that fellow's already in town and we're waiting for the papers to arrive."

"That so?"

"It is."

"And it'll be just like you done said? No questions asked?"

"None."

"No arrests?"

"Nope."

"Sounds too good to be true."

"It's true, all right," Dayton said. "I give you my word."

"What about the governor's word?"

"That too."

"I seem to remember them doing that to the Indians a whole passel of times, and we all know how that turned out." Bascom smirked.

"I can't speak to that," Dayton said. "I only know that the territorial governor's replied to me in writing that the amnesty papers are authorized and will be arriving." He reached into his shirt pocket, removed the telegram message, and handed it to Bascom.

The outlaw unfolded it and studied it in the faint light.

"Shucks, this ain't nothing. It's all hand-writ. Anybody coulda done it."

"It came from the governor."

Bascom was silent as he took in several deep breaths.

"Let me ask you something else," he said. "We gonna have to give up our guns?"

Dayton had thought about this. That would be the sensible thing to require, but it was hardly practical to expect these hardened outlaws to comply. Plus, he knew how he'd felt a little while ago when Bascom had ordered him to do the same thing.

Trust, he thought. *It's all about trust*. It had to start somewhere if this thing was going to succeed.

"I wouldn't be asking you to do anything I wasn't willing to do tonight," Dayton said.

This brought a smile to Bascom's face and he displayed the dreadfully crooked teeth once more.

He switched the bottle to his left hand, extended his right, and said, "Sheriff, you done got yourself a deal."

Dayton shook the outlaw's hand. It felt calloused, dry, and hard.

It looks like this has a chance of working out fine, he thought. *But you never know.*

ℰℑ

1913
Thunderhead Motion Pictures Lot
Near San Diego, California

Jim watched as the black man tied the paint's reins around the saddle horn and then dismounted from his horse, carefully guiding the reins over the animal's head. This horse was another stallion, but black as coal.

"What are you talking about, Henry?" Creighton asked.

The black man approached, giving the two Mexicans a quick glance.

"It wasn't the horse's fault," Henry said.

"What you talkin' about," the Mexican called Lobo said. "*Es loco*. Crazy."

"No," Henry shot back. "He ain't."

The black man reached into his shirt pocket with his left hand and pulled something out that looked tan and bristly.

Creighton's head jutted forward. "What in the hell?"

Henry rotated the bristly thing in his calloused fingers.

"It's a bur," he said. "And it was underneath the paint's saddle. Probably not enough to cause any pain or discomfort until Miss Faith mounted up. Then it cut into the animal's back, caused her to rear up and then run."

"A bur?" Creighton tapped his hat back and his forehead wrinkled. "How in the hell could that happen?"

"Better ask him," Henry said, pointing at the heavyset Mexican.

"*Dice que había una rebaba debajo de la silla del caballo*," Lobo said.

The fat Mexican's head began shaking back and forth and he started to respond in rapid Spanish.

"*No digas nada, estúpido*," Lobo said, cutting him off. He turned to Creighton. "*Señor,* Gordo say he don't know nothing."

Gordo, the heavyset Mexican, started to speak again, but Lobo held up an open hand to cut him off.

"He say it was Whitey and *el negro* that saddled the horse," Lobo said.

"I saddled her, all right," Henry said, his deep voice even and firm. "But I sure as hell didn't put no bur under no saddle. That had to be his doing."

Gordo began protesting in Spanish once more.

"You came and took the horse from the stable," Henry continued. "You walked her out to the street for Miss Faith to mount up."

Gordo must have understood, because he paused and licked his lips before uttering more Spanish.

"That's right," Faith said, still up on the stallion behind Jim. "He did walk the horse over to me."

Lobo turned and began conversing with Gordo again in their common language. The conversation started to get heated. Jim wished he could understand what was being said, but figured he was catching the gist of it through the tone and body language.

"Fire him," Creighton shouted.

Lobo paused and glanced back at the director.

"Get him out of here," Creighton said. "Tell him he's fired."

Lobo's dark eyebrows twitched and then he turned back to his heavyset companion.

"*Salga, chingado. Me ocuparé de ti más tarde.*" He backhanded Gordo across the face. The blow slashed open the obese man's lower lip, but he did nothing.

"*Vayas. Ahora*," Lobo said, taking another half-step in the heavy man's direction.

Gordo danced backward, his hand at the corner of his mouth now, trying to stem the flow of blood. He stumbled slightly, regained his footing, turned, and walked off at a quickening pace.

Lobo turned back to Creighton and flashed a smile. His teeth looked feral under his drooping black mustache.

"He *es* gone, *patrón*," he said. "He no come back."

Creighton nodded and turned to Tucker.

"See?" he said. "Tit for tat. We hire somebody, and we fire somebody."

The waspish man's mouth tugged into a straight line.

"Anyway," Creighton said. "Go take Lobo with you and pay the son of a bitch what he's owed. Take it out of petty cash. We haven't got time to go open the safe in the hotel. I want to get some filming in. We're still on a deadline."

Jim watched the heavyset Mexican walking off, pushing a few people out of his way here and there on the artificial western street.

There goes a bitter man, he thought. *But at least he's getting some severance pay.*

The thing with the bur was another matter, however. How had it gotten there?

It didn't appear to be some sort of freak accident, but why would Gordo do something like that?

Was it someone's idea of a real bad joke? Perhaps he'd anticipated Faith tumbling backwards and falling against him. It might be a sneaky way to be able to touch her body. She was a very beautiful woman with a figure like none Jim had ever seen. And for a guy as homely as Gordo, it would probably be like feeling up a goddess. Could that have been his motivation?

Who knows? Jim thought. *And who cares now? Looks like he's out of here and Larry and I are in.*

"Faith," Creighton said. "Get down from there and go get your makeup touched up. And you, young fella, get down as well. There are some forms to fill out and we'll get you and your friend on the payroll."

The big actor named Art stepped forward. Jim felt Faith stirring behind him, and he reached back and put his arm around her slim waist.

"Here," he said. "Let me help you, ma'am."

She giggled and pressed against him once more, giving him a shiver of delight. Then she slid to the ground with his assistance.

"Oooh," she said. "You're strong."

Art frowned.

"Come on, Faith," he said, slipping his arm around her. "Let's get back to work."

As they walked off with Creighton, Jim dismounted and patted the big horse's neck. Larry was pushing his way through the crowd and hobbled up next to Jim.

"Here," Larry said, handing Jim his hat. "That was really something."

"Much obliged," Jim said. "Where'd you find it?"

"Back yonder." Larry grinned. "Mr. Bierce give it to me. Still ain't found my sister's bonnet, though."

"That was damn good riding," the black man said. He held out his open palm. "Henry Jefferson."

Jim shook the man's hand. There was something about the black man's bearing that suggested both discipline and strength.

"Thanks. You look like you know horses pretty well yourself."

Henry smiled. "Yeah, I spent some time in the Tenth Cavalry."

This piqued Jim's interest. He'd heard of that outfit. "The Buffalo Soldiers?"

Henry's grin broadened. "Yep. Twenty years."

"You in the war?" Larry asked.

"I was. Against the Indians and then with Colonel Roosevelt when we took San Juan Hill." His right eye squinted slightly. "You served, too?"

Larry's head bobbled up and down vigorously.

"Yep. Me and Jim here was with the expeditionary force in the Philippines under Black Jack Pershing."

"See any action?" Henry asked.

"Plenty," Larry replied.

"We were in the Battle of Bud Bagsak," Jim added.

"That's where I hurt my leg," Larry said. "Jim here saved my life and won him a bunch of medals."

Henry's eyebrows rose in unison and he nodded approvingly.

"You had some of my people over there, too," he said.

"Sure did," Jim said. "And they fought real good."

Ambrose Bierce was approaching with a scowl on his face. Another man carrying a book was tagging along behind him, whose mouth was set in what looked to be an indelible simper. This second man was shorter and much younger than the author and seemed to be having trouble matching Bierce's long-legged strides. The younger man's brown hair was parted down the middle and in dire need of cutting. A pair of gold-rimmed spectacles sat on a large nose and his convex frame sported a rather narrow chest and rotund belly.

"I must say, Jim," Bierce said as he came abreast of the three of them. "No knight of the Round Table could have rescued the fair maiden in any less spectacular fashion."

Jim smirked and shrugged.

"Just lucky this horse was all saddled up and available," he said.

Bierce clapped him on the shoulder. "Well done, my boy. That fetching damsel could have been seriously injured or killed had you not interceded. It was analogous to Perseus rescuing Andromeda."

Jim shrugged again. "Well, I'm just glad I was able to help. And," he looked at his friend, "you and me got jobs after all."

"What?" Larry said.

"I'll be doing some riding in place of that actor fella," Jim said. "You can help Henry here with the horses."

"Golly, that'd be swell."

"Then it's good news all around," Bierce said. "I've been offered a stipend as well."

Jim glanced back at the author, who chuckled.

"This is Godfrey Monroe," Bierce said, making the introduction. "The screenwriter of this epic."

Jim shook the man's hand and introduced himself, as did Larry.

"It seems even here, just north of Baja, California, my reputation precedes me." Bierce slapped the bespectacled, shorter man on the back. "Godfrey here did an excellent con job on his employer, extolling the virtues of my past literary accomplishments, and convinced him that if I were to write an article about the filming of this project it would perk the public's interest in the motion picture." He winked. "Even though I told him my writing days were behind me now, he persisted and I grudgingly agreed, subject to certain stipulations and conditions, not the least of which was employment for the three of us, rooming and board, and a modest stipend." He uttered a harsh-sounding laugh. "But now I see my hard-fought negotiations were unnecessary. Your heroics already paved the way for you and Mr. Rush here, restoring my faith in the watchful benevolence of serendipity."

Jim wasn't sure what Bierce meant, but took the fact that they were all gainfully employed for the moment, and together, as a bit of good fortune.

"Just what is this story they're filming?" Larry asked. "My sister told me it really happened."

"It did," Monroe said. He held up the large book he'd been holding. "It's based on an actual event—a famous big shootout in a place called Contention City, Arizona."

"A shootout?" Larry said. "Anybody get killed?"

"Lots of people." Monroe flipped open the book and started paging through it. "There's some pictures in here. It tells the whole story, and then some."

"An arduous task," Bierce said.

Monroe shrugged. "I've read this book cover to cover. And I'm keeping it as close to the truth as I can."

"And I'm sure you will." Bierce grinned. "Give or take a lie or two to get it done."

Monroe blinked several times, as if he'd just been smacked.

"You best show them that stuff later, Godfrey," Henry said. "If they're gonna be a-filming, I'd best get this here horse's back brushed down some." He indicated the paint. "And then take 'em over to where they's supposed to be. And Jim and his partner need to go get put on the payroll."

Monroe looked up and readjusted his glasses on his nose.

"Yes, of course," he said. "I need to bring Mr. Bierce over to payroll as well. Come on, I'll take you there."

"We'll be needing to find us a place to stay, too," Jim said.

"Don't worry about that," Monroe said. "We've got a block of rooms at the hotel in town. You can stay there."

"Much obliged," Jim said. "But you sure there's rooms?"

"More than enough," Monroe said. "As I said, we reserved a block. We were anticipating having a lot of extras for the big shootout, but Lobo and his men spend most of their nights in the border town visiting the ladies, if you know what I mean."

He smiled sheepishly.

Jim mulled over the screenwriter's proclamation of "a famous big shootout" as they walked down the replicated street of what apparently was supposed to be a place called Contention City.

Odd name, Jim thought. *But at least in this skirmish we won't be dodging any real bullets. Or will we?*

As Jim walked behind Bierce and Monroe, they passed five camera stations, with the cameramen waving or yelling, "Nice riding" and "Good job," as he passed with the big horse. He was feeling pretty good until they got to the far end, near the place where he'd passed the Mexican, Lobo, smoking. A new figure emerged from a barn-like stable. This man was bowlegged and stooped over and sported a moderately long beard that was almost completely gray, except for a few dark streaks, but Jim could tell he was all cowboy and as hard as they come. The old guy pushed his worn brown hat back on his head and stared at Henry.

"What the hell happened over there?" he asked. "I heard a bunch of shouting going on."

Henry sighed. "That idiot, Gordo, musta somehow put a bur under Sasha's saddle. Spooked her as soon as Miss Faith climbed aboard. Horse went a-rearing and a-running."

The old cowboy spat and shook his head. "What the hell the damn idiot want to go and do a fool thing like that for?"

"Your guess is as good as mine," Henry said. "But anyway, it could've turned out real bad, if it wasn't for Jim here. He jumped on Champion and chased her down and rescued her."

"On Champion, huh?" The old cowboy snorted and shook his head. "Just what we need around here—another damn tenderfoot trying to play a hero."

"Hey, listen," Jim said, feeling the sting of the other man's remark. "I'm no tenderfoot."

The man canted his head to the side and smirked. "Is that a fact?"

"It is," Jim said. "And I was just trying to save the lady."

The old cowboy's mouth peeled back, exposing some spaced and weathered teeth as he laughed.

"Well, well, well," he said. "This one's got some spunk. At least we got us a stallion rather than a gelding."

Henry grinned. "He sure is. And he's a new hire, too. Him and his buddy. Gents, this here's old Whitey. Him and me run the stables."

Larry stepped forward and extended his hand.

"I'm Larry Rush. My sister and her husband run the food service."

The old cowboy spat again. "You gonna help 'em?"

"Maybe. But I think they said I was to help you, too, as needed."

"Help me?" Whitey assumed an indignant stance. "You know anything about horses?"

Larry shrugged. "Yeah, a little."

Whitey blew out a derisive breath. "Well, get ready to learn. And get ready to work. How'd you get that stiff leg?"

Larry's mouth puckered. He swallowed and said, "We was in the war."

"War? What war was that?"

"The Philippines," Jim said, stepping forward and offering his hand. "Jim Bishop."

The other man didn't reciprocate.

"Bishop? What kind of name is that? You a churchgoing man or something?"

Jim didn't answer. The fact was that he hadn't been to services since the Battle of Bud Bagsak.

Whitey blew out another derisive breath. It stank of tobacco and something more. Whiskey?

"You gonna be getting in my way, too?"

Jim shook his head. "Not if I can help it, sir."

The old cowboy seemed surprised and impressed by the courteous salutation.

"He's gonna be Mr. Arthur Weeks's stunt rider," Henry said. "And from what I've seen, he's not gonna have no trouble doing that. Oh yeah, and Gordo's fired."

Whitey huffed out the start of a laugh that turned into a cough. When he recovered, his eyes were moist but there was a smile on his face.

"Now that is some dern good news," he said, finally extending his hand for Jim to shake. "Them damn Mexes ain't worth a shit. None of 'em. All they talk about is *viva* their damn *revolución*. I say to hell with their damn revolution. It ain't gonna come to no good end anyhow."

"On that point, I tend to agree with you, sir," Bierce said. "As they say, in the end, the revolution always devours itself."

Whitey's eyes narrowed as he looked at the author and then to Monroe. "And who'd this feller be, Godfrey?"

"Mr. Bierce is a famous author. He's going to be writin—" Monroe started to say.

"Ambrose Bierce." The author made no effort to shake hands. "I'm just an interested party passing through. Don't pay me any mind."

The old cowboy snorted and cocked his head back.

"Don't expect I will, then," he said, and pointed a finger at Larry. "And you, stiff-leg. Don't you go thinking I'll be cutting you any slack, neither. Get ready to be shoveling shit, and the only thing I want to hear outta you is how much and where do I put it. Understand?"

Larry nodded, his face flushed.

"Come on, Henry," Whitey said. "We best ought to rub down poor Sasha to make sure she ain't got no more of that bur left on her. Git a move on."

Henry smirked and walked the paint into the stable.

"And you, hero," Whitey called back over his shoulder as he grabbed a brush. "Take that stallion in one of them stalls and loosen the cinch on him while we're doing this. Ain't you got no damn horse sense?"

What a cantankerous old coot, Jim thought. *Ordering everybody around. I wonder what his story is?*

Chapter 6

1880
Main Street
Contention City, Arizona

Dayton stopped to check his reflection in the window of Dally's General Store, shifted the bouquet of flowers to his left hand, and adjusted his hat on his head. The string tie and vest looked fine, as far as he could tell. It was closing in on eight in the morning and the promise of another unbearably hot day was already starting to come to fruition. He hoped the buttoned-up shirt and the vest wouldn't make him sweat too much, at least not until he'd given her the flowers and asked her out. Then, depending on what she said, he'd either be strutting back to his office like a proud rooster, or wrinkling up the extra garments into a ball of frustration and disappointment.

Glancing down the street he saw the children, mostly girls and a handful of boys, milling about in the yard in front of the schoolhouse. Dayton wondered if he should duck between the adjacent buildings and approach the location from the rear. That would spare him a curious "audience" of prepubescent youngsters.

Good idea, he thought and stepped into the space between Dally's and the barbershop. The area was about three feet wide and in shadow. The temperature seemed to be several degrees less as well.

More good fortune. He was sure he'd already sweated through his shirt, but maybe this brief respite from the sunshine would keep him from smelling too bad.

Another thought entered his nervous mind: What about Saturday, if she accepted? Even if they found a nice shady spot on the outskirts of town to picnic, the buckboard ride out there was certain to take its toll in the hot sunshine.

Well, he thought. *I'll cross that bridge if and when I come to it. First things first.*

And that meant he had to ask her and she had to accept.

At the building's rear he stepped over a substantial pile of discarded cans and a slew of empty whiskey bottles. Just before he lowered his foot all the way down on the other side of the detritus, he saw a pile of a different kind—several long, desiccated turds. Swearing, he angled his foot away from the feces, and this caused him to stumble into the filthy side of the one building. Dayton did a little dance step and emerged out in the open again. He'd dropped about half of the flowers. He paused to check the shoulder of his white shirt and found it smudged with a grayish-black stain. The dropped flowers were way too close to the fecal matter, so he decided to leave them.

Half a bouquet was sparse, but better than nothing.

Some dashing romantic I am, he told himself as he tried in vain to brush off the dirt.

At least he'd avoided the worst of it, or so he thought until he glanced down at his boots. Although he'd missed the human waste deposit, he saw that in doing so his other foot had squashed down on what appeared to be a second pile of crap.

He swore again and debated whether to try and wipe them clean, but with what? He certainly didn't want to use his handkerchief, and scrounging for some thick plant leaves to do the deed seemed highly unlikely. Plus, the blasted school bell would be ringing at any minute.

Swallowing his pride, he did a hasty trot around the back of the building and came up on the other side of the school just in time to find two boys pursuing an insect along the dirt. They both looked up with startled expressions.

"Golly, Sheriff," one of the boys said. "We almost run into you."

Dayton shot them both a quick smile and strode past them, hoping they wouldn't follow.

No such luck.

Then, to make matters worse, as he rounded the corner there was Miss April standing in her prim white blouse and long blue skirt, herding the kids into the classroom. When she saw him, she looked just as shocked as the two boys.

Dayton came to an abrupt stop and smiled, tipping his hat and then extending his hand with the depleted bouquet in her direction.

"Good morning," he said.

Her eyes moved down to the flowers, and then up to look at him.

"Goodness," she said. "What nice flowers."

He studied her face for a moment. Even devoid of those powders women were so fond of putting on nowadays, she had to be the prettiest girl he'd ever seen. And she was smiling at him.

"Oh," Dayton said after several seconds of awkward silence. "These are for you. I picked them myself."

Her hands reached out and took the bouquet from him. Her beatific smile radiated.

"Why, thank you, Sheriff. They're lovely. That's so sweet of you."

Dayton took in a deep breath, trying to muster up the nerve to ask her to go on the picnic with him. The two boys were still standing off to the side and one of them snorted a laugh.

"Hey, Sheriff," the boy said, tugging at Dayton's vest. "It looks like you stepped in a pile of horseshit."

"Or some other kind," the second one added with a snicker.

"And it's all over your boot," the first one said. "Can't you smell it?"

Dayton felt his face flush and wanted to smack the two little bastards.

"Timmy and Jed," Miss April said, her expression turning serious now. "Get inside and go sit at your desks. And Jed, don't you be using that kind of language."

"Yes, Miss Donovan," both boys said in unison as they made a quick dash for the door.

Dayton turned to watch them go and saw he had an audience of about ten other schoolchildren watching.

And listening, no doubt, he thought.

He turned back to Miss April and saw her compressing her lips.

Was she resisting the impulse to glance down at his boots?

Swallowing, he started to speak when she brought the flowers down to her side and gestured at the group of kids.

"All of you," she said in a stern-sounding tone. "Go on inside and take out your notebooks."

The mixed group of boys and girls were all smiling.

"Now!" she called out.

That spurred the group into motion and they filed inside the front door.

"They usually aren't so rambunctious this early in the morning," she said, bringing the flowers in front of her again.

They both stood there in silence, him trying to muster up enough gumption to ask her out, and her evidently waiting to reply.

Finally, she spoke.

"Well, I guess I'd better find a vase and some water for these."

Clearing his throat, Dayton agreed and reached out for them.

"I can do that if you don't have one handy in the school," he said.

"No, I have a pitcher and some cups inside. I'll see to it."

Dayton hoped the odor from his untidy footwear hadn't wafted its way up to her nose.

They lingered there a moment more and she sighed.

"I'd better go inside."

"Yeah, well, um . . ."

The words dribbled off and his vocal cords felt paralyzed. He tried to swallow again, but his mouth felt totally dry.

Her dreamy blue eyes stared up at him for a few more beats and then she smiled again.

Do it, dammit, he thought. *Ask her.*

But the words seemed caught in his throat.

"Thanks again for the flowers," she said, and turned and started walking toward the front door of the schoolhouse.

Dammit, he thought. *I've faced down bad men with guns in a shootout and I can't even do this.*

"Wait!" he called out. It sounded more like he was yelling out an order. He panted twice and said, "Ah, I was kinda hoping, if you were free this Saturday, if you'd like to go on a picnic with me."

There, he told himself. *At least I got it out. Now she can refuse me . . .*

"Why, I'd be delighted," she said.

"You would?"

"Yes. But I'm afraid I'm not a very good rider."

"I'll borrow a buckboard." He was still having a hard time believing that she'd accepted. "How's about I come by your rooming house at say, ten-thirty or so?"

"All right," she said, and began to turn away with a smile on her face.

"Wait," he called out again. "Could we make it eleven instead? I have to get everything set as far as the sandwiches and all."

"That's perfect. I'll be expecting you then."

Dayton felt on top of the world.

He watched her go up the steps to the front door of the schoolhouse, pause, turn, and wave to him. She looked like a real live version of one of those paintings of a beautiful woman that he'd seen in picture books. That she'd readily accepted made him feel that this could be the start of something good. Real good.

He was definitely on a roll.

"Hey, Sheriff," a malicious young voice called out from the open window of the school. "Don't forget to clean your boots first."

The admonition was punctuated by a chorus of snickers.

Damn little smart asses, he thought. *If I had the time I'd go in there and tan their damn hides.*

But what the hell, he couldn't complain. The amnesty deal with Bascom and his boys was set, and Miss April May Donovan was coming on a picnic with him. What more could he ask for?

Yeah, things were going mighty damn good.

☙

1913
Horse Stables
Thunderhead Motion Pictures Lot
Near San Diego, California

Jim hung his rucksack on a nail in the stall and went to work removing the big gold stallion's saddle and blanket. This horse had done well and deserved a rubdown just as much as the other horse did. He'd just finished unfastening the cinch when he heard the sound of voices. He lifted the saddle off the animal and set it on the stall's wooden railing. Larry and Bierce had left with Monroe to begin filling out their employment paperwork. Figuring it could wait until he'd seen to the horse, Jim had told them he'd be along in a minute.

The voices grew louder and more distinct. He couldn't understand what was being said, but he could discern the rolling syllables and distinctive rhythm of the words. They were speaking Spanish. Recalling Gordo, the heavyset Mexican who was fired, Jim closed the gate to the stall and crouched down. A group of five men approached, all vaqueros.

"*Hago migas a alguien este caballo,*" the one in front said.

It was Gordo, and he looked mad.

"No, no," one of the others said. "*Venga.*"

He tried to pull the fat Mexican's arm, but Gordo ripped it out of the other man's grasp. The other three laughed and said something Jim couldn't understand. All of them, including Gordo, wore gun belts with revolvers in the holsters.

As they passed through the barn entranceway to the stable, Henry came walking out to meet them.

"What you boys want?" he asked, a stern expression on his dark face.

The group stopped and stared at him.

"That damn *caballo es* what I want, *chingado*," Gordo said, lowering his tone to mimic Henry's deep voice.

At least his English has improved, Jim thought.

He stayed where he was for the moment, figuring that none of the Mexicans was aware of his presence.

"You fellas are drunk," Henry said. "*Baracho*. And *you* been fired, Gordo. Now get the hell outta here."

"*Chinga tu madre*, nigger," Gordo said.

Henry glared back at the man.

"It figures you'd know *that* word," he said. "I'm not telling y'all again. Get the hell outta here."

"Or what?" Gordo said, stepping forward.

He was bigger than the black man, but Henry's frame was solid looking. As the Mexican approached, Henry raised his hands.

"Y'all best stay back," he said.

"*Está asustado*." Gordo smirked and lumbered toward him.

Henry's left fist lashed out and smashed into the larger man's face. Gordo stumbled back two steps and wiped his nose. A torrent of red flowed down over his substantial mustache.

"*Hijo de puta*," Gordo yelled, and surged forward again.

Henry sidestepped and slammed a two-punch combination into the Mexican's corpulent body. The bigger man's knees sagged and he stumbled to the side, holding his gut.

Jim grinned. Henry could fight.

"Y'all want some more?" Henry shouted, his voice even but fierce sounding.

One of the other Mexicans jumped forward. Henry's fists lashed out once more, knocking this one to the ground. Two of the others jumped in as well.

I was afraid of that, Jim thought.

Without hesitation, he charged out of the stall and over to the group, knocking two of them down with a butting motion. One of them started to rise and Jim smashed an overhand right into the man's jaw. He took a wobbly two steps back.

"*Mata los*," Gordo shouted and straightened up, pulling his gun from its holster.

Jim instantly regretted hanging his rucksack with his Colt in the horse stall. What the hell had he been thinking, approaching a bunch of armed drunks without his weapon. He shot a quick glance back at the stall, decided it was too far away, and then dove for Gordo. He and the big Mexican rolled together on the ground like a mismatched pair of lovers, punching and kneeing each other. A flash of peripheral vision told Jim that Henry was engaged with one of the others, but a third man was reaching for his gun.

A loud shot echoed in the room, and then another.

The hat of one of the standing Mexicans tilted slightly askew. The other's sombrero tumbled off his head entirely.

"*¿Qué?*" the sombrero man said.

"Keep your hands away from them *pistolas, amigos*." Whitey marched forward holding a Colt Peacemaker in each hand and cocking the hammers of both weapons. Trails of smoke drifted from the barrels. "Or you'll be a-getting carried outta here feet first. *¿Comprende?*"

The other Mexicans now stood completely still. Gordo was frozen in place as well. Jim ripped the gun from the bigger man's hand and backhanded him across the face with it. Gordo's head jerked to the side, the sudden motion expelling several large droplets of blood. His eyes rolled back and his body twisted downward in a pirouette.

"Drop all your irons real slow like," Whitey said, "or I'll be dropping you."

The Mexicans apparently understood, and one by one tossed their guns onto the ground.

"Now pick up that piece of *mierdra* there and carry his sorry ass outta here," Whitey said.

The Mexicans cast nervous looks at one another.

Several people had gathered at the door and the crowd was growing. Monroe and Bierce were at the front. Lobo pushed his way through and stopped, glaring at the scene. He addressed the Mexicans in harsh sounding, rapid Spanish, gesticulating at the fallen Gordo. Two of the men helped Gordo to his feet.

"*Me ocuparé de ti más tarde, chigado,*" Lobo said to him. "I will deal with you later."

"*Lo siento, jefe,*" the stuporous man muttered as the others half-dragged him out. They stooped to pick up their hats on the way.

Lobo turned to Whitey and Henry.

"My apologies, *señores,*" he said. "I will see to it that this piece of shit does not return. *Nunca.* This never should *haf* happened."

"You're damn right about that." Whitey de-cocked the hammers on his two pistols. "And damn lucky I didn't decide to aim a mite lower. You'd be fixing a couple Mexican funerals."

"*Es* all right?" Lobo asked, turning to look at Henry.

"I reckon," Henry said, then glanced at Jim. "How about you?"

"No harm done."

Henry grinned and clapped Jim on the shoulder.

"*Por favor*," Lobo said. "*De* guns. I will take *dem*, eh?"

Whitey re-cocked the hammer of one of his Colts.

"Like hell," he said. "Them's our guns now and they're going to the studio armory. They're staying."

"No, no," Lobo said, his mouth forming a half-smile. "*De* guns are *nuestros*. Ours."

"Not any more they ain't," Whitey said.

"But—"

"But nothing," Whitey shot back.

Lobo raised his hands, palms outward. "*Señor*, we need *de* guns. *Para la revolución*."

Whitey spat. "That's what you can do with your *revolución*."

Lobo's face darkened but he did nothing. Whitey was still holding the Peacemakers.

Suddenly Creighton and Tucker pushed their way into the opening.

"What the hell's going on here?" Creighton said. "I thought we heard gunshots."

"You did, all right," Whitey said. "Them Mexes there come here looking for trouble, and they sure damn found it."

Creighton, his breath coming in pants now, glanced around and settled on the two men helping escort Gordo.

"Jesus H. Christ, Lobo," Creighton said. "I thought I told you to get rid of that bum?"

Lobo canted his head and gave a conciliatory shrug.

"I did, *señor*. He got ahold of some tequila and snuck back here."

"I've got a good mind to call the sheriff, dammit." Creighton tapped his hat further back on his head. "In fact, I think I'll do just that."

That didn't seem like such a bad idea to Jim. This group was obviously trouble and needed to be dealt with. He kept his mouth shut, however, not wanting to get in the middle of this situation any more than he already had.

"Frank," Tucker said, holding up his palm. "I'm not so sure we should do that."

Creighton glared at him. "Why the hell not?"

"We don't really need any adverse publicity, do we?" the waspish man said slowly. "And, if we play our cards right, we can get the press to instead write up something about that rescue today."

Creighton's face assumed a contemplative expression.

"The last thing we need is for Klayman to play up some kind of gunplay happening here," Tucker added. "Plus, we need all the extra riders we can get for the big scenes coming up, right?"

Creighton exhaled slowly and then nodded, but then pointed his index finger at Lobo.

"Now you listen to me," he said. "I want him out of here for good, understand. If I see him again, which I hope I never do, I will call the authorities and have him arrested."

"*Sí, señor*," the head Mexican said. "It will be as you say. He no come back."

Jim reminded himself he'd heard that before, but he hoped this time it would stick.

Lobo turned and shouted in Spanish to his group. Without further hesitation they began hustling Gordo away.

Lobo turned back and smiled.

"See?" he said. "*Está bueno ahora*. He *es* no more."

To Jim, that looked and sounded about as sincere as a politician's promise.

"All right, dammit," Creighton shouted. "Let's get these beasts over to the street set before we lose all of what's left of the daylight."

He turned and stormed off, with Tucker following close behind. The waspish assistant turned and glanced back at Jim and the others.

Jim saw Lobo grinning at him.

"*Adios, héroe*," the Mexican said before turning and walking away.

Jim wasn't totally sure of what the words meant, but the man's tone suggested sarcasm.

"I got a feeling that sooner or later me and him are gonna end up tangling," he said.

"It best be later if'n you want to keep working here a while," Henry said with a wide grin.

Jim sighed. "I reckon so."

Bierce placed a hand on Jim's shoulder. "*Illegitimi non carborundum.*"

Jim's brow furrowed. "Huh?"

"It's Latin," Bierce said with a laugh. "Don't let the bastards get you down."

Jim snorted a laugh as well.

I'm gonna have to remember that one, he thought. *And this guy sure knows a lot of stuff.*

❧

1880
Sheriff's Office
Contention City, Arizona

Dayton had gotten a bucket of water from the pump out back and had just settled down behind his desk with a wet rag and his dirty boot when the door burst open. He quickly dropped the boot and brought his right hand to the handle of his Colt Peacemaker, but relaxed when he saw the short, squat figure of Mayor Webber waddling inside. Behind him was the territorial governor's man, Martin Lipton, the railroad representative, Fred Dyer, and that reporter, William Bradford Cox. A fifth man, whom Dayton couldn't immediately discern, brought up the rear.

As the group fanned out in front of his desk, he saw the fifth man was Norman Burnside, the Pinkerton detective. Burnside was almost as rotund around the middle as the mayor, but he was a lot younger. Dayton estimated him on the far side of thirty. His skin was pallid, like he eschewed the sun, and his hands had an almost delicate look to them. A short, uneven little mustache graced the top of his upper lip like a forlorn caterpillar. All five of the visitors looked overdressed—suit jackets, white shirts, and string ties. The shirts were far from pristine, however. Their faces had that unshaven, bedraggled look, and they all stank of residual tobacco, booze, and body odor. Dayton figured they'd been at their poker table for the better part of the night.

Dayton stood, with the arch of his right foot extended to offset the unevenness of having on only one boot. With the desk between them, he figured the group wouldn't notice his lack of footwear.

"Lon," Mayor Webber said, "glad we caught you. We're heading down to get breakfast but wanted to check in with you first."

"What can I do for you?" Dayton asked.

The mayor turned slightly and held out his hand, indicating the fifth man who'd come in. "You remember Norman Burnside. He's with the Pinkertons. I want you to coordinate with him on this forthcoming amnesty thing."

Burnside stepped forward and stuck his hand out over the desk.

"A pleasure to see you again, Sheriff."

Dayton shook the man's hand, though it took some effort to keep his balance. He saw Burnside's eyebrow flicker, as if the man had noticed the awkward movement.

This fatso's not as thick as he looks, Dayton thought.

Assuming the others had noticed the abrupt shift in balance as well, and not wanting them to wonder if he'd been drinking this early in the morning, Dayton lowered himself into the chair and immediately regretted it. Seated, he had them towering over him. Yet to stand up again would make any misperception worse. He reached down and grabbed his loose boot and the wet rag, then leaned back.

"Had a little misstep this morning," he said. "Making my rounds and I stepped in a pile of shit."

To demonstrate this fact, he rubbed the rag over the soiled portion of his boot.

Webber laughed so hard his big belly shook. The others grinned, all except Burnside.

"Hell," Lipton said. "I thought I smelled something, but I figured it was Clyde here farting again."

The mayor bent forward slightly and grunted. A mellifluous, extended burst of flatulence immediately followed.

"Ask and ye shall receive," he said with an accompanying chuckle.

Dayton dumped the rag into the bucket and slipped his boot on. After working his foot into a reasonably comfortable fit, he stood up again. It felt better to be back on eye level with this crew.

"So what brings you fellas here this morning?" he asked.

Webber glanced at Lipton, who cleared his throat loudly.

"As the mayor said, we wanted to brief you on our plans for the Bascom gang capture."

Their plans?

Capture?

The word choice bothered Dayton somewhat. "I wouldn't quite call it a capture."

"All right," Lipton said. "An apprehension, then. Regardless of what we call it, it's got to be planned out. Thoroughly planned out."

Dayton noticed the gravity of the other man's tone.

"I'm working on that," Dayton said.

"So are we," Lipton shot back.

I'll bet you are, Dayton thought. Which was why they'd brought the Pinkertons in on it.

"Lon," Webber said, "this is way too big for you to handle alone. You already as much as told me that."

"And I also told you I'll need to recruit a couple of deputies. I've already talked to Elmer Abbey—"

"Nah, nah." Webber shook his head. "Abbey's a fine man, but we don't want a simple blacksmith doing the job that a professional ought to be doing."

"Elmer's a pretty fair shot," Dayton said. He didn't like having this discussion in front of the newspaperman, Cox. The last thing Dayton wanted was some kind of sensational account being spread around before the actual amnesty meeting was conducted. "And he's backed me up on many a bar fight. Plus, I was figuring on asking a few more of the boys around town. Maybe Kevin Fitzgerald, Big Rich Swafford. It would help if we could offer them a little incentive, say a five-dollar stipend."

"What?" Webber's face contorted into a frown. "Paying them that kind of money for some dubious support is not my idea of good fiscal management of city funds."

"So you're saying I have to ask them to volunteer at no pay?"

Webber pursed his lips and then nodded.

"What happened to our usual offer of two dollars?" Dayton asked.

Webber's frown deepened.

"What the mayor is saying," Lipton broke in, flashing a smile that looked about as sincere as a bar girl's expression of admiration, "is that something this big requires an element of professionalism."

Dayton looked at him.

"Meaning what?"

The governor's man's smile grew broader. "Now, we're not trying to impugn your fine performance as the sheriff here in Contention City. No, sir, not for one minute." He paused and coughed. "But you'll have to admit that this is a little bit above your usual capabilities."

"You've been sheriff here for what?" Fred Dyer said. "Going on eight years now? And in all that time Bascom's gang has been marauding the countryside, especially the railroads. You've never been able to catch him."

"No," Dayton said. "But the last time they robbed the bank here, I shot two of his crew. One fatally. That was three years ago and he ain't been back since."

He noticed Cox scribbling all this down on his notepad.

"Apples and oranges," Dyer said. "He merely switched his tactics to hit the stagecoaches and railroads more. Why, do you know how many times he's struck our rail shipments in the last three years?"

"Quite a few, I expect," Dayton said.

"Over a dozen," Dyer said. "And still you've done nothing."

Dayton wanted to mention the other ten wanted outlaws he'd brought in during that same time, as well as the dozens of bar fights, rowdy cattle drovers, and roving gunslingers who'd drifted into town looking for trouble. He'd faced them all down, not to mention the three murderers he'd brought to justice. Not that the killings had been all that difficult to solve—angry, drunken men beating each other and their wives and kids.

"Isn't that what you hired the Pinkertons for?" he asked. "Doesn't look like they've been too successful either."

From the corner of his eye he saw Burnside stiffen. Dyer's lower lip jutted out and his face flushed.

"Now, now," Lipton interjected. "Let's not get into a pissing contest here."

"That was the farthest thing from my mind," Dayton said. "Till you guys walked in."

Lipton smiled his typical politician's smile.

"All we're saying, Sheriff, is that we figured you could use a little help. Dependable, professional help."

"And that's why you've brought the Pinkertons here?" Dayton asked.

"Precisely," Lipton said.

"Me and my men are very well experienced in handling this type of criminal riffraff," Burnside said. "Believe you me."

Dayton had heard about some of the exploits of the Pinkertons. They were known for being good at their job, all right. And ruthless, not caring about innocent people who might get caught in the cross fire. Their duty was to their clients, not the public good.

Lipton patted Dayton on the shoulder and flashed a benevolent-looking smile.

"Clyde," Lipton said, "let's let the sheriff deputize some of his regular men if that's what he wants. We want all the help we can get, and it'll be a tribute to your leadership and the mutual resolve of the townsfolk here that they're willing to step up when needed."

Webber's lower lip jutted out as he considered this.

"And I'm sure the railroad will contribute to paying the deputies' stipends, right, Fred?"

"Absolutely," Dyer said.

Hizzoner grunted an approval.

Dayton was surprised and pleased at this change of heart.

"I appreciate that," he said.

"And to that end," Burnside continued, "we've got to get this planned out. I've taken the liberty of drawing some plans." He reached into the inside pocket of his jacket and withdrew a folded paper. Dayton caught sight of a nickel-plated revolver under the jacket in a shoulder holster. Burnside opened the paper, leaned forward, and spread it on the desk. "This is a diagram of your main street. If we put the amnesty tent here," he tapped a thick index finger on the drawing indicating the main thoroughfare, "that'll give us the advantage. We should have my men stationed here," he tapped the paper again, indicating a building, "here, and here. Additionally, I'll have two men with rifles on top of the buildings here and here. Naturally, they'll be staying out of sight until the right time."

Dayton gazed down at the diagram. There was a plethora of X's on the crudely rendered drawing of the buildings and streets. He wasn't liking this much at all.

"We'll route Bascom and his gang down this street here," Burnside said. "They'll then dismount and surrender their guns to you. Once that's done, my men will move in and we'll have them."

He paused, obviously pleased with his rendering, and grinned.

"Looks like the makings of a pretty good ambush," Dayton said.

Burnside's smile grew wider.

Dayton stared at him. "Which is why it ain't gonna happen."

"What?" Burnside said, the smile evaporating from his face.

"I gave Dutch my word that they could keep their guns," Dayton said.

"Your word?"

Burnside and Dayton locked eyes.

"You mean you've been in contact with him?" Lipton asked.

Dayton didn't reply for several seconds, and then said, "Yep."

"When was this?" Lipton said, his voice just falling short of a demand.

"Are you talking about that stupid note?" Webber asked. "The one you showed me?"

"This is ridiculous," Burnside interjected. "You can't trust a man like Bascom. He'll shoot you in the back the same as look at you."

Dayton shifted his gaze back to the Pinkerton man, then pointed to the diagram on the paper. "Sounds like that's what you've got planned for him."

Burnside's garbled reply consisted of a bunch of truncated words and syllables. He finally stopped, cleared his throat, and said, "This is absurd. You're asking for trouble. Or one of Bascom's bullets in your back."

"I don't think so," Dayton said. "He and his boys just want to take the governor up on his amnesty offer. Provided the papers get here as promised, by next Monday, the day after they'll be coming in to sign 'em."

Webber's mouth gaped.

"Tuesday," he muttered.

Dayton smiled, said nothing.

"You can't be sure of that," Dyer said.

"Actually, I can. Bascom had the opportunity to kill me last night, and he didn't."

The eyes of all four men widened as if on a cue from a stage director. The newspaperman was still scribbling, head bent over his notebook.

"You met him face to face?" Webber asked.

Dayton gave another slight nod.

"You were lucky it wasn't a trap," Burnside said. "You can't trust a man like Bascom."

"Building trust was what it was all about," Dayton said. "And we've got the whole thing worked out. Like I said, I'll need a couple of deputies standing by, and the tent's a good idea, but as far as Pinkerton men on the rooftops, no deal. And like I said, I already agreed that him and his boys could keep their guns."

"You're a fool," Burnside muttered.

Dayton glared at him. "What'd you call me?"

"Eh, eh, eh, eh." Lipton raised his hands, palms open, and stepped between the two men. "Let's not get into a pissing contest here. After all, we share a common goal. We want the same things."

"I'm not sure what he wants," Dayton said, pointing at the Pinkerton man. "And the last thing I want is some kind of shootout starting where innocent people could get hurt."

Burnside glared back.

"You incompetent rube," he said.

Lipton elevated his voice to just shy of a shout. "All right, all right. That's enough. Both of you." He shot a quick glance at Burnside and then looked toward Dayton. "We've all got to work together here."

"I'm fine with working together," Dayton said, "as long as we agree that I'm in charge and will be running this thing."

"Listen," the mayor said, his large gut encroaching into Dayton's personal space. "Your job is at my—"

"Clyde," Lipton said, flashing that politician's grin again. "Let's not be unreasonable here. The sheriff obviously has developed a relationship with these outlaws, and that's admirable. Let's not undo all the good work he's done up to this point."

Webber's lips pursed, but he remained silent.

The governor's man smiled benignly. "We've already made arrangements for the erection of the tent. And Detective Burnside and his men can stand by in reserve just in case of any mishaps. If Bascom and his group come in and act in a peaceable manner, then the papers will be signed and it'll be official." He paused and looked at Dayton and Burnside, then at Dyer. "And as for funding, I'm sure the railroad will be glad to provide that five-dollar stipend for the sheriff's deputies, right, Fred?"

The railroad man licked his lips. His cheeks twitched and he nodded.

"Sheriff?" Lipton asked, turning back to Dayton.

Dayton also nodded.

"Excellent," Lipton said. "And let it be known that should this matter be successfully resolved, Sheriff, a good portion of that substantial reward could be going to you. Five thousand dollars."

The way he'd emphasized that numeral amount made Dayton's gut tighten. With that kind of money, he could afford to turn in his badge, buy a little spread, and maybe even ask April to marry him. If everything went well on their first date.

But it wasn't really an official date, was it?

It was only a picnic.

And this promised offer felt about as solid as a pool of quicksand.

"How's that sound, Lon?" Mayor Webber asked, his face contorting into a smile that almost mirrored Lipton's.

"It sounds all right to me," Dayton said.

Lipton patted him on the back, uttering assurances of good fortune.

"Now," Lipton said. "You know Mr. Cox, correct?"

Dayton had never been formally introduced to the man, but said, "I do."

"Good, good," Lipton said. "He's writing a book about the area and wants to include a chapter on this upcoming event."

Cox slipped the notepad in the inside pocket of his suit jacket. He looked like a beanpole in a striped suit as he stepped forward. His hand jutted out and Dayton shook it.

"I've got my associate, Herman, standing just outside with the camera," Cox said. "I'd like to get a few photos of you, Sheriff."

Dayton frowned and thought about asking if he had time to finish cleaning his boot off.

"If that's all right," Cox said, as an afterthought. "Won't take more than a minute or two."

Without waiting for an answer, he went to the door and opened it. Herman Farrell, who was a photographer for the town newspaper, in addition to being a part-time bartender at the Brass Cupcake, entered and flashed a grin at Dayton, who acknowledged it with a fractional nod of his head.

He wasn't liking this much.

"I'd like to get one of you sitting behind your desk," Cox said. "Maybe one standing, too. And then we'll move outside. Do you have a coat you could put on to go with the vest?"

"No," Dayton said. "I don't."

"No matter, no matter," the newspaperman said, fluttering his hands. "It'll be better that way. They'll be able to see your six-guns. You do have more than just that one, don't you?"

Dayton took a breath and said, "Yeah."

"Fine, fine." Cox stepped back and held up his hand as if framing the photograph. He turned to Herman and they began conversing in hushed tones as Herman sprinkled what Dayton figured was flash powder onto a tray.

"Hey," Hizzoner said. "What about me? I'm the mayor, after all."

"We'll most certainly get you in the picture." Cox's head was jerking up and down like a fisherman's bobble. "You other gentlemen as well, of course." He smiled at the rest. "But let me get a few of the sheriff first. I want to have them in case something untoward happens."

Untoward, Dayton thought. *Such as me meeting an untimely demise?*

Cox positioned him behind the desk, turning him slightly so his Colt Peacemaker was prominently displayed.

Dayton frowned. Perhaps he should contact Dutch and call this whole damn thing off, or at least put it on the back burner for a while.

But thoughts of that five-thousand-dollar reward and owning his own spread danced in his mind's eye.

September Gun . . . He wasn't getting any younger.

The photographer spread the tripod legs of his camera and ducked under a black sheath attached to the camera's back. Herman's somewhat muffled voice came from under the curtain: "Hold real still now and say cheese."

Dayton's thoughtful frown deepened.

The flash powder ignited with a sudden pop and a smoldering burst of smoke. Herman ducked out from under the black sheath and pulled a rectangular frame out of the camera.

"Let me change the film and we'll get another one," he said. "And then we'll do the group shots before we go outside."

Another one?

Damn. Dayton was still seeing stars from the ignescent powder blast. Gradually, his vision cleared and he could see the two politicians, the railroad man, and the Pinkerton standing by the wall staring at him and smiling.

Wolves in suits.

"Do you have another gun you could stick in your belt, Sheriff?" Cox asked. "I'd like to get a picture that looks like you're loaded for bear."

Dayton sighed, pulled open his desk drawer, and removed the Colt Lightning. As he jammed it into the left side of his gun belt, Cox made a tsking sound.

"Can't you put it next to the other one?"

Dayton's brow furrowed. "What?"

"We won't be able to see it if it's on the left side," the newspaperman said. His voice had a whiny quality to it that set Dayton's teeth on edge.

"Maybe he can just hold it," Burnside offered, and then chuckled.

"My gun stays where it's at," Dayton said. "Or better yet—" He pulled the Lightning out of his gun belt and put it back in the desk drawer. "I'm done here."

"Aw, come on," Mayor Webber said. "Do it for the sake of the town, Lon."

Burnside emitted another low chuckle.

Dayton glared at him but said nothing.

This was turning out to be one hell of a long morning. But as long as it all worked out all right in the end . . .

If it does, he thought.

Chapter 7

1913
Contention City Set
Thunderhead Motion Pictures Lot
Near San Diego, California

The afternoon's "work" seemed rather monotonous and unproductive to Jim. Mostly he and Henry just stood around holding the horses or mounted up and rode up and down the phony street. Larry's sister had come and whisked him away to help with the evening meal's preparation, and Bierce and Monroe stood off to the side engaging in periodic conversations, with Bierce doing most of the talking.

Monroe seemed in awe of the author, and Jim could hardly blame him. For a fledgling writer, being around someone so famous had to be an enviable position. The two stars, Faith and Weeks, were joined by a host of other actors and they all sat in the shade of a tent erected between two of the ersatz western town buildings. Periodically, Creighton would summon one or all of them to do some kind of scene. At various points along the street the men operating the cameras twirled little handles on the sides of the machines. Platforms had been erected in several places for them to stand upon.

It seemed incredible to Jim that only a short time ago, he'd ridden down the same street and rescued the beautiful actress.

His heroic deed had seemingly been forgotten. He cast a wistful look at her as she sat next to the big actor, Arthur Weeks, and leisurely indulged herself in a cigarette. He wondered if she even remembered him now.

"She sure is pretty, ain't she?" Henry said, casting a sideways glance at Jim and grinning.

Embarrassed that the other man had caught him stargazing, Jim felt himself flush, but then nodded.

"Yeah, she sure is," he answered. "But she don't know me from dust."

"Don't be so sure about that," Henry said. "That was a mighty fine thing you done saving her this afternoon. She ain't gonna be forgetting."

He'd just finished making himself a cigarette, and he offered the small bag of tobacco and rolling papers to Jim.

"Thanks," Jim said, and took the makings. "Don't mind if I do."

He quickly poured some tobacco onto a rectangle of paper, rolled it tight, and sealed it with a lick.

Henry flicked his thumbnail over the primer of a wooden kitchen match and held it to the end of Jim's cigarette first, and then his own. The smoke tasted dirty and hot, and Jim reminded himself that he'd vowed to quit the last time Bierce had offered him one.

Have to make this one my last, he thought. Besides, with his pocket empty and not knowing when he was going to get paid for this gig, he decided he just couldn't afford any luxuries. He'd be lucky to scrape together enough coins to purchase a bath when the weekend came.

He drew the smoke into his mouth and blew it out immediately, without forcing it into his lungs, remembering the persistent and nagging coughs of his father and uncles back on the farm. They'd all smoked consistently their whole lives and continually railed against the practice, advising him never to start. He'd smoked occasionally in the army out of boredom, and had never enjoyed it.

"Don't smoke much, does you?" Henry asked.

Jim smirked and shook his head. "You can tell, can you?"

Henry laughed. "It's a mighty good habit to avoid. I only allows myself four cigarettes a day. Did me some boxing in the Tenth. Was regimental champion for a time."

"Boxing, huh? I could tell you knew how to handle yourself back at the stable." Jim smiled. "Sure took those Mexicans to task."

Henry grinned. "You didn't do too bad yourself."

"Us veterans got to stick together."

"You got that right." Henry held up the cigarette and motioned with his head. "Smoking cuts down on your wind, your endurance, 'less'n you smokes a pipe, and I can't afford that."

"Me either," Jim said and took another light drag on the cigarette. Through the haziness of the smoke he saw the man named Tucker staring at him. His head was canted to the side and his eyes were framed in twin squints.

Jim got the distinct impression that the man didn't like him. Or maybe the hostile gaze was being directed at Henry.

"That fella Tucker's sure giving you and me the evil eye, ain't he?" Jim said. "What's his game anyway?"

"Hard to say." Henry let twin plumes of smoke drift out of his wide nostrils. "Sticks mostly to himself when he's not standing by with Mr. Creighton. His right-hand man. He's good at pinching pennies, that's for sure, but I gots me a feeling there's more to him than that. Got some kind of bitterness inside."

When Jim looked back, Tucker was removing a long, thin cigarette from a silver-colored case. His smokes looked store bought.

Two thin men dressed in non-western gear came up to them carrying a large cloth sack. They looked at Jim, then at each other, and then nodded.

"Here," one of them said, shoving a light blue shirt toward Jim. "Put this on."

"Huh?" Jim said.

"Just do it," the other man said. "We're from wardrobe."

He set the sack on the ground.

"Wardrobe?" Jim asked.

"Yes," the other one said, his tone petulant. "Wardrobe. And it's on Mr. Creighton's orders."

Henry chuckled, took one more drag on his cigarette, and tossed it way.

"Better do it, Jim," he said. "Here, I'll hold your horse. Look like they're gonna be making you a star."

A star?

What did that mean?

Jim tossed his cigarette away without even sampling a final taste and handed the animal's reins over. As he stripped off his shirt he saw one of the thin wardrobe men holding the new, light blue shirt by the shoulders, waiting for him to slip it on. The entire front section was folded outward, with a row of buttons up the left side and across the top. He realized then that it was identical to the one the big actor, Arthur Weeks, had on.

After Jim had stuck his arms into the sleeves, the two wardrobe men went to work affixing the buttons. One of them ripped Jim's hat off his head and replaced it with a tall, white Stetson—the same type as the movie actor's.

"Not bad, not bad," one said. "I told you it would fit."

The other's face contorted.

"Yes, but the pants," he said. Without another word he sniffed Jim's old shirt, frowned, and tossed it onto the ground.

"Hey," Jim said.

The wardrobe man made a tsking sound and dropped to one knee, pulling a cloth tape-measure out of his pocket. His left hand pinched Jim's crotch as the tape slithered between his right thumb and forefinger, traveling downward to Jim's boot.

"Oww," Jim said. "Watch it, will ya?"

"My mistake," the kneeling man said. He muttered something more and the other wardrobe man jotted notes down on a small notepad.

"We'll never be able to get this altered today," the kneeling wardrobe man said.

"Correct," the other said. "So we'll use the chaps, just like I suggested."

The kneeling one stood up and removed a pair of leather chaps from the sack.

"Put these on over your pants," he said. "Do you know how to do that or should I—"

"I think I can manage," Jim said, grabbing the chaps.

"Very well. Then report over to the boss. And make it snappy."

Make it snappy?

Jim glanced at Henry, who was having a good chuckle.

"Your star awaits, my prince," a voice said. Jim whirled and saw Bierce and Monroe standing only a few feet away.

"And I must admit," the author said. "Cerulean is definitely your color."

As soon as Jim had secured the leather riding chaps over his pants, he walked over to where Creighton, Tucker, and the group of actors were standing and saw they'd outfitted him in an identical costume to Arthur Weeks, at least from the waist up. The wardrobe team strode over to the actor and stood holding a pair of leather chaps toward him. Weeks sighed theatrically and rolled his eyes.

"Do I really have to subject myself to this indignity?" he said, in a plaintive whine.

Creighton frowned. "You do if you want to get paid."

Weeks heaved another exaggerated sigh and grabbed the chaps out of the wardrobe man's hands.

"Oh, just do it, Artie," Faith said. "I think it'll look fetching."

She cast a quick glance at Jim and winked.

He was stunned.

"The idea is to make him look like you," Tucker explained, gesturing toward Jim. "On camera, anyway."

The actor regarded Jim with an elevated-eyebrows expression of distaste and blew out a sonorous breath.

"Talk about trying to make a sow's ear into a silk purse," he said. "Not to mention the heat. I hope I won't have any sweat stains under my arms for the close-ups."

What a spoiled idiot, Jim thought. *If he'd been over in the Philippines with us, he'd know that the last thing to be worried about would be sweat stains.*

He felt like telling Weeks off, but then figured he and Larry had just gotten hired, so that wouldn't be very prudent. This was a land of make-believe, after all.

Everyone acted like Jim was just part of the scenery, or better yet, just another horse to be ridden and put away wet.

Faith, however, was different. She eyed Jim up and down, smiling, and complimented him on how handsome he looked. Her smile was like seeing one of those paintings in a museum or in a picture book.

Maybe she does like me, he thought.

But she kept being whisked away by Creighton to pose for more time in front of those cameras. Faith and Weeks were strategically positioned on the ersatz boardwalk in front of a building labeled *SHERIFF'S OFFICE* in big black letters against a white background. Creighton stood off to the side, out of camera range, and yelled directions through a megaphone. They played the same scene, Weeks standing there talking and Faith fawning up at him, looking captivated by every word.

Jim felt a pang of jealousy.

Some guys have all the luck, he thought. Even spoiled bastards who were born with a silver spoon in their damn mouths. He wondered if the actor had ever put in a hard day's worth of honest work.

Creighton called out they were going inside and told everyone, including the extras, to move into what was supposed to be a bar. After the cameras were strategically set in numerous places, the cameramen stepped back. Creighton went to each one, put his eye to the viewfinder, and called out orders positioning people in different spots, and then called over his shoulder to the fellows who would be operating the cameras, telling them how he wanted it filmed. Tucker followed behind him with a scowl plastered over his face. Finally, Creighton moved to the front of a long bar and called to Weeks and another man, a big burly fellow.

Jim had been standing off to the side when Creighton looked around and said, "Where the hell's my new stuntman?"

Tucker, his aquiline nose jutting out from under the brim of his Panama hat, slapped Jim's shoulder hard.

Jim turned and glared at him.

Before Jim could say he didn't like being manhandled, Tucker whistled and pointed. "Here he is, boss."

"All right." Creighton waggled his fingers in a come-hither gesture. "Get over here."

It was like he was issuing commands to a dog, but Jim reminded himself that he and Larry had just gotten hired and they needed these jobs. Very much. They were still skating on thin ice.

He swallowed his resentment and strode over to the three other men. The bar was slightly below chest height with a polished top counter just like one in a real tavern. Beyond the aisle, a row of bottles was lined up in front of a mirror that ran the length of the bar. In the reflection, Jim could see the main actor, Weeks, standing there smoking a cigarette and appearing utterly bored.

The burly guy took a look at Jim's size and build and gave a minute nod. "He sure looks like he can do it." His lips parted, displaying a gap-toothed grin.

"All right, then," Creighton said. "Here's the way we're going to do this. Baker, you take a looping swing at Art here. And Art, you duck and let the blow go over your head." The director turned back to Baker. "Make sure you don't knock off his hat. Got it?"

Baker grunted an affirmation.

Creighton turned back to Weeks.

"Then we'll freeze it, and you," he tapped Jim on the chest, "will take Art's place. Just make sure you keep your face turned away from the camera, got it? Don't look back."

Look back at what? Jim thought.

"Then," Creighton said, "you bend down and grab Baker by the legs here, lift him up, and throw him over the bar. Got it?"

"Better make sure he can lift him," Tucker chimed in. "Think you can handle that, hotshot?"

Hotshot?

Jim was about to say something in reply but hesitated, reminding himself once again that he and Larry really needed this job. He happened to glance over and saw Faith standing off to the side on a stairway to what was supposed to be the second floor. She was watching the scene unfold and seemed to be focusing on him.

Guess I'd better make a good showing of myself, he thought, allowing himself a mental dalliance of him and Faith someday sharing a drink at a real establishment like this.

Jim exhaled as he sized up Baker's girth.

"Let's see," he said, and bent over and grabbed the other man's legs as he sunk his right shoulder into Baker's soft gut. Then he bent his own legs and straightened up. The other man was heavy, but it was nothing Jim couldn't handle after hoisting all those rifles, machine guns, ammo boxes, and other stuff over in the Philippines.

"Where do you want me to put him?" he asked with a grin.

Creighton chuckled and pointed to the other side of the bar. "Can you dump him over there?"

Jim hoisted Baker higher, leaned over the bar, and started to drop him on the other side. The actor behind the bar ran over and held up his hands.

"Hold on," he said. "There's no mattress down there."

Jim felt Baker's hands grip him and he stopped.

"Goddammit," Creighton shouted. "Where the hell's the mattress?"

The bartender bent down and began pulling at something under the bar.

"It's rolled up here," he said.

"Well, spread it out, then," Creighton said. He turned back to Jim. "You might as well set him down, son."

Jim checked to see if Faith was still watching. Seeing that she was, he stood straighter and smiled, trying to make the human burden on his shoulder appear effortless as he set him down.

After the mattress was unrolled, Creighton told Jim to pick up Baker again and do a practice drop.

Baker's body seemed to have gained thirty pounds in the interim, but Jim did his best to hoist the man up and over the bar. Baker's cascading body caused Jim's tall white Stetson to take the plunge with him.

"No good," Tucker shouted. His aquiline nose jutted outward in an accusatory fashion. "Your damn hat fell off, you cretin."

Jim wasn't sure what a cretin was, but he was pretty sure it was something bad. He rotated his head and looked back at the hawk-nosed assistant director.

It was getting harder and harder not to tell this little son of a bitch off.

Baker popped up from behind the bar, grimaced as he rubbed his shoulder, and handed Jim his hat.

Creighton was standing back, his thumb and forefinger stroking the corners of his mouth. "You know, that might not be such a bad thing," he said. "Art, take off your hat and turn around."

The actor was in the process of smoking another cigarette, having just thrown the first one away. He heaved an exaggerated sigh, took a copious drag on his smoke, and removed his hat.

Creighton looked from him to Jim and then back again.

"Turn around, both of you," the director said.

Jim did so and saw their reflection in the mirror again. He searched for a glimpse of Faith but couldn't see her at the angle he was standing.

"Ah, dammit," Creighton said. "His hair's too short."

"And don't expect me to cut mine," Weeks said. "I'm not going to walk around looking like that simpleton."

This simpleton might just kick that smart mouth of yours all the way down to your ass, Jim thought.

But still, he said nothing, not wanting to get hired and fired in the same day. Peripherally, he saw Faith looking at him askance with a sly smile.

Jim heard Creighton grunt, and then the director snapped his fingers. When he spoke, his voice rose to a new level of excitement. "This is what we'll do. You've both got pretty much the same build." He tapped Jim on the shoulder and said, "Get over to the makeup tent and have them give you a wig."

"A wig?" Jim said.

The idea didn't set real well with him. Wigs were for women, weren't they?

"It'll certainly be an improvement," Arthur Weeks said with an accompanying laugh. He puffed on his cigarette and yawned. "Are we going to break for dinner soon? All this work has gotten me famished."

Work?

That dandy probably never did a hard day's work in his damn life, Jim thought, recalling the hardships he'd endured in the Philippines. *This ain't nothing. The son of a bitch don't know how good he has it.*

"Oh," a feminine voice said from across the room. "I think he'll look very handsome in that wig, Arthur."

Jim glanced over and caught another glimpse of Faith on the stairway. She was smoking a cigarette now, too, and leaning over the banister so that the front of her blouse spilled open a bit, exposing some of her cleavage. Jim couldn't tear his eyes away from the sight.

She apparently noticed his gaze and thrust her shoulders back slightly, exposing more of her soft flesh as her red lips drew back over her straight white teeth.

Her smile told Jim she knew what he'd been looking at, and in embarrassment he averted his eyes. But his mind raced. She'd complimented him . . . And she was smoking. The old adage he'd heard spoken by the older, more experienced boys of his youth resounded in his head: *If she smokes, she drinks. And if she drinks . . .*

Fat chance of that, he thought.

He swallowed and stole another glance at her.

But man, what a woman, he told himself.

Creighton emitted a sigh and dug his index finger inside his collar, rubbing it around.

"All right, all right," he said. "What the hell time is it, anyway? Somebody got a watch?"

"I do," Ambrose Bierce said. He and the scriptwriter, Monroe, had been standing on the fringes of the crowd, next to one of the cameramen. Bierce reached into his vest pocket and pulled out the gold watch Jim had seen before.

There's that watch again, he thought. *Someday, if I ever get the money, I'm going to get me a real special watch like that.*

"It's a quarter of five," Bierce said and snapped the lid closed.

Creighton nodded and blew out a long breath.

"It's a wrap for today," he said. "Tidy things up and then go eat. But, we resume right here tomorrow morning. Eight sharp. And you—" The director turned and pointed at Jim, "be in this same outfit and with your wig. Got it?"

Got it, Jim thought. He nodded and answered, "Yes, sir."

Creighton's eyebrows flickered slightly and he smiled, clapping Jim on the shoulder.

"This boy's nice and polite," he said, turning to the waspish Tucker. "Good manners. See, Don? I told you it was a good idea to hire him."

Tucker's frown deepened as he and the director walked away.

The two wardrobe men trotted over to Jim, demanding he remove his shirt.

"My shirt?" he said. "What for? I just put it on."

"And we'll have no time to launder it before tomorrow," one of the wardrobe men muttered, fluttering his hands. "Now take it off, take it off." He reached up and began undoing the buttons but Jim shoved the probing fingers away.

"I can undress myself, dammit," he said.

The wardrobe man pursed his lips.

"Who would have thought you'd be starring in a burlesque show," Bierce said with a laugh.

Jim laughed too as he slipped out of the fancy shirt.

The other wardrobe man shoved Jim's old shirt at him and both of them turned and scurried off, chattering to themselves.

Jim shook his shirt a few times, trying to rid it of the dust it had accumulated from being tossed on the ground. He was cognizant that it smelled a bit, too, and made a mental note to wash it out tonight when he got to their hotel room. As he did so, he caught a glimpse of Faith watching his shirtless performance. Their eyes met and she smiled.

A group of extras and what looked like maintenance men dressed in nondescript brown clothes began cleaning up and stacking the chairs on the tables. Weeks turned and walked away without a word. He was met by Faith, who took his arm, but not before shooting another smile and quick wink in Jim's direction.

Jim walked over to Bierce and Monroe, wondering what she'd meant by the flirtatious winks.

Bierce had an expression of amusement on his lined face as he locked eyes with Jim.

" 'Shall I compare thee to a summer's day?' " the author said. " 'Thou art more lovely and more temperate.' "

Jim's brow furrowed.

"Shakespeare's eighteenth sonnet," Bierce said. "Reflecting the state of a young man smitten by Aphrodite incarnate."

Smitten . . . Jim smirked. That was him, all right.

"But," the author continued. "It's wise to remember the remaining verse. 'Rough winds do shake the darling buds of May, and summer's lease hath all too short a date.' "

He clapped Jim on the shoulder.

Jim considered Bierce's words carefully. *I guess he's trying to remind me not to be making much ado about nothing.*

ϛ

1880
Main Street
Contention City, Arizona

After getting numerous pictures of Dayton in different poses and then some more of the interior of the sheriff's office and the cells, the minute or two that Cox had mentioned would be enough to finish the photo shoot was turning into an extended session that was bordering on forty-five minutes or so.

"These look pretty sturdy," Cox said, running his fingers up and down the smooth bars. "You get to use them a lot?"

"Some," Dayton said, aware that Hizzoner the mayor had positioned himself in the doorway separating the cell block from the office area.

"How about getting one of me in there, standing out here beside the sheriff?" Webber said. "Maybe holding one of them shotguns."

"Sure," Cox said. "That'll look real good."

"Lon," Webber said. "Can you get me one of them guns? They're all chained up."

The last thing Dayton wanted to do at this point, besides posing for more pictures, was to go grab the key out of the special hiding place in his desk and unlock the gun rack, but it was obvious that Hizzoner wanted his moment in front of the camera.

Dayton blew out a slow breath and strode over to the door, pausing while the mayor stepped back to allow him passage. Lipton, Dyer, and Burnside were all standing in a semicircle in the office, conversing in hushed tones. They stopped talking as Dayton entered and went to the desk. He opened the top drawer, pulled it all the way out, and set it on top of the flat surface. Stooping down, he extended his arm underneath and plucked the key from the metal hook he'd fastened to the underside. Then he rose, went to the rack of rifles, and inserted the key into the padlock.

"You keep those under lock and key, I see." Burnside flashed a grin. "Smart move. You keep them loaded?"

Dayton twisted the key and felt the lock release.

"All except the shotgun," he said, carefully pulling the chain through the trigger guards.

"Why not that one?" Dyer asked. "I've usually found that's a pretty good weapon for handling trouble."

"It is." Dayton removed the double-barreled shotgun from its perch, broke it open, verified that it was empty, and then slammed it closed. "It's also the easiest one to accidentally fire if you mishandle it."

"That's true," Burnside said. "I saw a hick lawman's deputy blow his foot off grabbing one of those once."

Dayton said nothing.

"Where do you keep the ammo?" Burnside asked.

"In a safe place," Dayton said, thinking that he was going to have to find a new hiding spot for the key now.

He stepped over to the mayor and handed him the shotgun.

Webber accepted it with a wide smile and immediately shouldered it, pointing the barrels at the cameraman.

"Reach for the sky," he bellowed.

Herman's face twisted in a frightful expression and he gasped.

Dayton's hand shot upward and grabbed the end of the barrel, pointing it at the ceiling.

Webber regarded him angrily.

"What the hell?" the mayor said. "I wasn't going to shoot him or anything."

Still holding the barrel in his iron grip, Dayton stared down into the mayor's eyes.

"Never point a gun at anything you don't intend to shoot," Dayton said, his voice a low, even growl.

"Oh, for Christ's sake, Lon," Hizzoner said. "You just finished saying it wasn't even loaded."

"You treat every gun as if it's loaded." Dayton kept staring at the shorter man until the latter's face flushed.

"Hold the weapon at port arms," Dayton said. Noticing the look of confusion on the mayor's part, he took the shotgun and demonstrated. "Like this. You always want to keep the barrel pointed in a safe direction. Got it?"

Webber seemed to be chewing the inside of his lip as he listened. The flush spread downward onto his heavy jowls. He quickly lowered his head with a jerking motion that indicated agreement, obviously embarrassed at being chastised in front of his poker buddies.

Herman picked up the camera, walked backwards, and gently set the contraption down again.

"This is going to be a tight shot," he said. "Sheriff, you and the mayor go stand over by those *Wanted* posters, will ya?"

They did, with Webber continuing to hold the shotgun across his chest.

"That's good," Herman said. "Now, take a step closer together, will ya?"

They did and Dayton once again caught another unpleasant whiff of the mayor's pungent body odor.

"Is this going to take much longer?" Dayton asked. "I got some things to do."

"Like finishing getting the rest of that horseshit off your boot," Burnside shouted.

The rest of the group laughed.

Dayton's frown deepened.

"How's that look, Bill?" Herman asked. "That what you want?"

"Perfect," Cox replied. "Now, Mr. Mayor, why don't you get a real mean expression on your face."

Webber did and then a sudden loud burst of flatulence broke the silence.

Dayton recoiled and the mayor laughed.

"I thought you said it wasn't loaded?" Hizzoner said, still chuckling.

The others all laughed, too.

Herman ducked under the black hood again and raised the tray with the flash powder. "Hold still now," he said. "And remember, this is for posterity, so look stern."

The combined odor hanging in the air made Dayton want to gag. His lips visibly tightened as he stood holding his breath.

"Ah," Herman said. "Sheriff, you want to take your gun out of the holster?"

"Just take the damn picture, will ya?" Dayton's voice was a low growl.

The flash powder ignited, blinding him for a split second. Gradually his vision returned and he saw Burnside standing several feet away with a smart-aleck grin plastered on his round face.

"You're going to need our pictures, too, ain't ya, Bill?" Lipton said. "Maybe a group shot of all of us?"

"Sure thing," Cox said. "Herman, let's move this outside."

Herman ripped off the black cloth, smiled, and then caught a whiff of the mayor's residual stench. The smile disappeared.

"That sounds like a good idea," he muttered, and lifted the camera and collapsed the three long wooden legs.

"It shouldn't take much longer," Cox said. "And then we can do some more after lunch."

What a lousy end to what should have been a nice morning, Dayton thought. *And I still have to figure out who all I should be able to deputize.*

℘

1913
Stable Area
Thunderhead Motion Pictures Lot
Near San Diego, California

After taking care of the horses Jim, Henry, and Whitey made their way back in the fading late evening light toward the main entrance and the food tent. Bierce had elected to remain with them, spouting off more Shakespearean quotes after hearing that Henry had served in the army as well.

"And what about you, my good man?" the author asked Whitey in a friendly tone as the four of them walked abreast.

Whitey snorted. "You'd better go see about getting yourself some of them eyeglass spectacles, mister, if'n you're gonna be referring to me as a 'good man.' "

Bierce laughed.

"A mere colloquialism," he said. "And certainly not intended with any facetiousness."

Whitey glanced at him. "You ain't making fun of me, is ya?"

"Why, certainly not," the author said. "But, I must contend, a particularly appropriate designation after witnessing your prowess with a pistol during that little fracas earlier."

Whitey snorted again and glanced at Jim and Henry. "One of you two want to tell me what the hell he's saying?"

Henry laughed. "He's talking about how you shot that Mexican's hat off back at the stables."

Twin creases appeared between Whitey's bushy eyebrows. "And what of it?"

"He's saying you're a pretty fair shot with a pistol, Whitey," Jim said.

"Pretty fair?" Whitey's mouth twisted into a frown.

"Unless you meant to aim a mite lower," Henry added with a chuckle.

Whitey stopped walking and squinted at him. The others stopped walking as well.

Whitey's head swiveled from side to side, and then he pointed with his non-gun hand at the side of the dirt path.

"One of y'all go pick up that piece of tin over there," he said.

Jim saw a discarded can of chewing tobacco lying in the dirt.

"What the hell for?" Henry asked.

"Just do it, dammit." Whitey's voice sounded gruff.

None of the others was moving, so Jim stepped over and picked it up.

"Now what?" he asked.

"Toss it up in the air," Whitey said. "Good and high."

The request took Jim by surprise, but he drew back his arm and gave the tin can an underhanded toss.

Raising up the tails of his untucked shirt, Whitey pulled out one of the Colt Peacemakers that had been tucked into his belt, cocked back the hammer, and fired.

The sudden sound of the pistol was like someone unexpectedly clapping both hands over Jim's ears. His hearing disappeared for a moment, and then gradually returned, accompanied by a constant ringing sound.

The tin can hit the soft dirt a few feet away. Whitey stuck the Peacemaker back in his belt and covered it with his shirttail. Henry strode over, retrieved the fallen tin can, and held it up for the others to see. A round hole was right through the center.

Jim emitted a low whistle.

"Damn, Whitey," he said. "That was some good shooting."

"Very impressive indeed," Bierce added.

Whitey's rickety teeth appeared under his bushy mustache.

"Hell, I woulda put two rounds through it 'fore it hit the ground," he said. "But I didn't want to waste the ammo."

Henry laughed out loud and handed the perforated can to Jim.

"You best keep this, 'less'n he decides somebody else needs convincing. You can just show 'em that, and he won't have to fire no shots."

Jim grinned and slipped the can into his rucksack. It would be a good conversation piece, and it was also a reminder that there was clearly more to Whitey than he'd thought.

A whole lot more.

Chapter 8

1880
Blacksmith's Shop
Contention City, Arizona

Dayton entered the blacksmith shop silently and stood off to the side watching, not wanting to disturb the blacksmith in the midst of his work. Elmer Abbey used the metal tongs to pull one of the red-hot horseshoes from the heated embers and transfer it to the anvil. His right hand, the one with the heavy sledgehammer, came up and slammed down onto the heated metal, the massive biceps of his huge arm standing out in bas-relief. He banged the hammer down several more times, leaned forward to inspect the shoe, and then dropped it into the bucket of water, causing a hissing sizzle.

"What can I do for you, Sheriff?" Abbey asked.

Dayton stepped closer. The blacksmith's pungent sweat mixed with the sharp, metallic odor of the other horseshoe on the hot coals.

"I need your help for an upcoming event," Dayton said.

"As a deputy?"

"Right." Dayton debated how much to tell him. At this point he didn't want a lot of rumors swirling around about the amnesty proposal plan, but on the other hand, the way the mayor and his cronies were bustling about taking pictures, it wouldn't stay a secret for long.

Abbey used the tongs to rotate the horseshoe on the coals.

"What event is this?" he asked.

"You heard about the territorial governor's proclamation of amnesty?"

Abbey nodded.

"Well," Dayton said, "I've got Dutch Bascom and his gang coming in a week from tomorrow to sign up for it."

Abbey's face registered surprise. "Dutch Bascom? The last time he was here, they shot up the town."

Dayton nodded, letting the information settle. "That was a while back. I think he knows his time's about up. He either takes the amnesty or they hunt him down."

Abbey licked his lips and then blew out a heavy breath. "I reckon you're right. That seems to be the way for those who live by the gun. Time always catches up to them."

The words hit Dayton like a punch to the gut. Was time catching up to him too?

September Gun.

"I talked face-to-face with Bascom," Dayton said. "He's the one contacted me about it. I don't think he's looking for any trouble."

Abbey said nothing.

"And the pay's up from two to five dollars now," Dayton added.

"Five dollars." Abbey raised his eyebrows. "Damn."

The blacksmith rotated the glowing horseshoe a bit more, and then transferred it to the anvil as well. He brought the hammer down hard, tapped it several times, and then smashed it down again. The ringing was still echoing in Dayton's ears as Abbey dropped the second shoe into the bucket.

"Yeah, I reckon I can do that." He grinned. "Can't expect you to face up to them ne'er-do-wells by yourself. And I can't complain about making that kind of money."

Dayton felt relieved. Not only was Abbey one of the strongest men in the town, but he was level-headed and a pretty good shot as well.

"Who else you got?" the blacksmith said.

"I'm fixing to ask Big Rich Swafford and Kevin Fitzgerald."

Abbey's head rocked slightly to and fro.

"Both good men. They done pretty good the last couple times we worked with 'em."

That had been when a bunch of wild-acting cowboys fresh off of a cattle drive had come sauntering into town to blow off steam. Dayton had laid down the law early and tossed a bunch of them in jail. The others quieted down real quick after that and no one was shot, nor any substantial property destroyed, except for a broken mirror at the Brass Cupcake saloon.

Dayton felt he should tell Abbey the rest of it. "Mayor Webber's arranging for some Pinkerton detectives on hand, too, just in case. But like I said, I don't think there'll be any trouble."

Abbey was placing another horseshoe onto the reddish-orange embers.

"We should be in for a real easy day," Dayton said.

"Sounds like easy money, then."

"Easy money," Dayton repeated, the thoughts of a portion of that five-thousand-dollar reward dancing in his mind's eye. "Let's hope so."

He was feeling pretty damn good as he exited the blacksmith's shop and started over toward the center square, trying to figure where he might find Swafford and Fitzgerald. The former owned a general store but was purported to have been in some heavy fighting in the Civil War, so he knew how to handle himself. Fitzgerald had several jobs, the most regular of which was bartender at the Brass Cupcake. That hadn't stopped him from assisting Dayton from time to time when he wasn't working. And if this amnesty deal was going to occur at ten o'clock in the morning, Fitz should be available, provided he hadn't had a prior late night.

Just as Dayton was about to turn in to Swafford's shop, he heard someone call his name.

"Lon."

He turned and saw Mayor Webber, Lipton, Dyer, and Burnside, followed by the reporter, Cox, and the hapless Herman toting his camera, his flash powder and T-square, and the heavy black veil.

Dayton blew out a slow breath.

What more could these idiots want?

He stopped while they made their way over to him.

"Glad we caught you," Hizzoner said. "Where'd you disappear to?"

"I've been trying to line up them deputies," Dayton said.

Webber frowned and pursed his lips. "Never you mind about that now," he said. "Mr. Cox wants one more picture of you."

"Another one? How many do you need?"

Cox made an attempt at what Dayton took to be a fair imitation of an apologetic shrug.

"I realized that we didn't have one of you and Mr. Burnside standing side by side." He licked his lips and pointed to the boardwalk in front of the barbershop. "This looks to be a good solid backdrop. Right next to that red and white pole."

Dayton silently reflected that the red and white pole once symbolized a medical treatment station, back when barbers often acted as doctors.

And this son of a bitch is gonna need one before too much longer, he thought. *If he doesn't quit bothering me.*

"Mr. Burnside," Cox continued. "If you'd be so kind as to step up there next to the sheriff."

It was a small consolation that Burnside looked as bothered and bored as Dayton was.

"All right, let me see." Cox held his hands out in front of him as Herman was spreading open the three stick-legs of the camera. "Sheriff, you're a bit taller than Mr. Burnside here." He bit his lower lip and spoke over his shoulder to his photographer. "Herman, can you get closer and make this one a three-quarter shot? Not showing too much of their legs?"

Herman rolled his eyes and picked up the camera. The sweat was pouring off of him as the sun rose to midmorning.

"Now," Cox continued, "Sheriff, can you kind of squat down a tad? So your heads are about level with each other?"

Dayton didn't make the requested move.

"Sheriff?" Cox repeated.

"I've just about had enough of you, Cox," Dayton said. "Take the damn photo or I'm walking away. I got work to do."

"Lon," Webber said. "This is for posterity. For the history of Contention City."

Dayton stood rigid beside the shorter Burnside, who looked equally disgruntled.

"Mr. Burnside," Cox said. "Show us your gun, please."

Burnside obliged by tucking the tail end of his long jacket behind his holstered weapon. Dayton glanced down at it and saw it was a big double-action Remington, and wondered if Burnside knew how to use it.

Herman ducked under the black veil again and held up his T-square with the flash powder.

"Smile," he said. When neither man did so, he added, "Or not."

The flash powder ignited with an accompanying loud thump. The sudden burst made Dayton close his eyes as the image of residual starlike brightness danced over his retinas.

"There," Cox said, sounding triumphant. "That wasn't so bad, was it?"

Without another word Dayton turned and marched away from the six of them.

What a parade of fools, he thought.

ळ

1913
Food Tent
Thunderhead Motion Pictures Lot
Near San Diego, California

After getting their plates, silverware, and cups, Jim, Henry, Bierce, and Monroe moved through the serving line at the food tent. It appeared that they were the last to be served. Jim looked around. The rows of tables were filled with a variety of workers, most of whom he'd seen operating the cameras and arranging things on the set earlier. There was one conspicuous absence, however.

"Where's that Lobo fella and his boys?" Jim asked.

"They're most likely already over in *La Fronteriza*," Henry said. "They usually just grab something and scurry across the border."

"And good riddance, too," Whitey added. "They better hope I don't see 'em if 'n I decide to meander over there myself tonight to get me a little Mexican tail."

"That sounds like a proposition I might be interested in," Bierce said with a lascivious grin.

It sounded like a dangerous proposition to Jim. He'd already had enough trouble with Lobo and his boys for one day. He looked over and saw the pretty Mexican girl, Teresa, he thought her name was, standing behind a large metal pot with a ladle in hand. He hoped she hadn't heard Whitey's comment. Next to her was an older man in a white chef's uniform and matching hat. The front of his apron, which was pushed outward by his substantial stomach, had several stains on the front, but was otherwise immaculate. Larry stood off to the side behind the serving table holding his plate as well. He grinned at Jim who brought up the rear.

"Been waiting to eat with y'all," Larry said. "Then I gotta help Donna and Richard with the dishes."

As they stepped forward, Larry said, "You remember Teresa."

Jim smiled and nodded. "I sure do."

She smiled at him, then turned and placed her hand on the arm of the man in the cook-whites.

"Jim, this is my father," she said, and then made some comment to the man in what Jim figured was either Spanish or French. From what he knew, he figured on the latter.

Teresa's father's head bobbled slightly and he smiled.

"François Delacroix," the man said, straightening his body as if coming to attention. "At your *service*. *Et es* my *plaisir* to meet you, *monsieur*. I *haf* heard much about *choo* from Teresa."

The girl quickly compressed her lips and shot a mean glance at her father.

Jim gave him an acknowledging nod. Everything seemed to have worked out pretty well. He and Larry were both employed and had a place to stay.

Not bad so far, he thought as he held out his plate.

Teresa turned back and smiled at him as she dipped the ladle into the pot of stew and then poured it onto his plate. A delicious smell wafted upward and Jim thanked her.

"Anything for our big hero," she said, handing him two biscuits. Those smelled good as well. "I heard you saved the day."

Jim shrugged. "It wasn't much. Just did what anybody would've done."

"That's not what I heard," Teresa said.

"It sure wasn't," Larry interjected. "Why, Jim here's a real live hero. Remind me to tell you what he done over in the Philippines sometime."

"Larry," Jim said, letting some harshness enter his tone.

"What? It's true." Larry turned back to Teresa. "Why, he saved my life. I wouldn't be here if'n it wasn't for him. And they give him a bunch of medals, too."

Jim felt himself flush as the pretty girl's smile broadened.

"A veritable modern-day Sir Galahad," Bierce said, stepping over to them. He looked at Teresa and said, "*¿Y el es muy guapo, también, no?*"

Her smile broadened further, and Jim thought he detected a glimmer of adulation in her dark brown eyes.

"*Sí, es verdad,*" she said.

"*Muy verdad,*" Bierce added, casting a knowing glance at Jim.

"You speak Spanish, Mr. Bierce?" Larry said. "I didn't know that."

"A smidgen here and there," the author said. "Come on, let's go eat."

Jim caught a glimpse of Teresa watching them as they started to walk away. "What'd you say to her?" he asked.

Bierce grunted a laugh. "Just attesting to your good looks," he said, then leaned closer and added, "She likes you. And she's very pretty, too."

Before Jim could agree, he heard a voice call out to him. A feminine voice. Faith sat at the closest table, next to Arthur Weeks. Creighton and Tucker sat on the opposite side.

"Jim," Faith said again. "Come join us."

"Oh, *puhleeze*." Weeks held his hand up and gripped the end of his nose. "The last thing I want is to be sitting across from someone that smells like a stable, and that's putting it kindly."

Jim self-consciously turned his head and did a surreptitious sniff. He had to admit, he didn't smell very nice. He made another mental note to take off his shirt and wash it when he got to the hotel. A bath would be preferable, if one were available. It had been several days since he'd washed.

More like a week's worth, he added mentally.

Over in the Philippines he'd gone for much longer than that and smelled a lot worse, but back then he wasn't going to be within smelling distance of someone as beautiful as Faith.

"He doesn't have to sit next to you, Artie," Faith said. "He can sit next to me."

She turned her head back toward Jim, smiled, and patted the back of the chair on her right side.

"Listen, my sweet," Weeks said, his eyes hooded as he looked down at her. "A leading man, and his leading lady, do not mingle with the hired help." He raised his gaze to Jim and the others. "Especially if their ranks include the lower social classes. Those two sleep in the barn, for Christ's sake."

Whitey nudged Henry and they both started walking toward the far row of tables.

Jim felt like going over and belting the fatuous actor, but remained frozen in place, reminding himself that this was their first day, and he didn't want to do something that would make it their last.

Tucker glared at them and jerked his thumb in the direction that Henry and Whitey had gone. "Beat it. We got private matters to discuss. And Monroe, you stay here."

Monroe glanced at Bierce and Jim, then slowly started toward the seated array of very important people.

"Mr. Bierce," Creighton said. "You can stay if you want."

Bierce raised an eyebrow and surveyed the seated individuals, then shook his head.

"I think not." The author smiled. "I've been traveling for several days and am a trifle bit odiferous myself. I shouldn't want to upset Mr. Weeks's delicate sensibilities."

Weeks frowned.

"Besides," Bierce continued, "I share a certain comradeship with Jim here, and the black man as well. We're veterans of three separate wars."

With that, the author started walking away. Monroe said, "Wait, Mr. Bierce. Here."

He handed Bierce a large hardbound book, which the author slipped under his arm. "Ah, yes," he said. "I'd almost forgotten. Thank you."

Tucker was still glaring at Jim. Not wanting to say anything in reply and cause a ruckus, Jim reached up and tipped his hat to Faith, and then followed Bierce. After a few long strides, he caught up to the author.

"I think it'll be much better company over yonder," Jim said.

"Undoubtedly."

After they sat at the table with Henry and Whitey, the black man grinned. "Come to join us lower social classes, I see."

"One's self-perceived social status is nothing more than a figment of a fool's own self-aggrandizement," Bierce said, settling into his chair.

Henry shook his head. "I don't know what you just said, but I gots me a feeling I oughta agree with it."

Bierce chuckled.

Larry came ambling over along with Teresa, who was carrying a coffeepot in one hand and a carafe of what appeared to be water in the other.

"My sister says I can eat with ya," Larry said, setting his plate down and swinging his stiff leg in front of a chair on the other side of the author. "And Teresa's brung us some coffee."

"I have water too," she said. "If you'd rather have that."

"Coffee for me, please, fair maiden," Bierce said.

She poured some of the dark liquid into his cup and then immediately looked down at Jim and smiled. "And which would our white knight prefer?"

Jim smiled back at her and asked for water.

As she leaned forward to pour, Jim couldn't help but notice the delicate smoothness of her skin and the exquisite symmetry of her features. He noticed that she had a nice shape to her as well.

"*¿Si el es Don Quixote*," Bierce said, "*entonces quisas eres Dulcinea?*"

Teresa stared at him, but said nothing. Jim felt that some sort of foreign communication had occurred between the two of them and he sensed that she was upset.

Bierce must have noticed it too, because his face took on a strained expression and he said, "*Lo siento, señorita. Soy muy tonto. Estoy culpable y no fue divertito.*"

She gave a slight smirk and rolled her eyes, moving around the table offering the two choices to Larry, Whitey, and Henry.

After she'd served each of them she took one more look at Jim and then headed back to the main serving table.

"I'll be along in a couple of minutes to help ya," Larry called out and then looked at Jim. "She's sweet on you, ya know."

Jim said nothing.

"He knows," Bierce said. "Gentlemen, we are in the presence of a modern-day Don Juan."

Jim dipped his spoon into the stew and sampled it. Although it wasn't very hot now, it still tasted great.

"What did you say to her that time?" he asked the author.

Bierce ate a spoonful of his stew, broke off a chunk of biscuit, and then frowned. "Just another example of Bitter Bierce making another of his faux pas. An old man's feeble attempt at humor in a putrid effort to impress a young maiden."

Jim found the author's explanation confusing. "Who's Dulcinea?"

"I see you've never read Cervantes. *Don Quixote.*"

"Who's that?"

"Another knight." The author dropped the fragment of bread into his stew and snared the mixture with his spoon. "But I daresay my comparison was a poor and inappropriate jest. In fact, *Señor* Cervantes's creation, Quixote, is more reminiscent of me than you, and she is certainly no Dulcinea."

Jim made a mental note to look up that book when he got the chance.

They all ate in silence, devouring their food. When he'd finished his, Larry emitted a hefty sigh and grinned.

"Donna always was good at making biscuits," he said. "But I guess Teresa and her father do most all of the other cooking."

"Her father?" Jim asked. "He's a cook, or something?"

"Calls himself a chef. Name's François Delacroix," Henry said. "He's a Frenchman that settled in these parts. Married

Teresa's mother, but she done passed a few years ago. Now he wants to open a restaurant around here, if'n he can."

So she's half Mexican and half French, Jim thought. *That's quite a combination.*

"Nice fella, too," Larry added. "Say, I thought I heard a gunshot 'fore y'all walked up. Was there some more trouble?"

The other four exchanged knowing looks and Jim reached into his pocket and withdrew the perforated tin can.

"Take a look at this," he said, setting it on the table.

Larry's eyes widened. "Damn, who done that?"

Jim glanced at Whitey, who said nothing.

"And he shot it out of the air, too," Henry said. "This man's a real live western gunslinger."

"A gunslinger?" Larry's mouth gaped. "No kidding."

Whitey picked up his cup and slowly sipped the coffee in it.

"When we was coming back on the ship from the Philippines," Larry said, "Jim here musta read me all the books in the ship's library. A couple of them was yours, Mr. Bierce, but most of them was western stories about gunfighters. You one of them, Whitey?"

The other man didn't reply.

Larry looked at the hole in the tin can, and then back to Whitey.

"Outta the air, too," he said. "Whitey, you ever been in a gunfight?"

Whitey set his cup down and exhaled. "A time or two."

Larry's eyes darted around the seated group, and then he asked, "Ever killed a man?"

Whitey considered the question, blew out a long breath, and then said, "Yep."

"How many?"

"Enough of 'em," he said. "And I'm fixing to kill another one not too far down the road, too."

Larry grinned. "Well, I guess that's my cue to stop bothering you with so many questions, huh?"

That brought a series of chuckles all around.

Bierce picked up the good-sized book that Monroe had given him and plopped it down in the center of the table.

"There's some authentic, old-time gunfighters in here," he said. "It's called *The Contention City Shootout*, and tells the sad tale of the real occurrence. Godfrey loaned it to me. He's using it to write the script for the motion picture, trying to keep it as authentic as possible."

He opened it to a bookmarked section with a photograph of two men standing side by side. One was taller and wore a star above the left breast pocket of his shirt. The other was heavyset and shorter, with a suit jacket on, the tail tucked over the handle of his big six-gun.

"Shucks," Larry said. "Them two fellas don't look none too happy, do they? Especially that one."

He laid a finger on the tall man in the photograph.

"That's Sheriff Lon Dayton," Bierce said, "whom our illustrious Mr. Weeks is portraying in the film. He's still alive and purportedly was involved in this big gunfight with a gang of outlaws back in eighteen-eighty."

"A gunfight?" Larry said. "A lot of people get killed?"

Bierce nodded. "Quite a few, according to this book."

Whitey snorted and spat off to the side.

"Godfrey has told me this man, Dayton, was a genuine hero, along the lines of Wyatt Earp." Bierce looked up from the book. "They're paying for him to make an appearance here next week, upon the motion picture. Creighton's asked me to make sure I put that in the article I'm writing."

"You got a title for it yet?" Jim asked.

Bierce rubbed his chin. "I'm leaning toward, 'Code of the West.' That's the title of the motion picture."

Whitey spat again.

"Gosh," Larry said. "An actual gunfight . . . And a real live hero lawman, too. I can't wait to meet him." He stood and collected everyone's dishes and cups. "Guess I'd better get these over there and start to washing. Just like pulling KP in the army, huh, Jim?"

Jim got up. "Let me give you a hand."

Before Larry could reply, the loud blast of a car horn sounded and a sleek, shiny, black automobile pulled up on the outskirts of the serving tent. Two men were inside the car, and the one in the passenger seat looked gigantic. He had a huge, elongated face with a mean-looking expression. The black hat he wore looked somehow too small as it sat atop his enormous head. The guy behind the wheel was a much smaller, corpulent fellow who was wearing a cream-colored suit and a soft, wide-brimmed hat in a matching color. A leering grin was fixed on his fleshy visage, and he reached over and squeezed the horn again. There was one on each side of the vehicle.

"Uh-oh," Henry said. "Here comes some trouble."

Jim turned and looked at the two men in the car and felt a growing uneasiness.

"Who's that?" Larry asked.

"Wade Klayman," Henry said. "He runs his own movie studio. Been trying to buy Thunderhead from Mr. Creighton for the longest. Nobody 'round here likes him much."

Larry whistled. "Man. What kind of automobile is that?"

"If I'm not mistaken," Bierce said, "it's a seven-passenger Cadillac limousine."

Jim watched as the man in the cream-colored suit squeezed the horn on the automobile once more and grinned. The door on the other side opened and the giant got out, hustled around the car, and opened the driver's door. Klayman slid out from behind the steering wheel and plopped his feet onto the ground. He was at least a foot and a half shorter than the other man.

"Who's the big one?" Larry asked.

"His name's Maynard Hogan," Whitey said. "Bigger than a buffalo and meaner than a rattlesnake."

"Nobody likes him, neither," Henry added. "But they's all too afraid to say so."

Jim shook his head and watched as the mismatched pair sauntered toward the food tent and the table where Creighton and the others were sitting.

Were things ever going to settle down around here?

*

1880
Swafford's General Store
Contention City, Arizona

"Then I can count on you, Rich?" Dayton asked as he stared across the counter at the big man on the other side. Swafford had a barrel chest and was even taller than Dayton himself. His shaggy brown hair hung down over his ears, matching his drooping mustache. The massiveness of the man was offset somehow by a delicate pair of round, gold-framed spectacles that sat on his nose.

"The Bascom gang." Swafford shook his head and took in a deep breath. "Who'd believe it?"

"Believe me, it's true. So, you with me?"

Swafford slowly exhaled. "All you've done for this town, Lon, I can't rightly refuse. And I guess I got enough left in me for one last battle."

"Ain't gonna be no trouble," Dayton said. "The territorial governor's offering amnesty to them. And they want to take advantage of it."

"I hope that's the only thing they're going to take advantage of. Who all you got again?"

"You, Elmer Abbey, and me so far," Dayton said. "I'm fixing to run over to the Brass Cupcake in a bit and see about getting Kevin Fitzgerald, too."

Swafford removed some canned goods from a box and set them on the shelf behind him.

"He's a good man," Swafford said. "So long as he's got a scattergun. Can't shoot for shit."

Dayton chuckled. He was as concerned about the possible danger as Swafford was, but felt that he had to believe there wouldn't be any trouble.

"I've already met with Dutch Bascom," Dayton said. "And he's tired of fighting. Him and what's left of his boys know their days as outlaws are numbered."

Swafford's head swiveled. "You met with Bascom?"

Dayton nodded.

"When?"

"A couple of nights ago. He sent me a letter asking about the amnesty. I confirmed it with the territorial governor and then met with him."

The large man seemed to ponder this and then nodded.

"And he didn't try to shoot you?"

Dayton smiled. "He had the opportunity, if he'd been of a mind to, but he didn't. It convinced me him and his boys intend to give themselves up."

"Who'd a figured it?"

"So, can I count on you to back me up?" Dayton asked. "Wear that deputy's badge one more time?"

Swafford finished putting the cans in place, turned, and extended his big hand across the counter. "Like I told you, Lon, I'd follow you to hell and back."

Dayton smiled and the two men shook.

As he stepped out into the sunshine Dayton was feeling cautiously optimistic. So far, two of the three men he wanted as deputies had agreed. And he wasn't expecting trouble, just like he'd told Swafford. If he could get Fitz to come along, Dayton felt the show of force would be more than adequate to ensure a smooth and orderly process.

A process . . . Was that the proper terminology?

Burnside had called it "a capture."

Dayton shook his head. Leave it to that fat, self-centered idiot to toss some dirt into the gears instead of oil. He made another note to make sure he made it clear to Lipton and Hizzoner that he was in charge, not Burnside, and for safety's sake, the Pinkertons were to stay out of sight.

He felt he had gained Bascom's trust, and that the outlaw would keep his word. Bascom and his boys were the ones with everything to gain by the amnesty. And they had to know that if they turned things sour, they would lose.

But things weren't going to turn sour. Dayton was sure of it. As long as things went smoothly, and they saw three big men like Elmer, Rich, and Fitz standing there holding their rifles at port arms . . . Their size would be an intimidation factor. So would their rifles.

And I intend to be wearing my two guns, Dayton thought. *With Dutch and his boys able to keep theirs, it'll be a kissin' cousin to a Mexican standoff. They'll ride in, we'll meet them at the tent, Lipton or whoever can present them with the amnesty papers, and then it'll be all over with and it'll be one for the record book.*

Burnside and his Pinkertons could stay in the background and out of sight, and then come up later and pose for all the photographs they wanted with Cox and his photographer. Him and his damn picture book. He wondered if Cox had a title for it yet.

But what the hell did it matter?

The parade of fools could march all over town proclaiming victory and claiming the amnesty deal was of their making. So could the territorial governor. Nothing mattered to Dayton except seeing this deal through to the end without any trouble. And with no one getting hurt.

As he approached the Brass Cupcake, he saw the boardwalk in front of the place was deserted. Hopefully he could catch Fitzgerald inside polishing glasses or something.

Hell, Dayton thought. *I don't care even if he's nursing a hangover. So long as he agrees to be deputized.*

And he knew that once that was done, he could allow himself to think about his upcoming picnic with April May, and maybe, just maybe, what he was going to do with his portion of the promised five-thousand-dollar reward.

But I don't want to get too far ahead in my thinking, Dayton told himself.

There was still a whole lot of stuff that could happen.

ℰℭ

1913
Food Tent
Thunderhead Motion Pictures Lot
Near San Diego, California

Jim carried a stack of dishes toward the front and watched as the mismatched pair, the lumbering giant and the officious-looking pipsqueak, waddled toward the VIP table inside the open tent.

"Aren't you going to invite me and Maynard to sit down and join your dinner, Frank?" Klayman asked, puffing on a cigarette. The sly smile on his face made the inquiry appear rhetorical.

"Dinner time's over," Creighton said in a flat tone. "What do you want?"

Klayman's head canted to the side, the smile on his undersized mouth suspended between two bulbous cheeks above it.

"Now is that any way to treat the man who made a special trip down here to offer to save your ass?"

"Save my ass from what?"

The tip of Klayman's cigarette glowed brightly and the unctuous little man blew out a cloudy breath.

Creighton looked obviously disturbed. He put a cigarette between his lips and started patting his pockets for a match. Tucker, who was still seated next to him, drew a long wooden one out of his pocket, flicked the primer with his thumbnail, and held it in front of Creighton's face.

Nodding thanks, Creighton leaned forward and put the tip of his cigarette into the flame. Puffing a few times, he blew out a plume of smoke and glared over at the two would-be intruders.

"I asked you what you wanted?" he said.

Klayman expelled a burst of air that resembled a laugh.

"What do I *want*?" His voice rose half an octave on the last word. He chuckled and his grin grew wider. "What I want is to save you from certain financial ruin. Save your current motion picture project as well." Klayman paused and gripped the lapels of his suit jacket with both hands, then leaned back. "The way I see it, I'm your only way out."

"Out from what?"

"From financial ruin, as I said. You'll never get this monstrosity of yours completed on time. Add to that, your whole proposal is wrong."

Creighton blew twin plumes of smoke out his nostrils.

"Bullshit," he said. "And how the hell would you know?"

Klayman's mouth turned downward at the edges as he shook his head.

"It's too damn long, for one thing. Nobody's going to want to sit in a theater long enough for a four-reeler."

It was Creighton's turn to frown. "That's where you're wrong. It's going to be the coming thing, and Thunderhead's going to be leading the charge."

Jim watched as Klayman's face scrunched up.

"I heard you had some trouble on the set today," he said.

"Where'd you hear that?"

The other man laughed. "I've got my ways."

Jim was standing by the main table now, holding a stack of the dirty dishes and cups he'd gathered and trying to gauge Faith's reaction to all this. She seemed pretty much unaffected, leaning against Arthur Weeks's big shoulder. The actor, along with all of the other seated individuals, was totally silent.

Guess they're waiting to see how this one plays out, Jim thought. *Just like me.*

Teresa was suddenly in front of him, smiling as she gently touched his arm and guided him toward the rear of the serving table where a large tub of soapy water was perched on top of a wooden stand. Teresa's father and Donna stood next to it.

"You going to hold those all night?" Teresa said, her voice imbued with merriment.

Jim smiled reflexively. "I reckon not."

"Larry, *por favor*," Teresa said. "Help Richard get the rest of the dishes, would you?"

Larry had finished placing his plates in the water and quickly hobbled after his brother-in-law, who was already at the VIP table. Phipps had most of the dishes stacked up against his chest with his one good arm, walking with cautious steps as he worked his way around the table.

The big man, Maynard or whatever his name was, seemed to take notice of this and ran his tongue over his teeth with a sucking sound. Just as Phipps rounded the far corner of the table, the giant took a lumbering step forward and bumped hard against him. Both Phipps and the dishes went scattering over the tabletop, upsetting a couple of the coffee cups that remained there and spewing the dark liquid on top of the white tablecloth.

"You damned one-armed son of a bitch," the huge man bellowed. "Why don't you watch where you're goin'?"

"Hey," Larry shouted as he helped Phipps up. "You done that on purpose, mister."

"Another cripple?" Maynard said. "That all they hire around here?"

"You best shut your mouth," Larry said. "Or I'll shut it for you."

Half of Maynard's face twitched with a smirk. He reached out and grabbed Larry's shirt front and lifted him up off his feet.

"No, you better shut *your* damn mouth, crip," Maynard said, and then shoved Larry backwards.

Larry tried to maintain his footing, but his stiff leg made this impossible and he fell onto his side. Jim rushed over just as Larry was getting to his feet and balling up his fists.

Maynard saw this, grinned, and spat into each of his big hands and rubbed his palms together before clenching them tight. His fists looked the size of twin cantaloupes.

Jim managed to grab Larry's shoulder before he could step into punching range. "Settle down, Larry," Jim said.

The big man squinted and laughed.

"That's all right," he said, his voice a low growl. "I ain't a-feared to take on both of y'all at once. Come on."

Larry tried to surge forward but Jim held him back.

The giant uttered another taunt, this one laced with profanity, and ending with, "You yellow-bellied bastards. I told ya, come on."

As the big man was muttering this, Jim was working his right hand into his rucksack, which he'd kept looped over his shoulder. He withdrew the Colt 1911 from the canvas container and leveled it at the oversized adversary.

"How about we end this peaceably?" Jim said, keeping his thumb on the safety lever. He'd snapped it on after he'd chambered a round, and didn't want to disengage it until he was ready to fire. The single-action trigger required only the slightest of pulls.

Maynard's eyes widened as he saw the weapon. He straightened up and lowered his big fists to his waist.

"Disgraceful!" Klayman shouted. "You've got nothing but a bunch of hooligans working for you, Creighton, ya hear? A bunch of hooligans."

Creighton was sitting back now with a large grin on his face.

"The only hooligans around here are you and your trained gorilla, Klayman," he said. "Now get in your fancy roadster there and get the hell off of my lot."

Klayman blinked twice, his lips drawn together tighter than a miser's purse, and turned toward the automobile.

"Come on, Maynard," he said. "Send me a telegram when you're ready to talk price, Frank. And it can only go down from here."

Creighton glared at him, but said nothing.

Tucker touched Creighton's arm. "This may be a mistake, Frank. Maybe we should hear his offer at least."

Creighton shook his head.

The giant kept his scowl directed at Jim as he dropped his hands the rest of the way and turned toward the roadster.

"This ain't over, buster," he muttered. "And next time I'm gonna bring *my* gun."

"You do that," Jim said, and slowly lowered the forty-five. He kept his gaze directed at the other man.

Everyone was silent as the unlikely duo got back into their roadster and departed. As it rolled away, Jim heaved a sigh of relief and replaced the Colt in the rucksack.

Two near-gunfights in one afternoon, he thought. *What a way to start a new job.*

"You shoulda let me stomp him, Jim," Larry said.

His brother-in-law was busy regathering the dishes.

"That fella's so big it would probably take a whole regiment to do that," Jim said. "Let's help Richard get them plates and cups."

Creighton was standing now, the wide grin still on his face. "I'm starting to take quite a shine to you, my boy," he said. "That's the second time today you've come through for me and Thunderhead. You're definitely my good luck charm."

Tucker moved beside him and cast a piercing glance at Jim and Larry.

Arthur Weeks blew out a derisive breath and stood, pulling at Faith's arm. "Come on, let's get out of here and let the scullery crew clean up," he said.

She rose reluctantly and flashed a luscious smile at Jim as they walked away.

He stood there momentarily transfixed by her radiance until he felt a semihard slap on his back.

It was Creighton.

"Stick around here long enough," the motion picture man said in a booming voice, "and I just might decide to make you into a star."

A star, Jim thought. *Maybe then I'd have a chance with Faith.* Maybe . . .

He watched her and Weeks walking away, the big actor's arm around her waist in proprietary fashion.

Chapter 9

1880
Outskirts of Town
Contention City, Arizona

It was approaching the early afternoon of what Lon Dayton considered was turning out to be damn near a perfect day. Miss April May Donovan and Dalton both sat on the blanket he had laid out on the ground under the shade of the glade of trees.

Oak trees, Dayton surmised, but he couldn't be sure. The fan-shaped leaf he'd plucked from one of the lower branches was as big as a pint-sized flask. He was sorry he hadn't brought one of those, filled with a bit of liquid courage to loosen his tongue a little while trying to make conversation with April May Donovan. Talking to a rowdy drunk or a mean-tempered man with a gun was easier than trying to impress a pretty girl. He twirled the leaf between his fingers.

"Guess this is an oak tree," he said. He could think of nothing else to say.

They'd ridden out here in the buckboard, and he'd secured the wagon and tethered the horse over by a patch of grass, near enough that they didn't have to walk far, but enough distance that the smell of any road apples the animal might decide to drop wouldn't spoil their appetites, or the pleasantness of the moment.

"Actually," she said, "it's a burr bur oak."

He looked at the leaf and twirled it, feeling stupid.

April May laughed.

"One of those useless things a schoolmarm knows," she said.

He thought her laughter sounded like graceful melody coming from some fine wooden instrument, like a violin or maybe a guitar.

"I wouldn't say knowledge is useless," he said.

She smiled. "Me neither. It's just some things are more important than others. Especially out here."

What a beautiful smile, he thought, struggling for something else to say.

"You ain't from around here, as I recall," he said. "Missouri, ain't it?"

He already knew, recalling his memory of the ladies' gossip three months ago about the spinster schoolteacher coming to town by way of St. Louis. Dayton had never been to a big city like that, and wondered what it might be like.

"St. Louis," she said.

She was still smiling, which he took as a good sign. They'd dined on the turkey sandwiches that he'd picked up from the restaurant earlier that morning. He'd made a small bonfire out of some twigs and a bit of the long grass and set the coffeepot on top of it. The basket contained two cups that young Sally had packed for him.

"I'll put a couple of sugar cubes in the napkin," she'd said. "To sweeten that coffee."

Dayton set the two cups on the blanket and picked up the coffeepot. The metal handle was hot and he retracted his hand way too fast. The pot fell over, some of its contents washing over the sparse flames and extinguishing the fire.

"Damn," he said under his breath.

Could anything more go wrong today?

He grabbed the napkin to shield his grip and the four sugar cubes went flying into the dirt as he managed to right the pot before all the coffee escaped.

He heaved a frustrated sigh, but to his surprise, April May was laughing.

"What a day," he said.

"Yes," she said, the smile still in place. "It's been a beautiful day."

Not knowing how to respond, he held up the pot and asked if she'd like some coffee.

"Yes," she replied. "With sugar, please."

Her comment stunned him and she giggled again, holding out her empty cup.

"And I wanted this to be so perfect," he said as he poured.

"Oh, it has been," she said. "I was only joking about the sugar. It's a lovely afternoon."

Dayton wondered if she really thought so, or was just trying to spare his feelings. He poured the remainder of the brew into his cup. It was barely half full.

"You really think so?" he asked.

"Of course I do."

He compressed his lips, then decided to take a sip. The hot liquid scalded his tongue and his head jerked.

"Careful," she said. "It's hot."

He emitted a grunt in affirmation.

A trail of grayish smoke rose from the extinguished fire.

"At least we won't have to worry about putting that out when we leave," he said, staring at the dead embers. A group of ants had already found the sugar cubes and were busily attacking them.

Up close, she was even more beautiful than he'd realized. Or was it her sparkling personality? She seemed to make everything better just by being there. He searched for the right words to say.

"I'm glad," he said haltingly, "that you . . . came with me today."

I'm sounding like one of her dumb schoolboys, he thought.

"I am, too." She took a tiny sip of her coffee, looking at him over the rim of her cup. "I turned down another invitation to be here, you know."

Another invitation?

What did that mean?

Dayton swallowed hard and asked, "From who?"

"Martin Lipton."

Lipton, he thought. That slick son of a bitch had his eye on April May?

Dayton felt his breathing quicken. "I didn't know you knew him."

She nodded. "I saw you talking to him the other day. Weren't you posing for pictures with him?"

"Ah, yeah, I was. But it wasn't my idea. He's got some fella writing a book about Contention City."

"That would be William." Another slight smile, followed by a delicate sip.

"You know him too?"

"Yes. He came by the school to talk," she said. "About his plans for the book."

Were there any eligible bachelors in town who weren't after her?

Dayton brought the cup to his lips and drank. The liquid had cooled a bit and no longer burned on the way down.

"How well do you know them fellas?" he asked, and then a second later wished he hadn't.

Her head canted slightly and her eyebrows flickered.

"Not that well," she said. "Although . . ."

"Although?"

She took another sip from the cup, brought it down to her lap, and said, "Martin's asked me to marry him."

Marry him!

The words hit Dayton like a giant fist plunged into his gut. He sought for a response, but had none.

"What," he said, "did you say?"

Her blue eyes stared back at him. There seemed to be something, some emotion, lurking behind them, but what it was exactly, he couldn't figure.

"I told him I needed to think about it some." She took in a deep breath. "Lord knows, a spinster schoolmarm here from St. Louis isn't going to get too many offers."

And no doubt Lipton played up his damn position with the territorial governor, Dayton added mentally. The son of a bitch.

He felt his heart racing, his breathing speeding up.

I have to ask her now, he thought. *Get my hat in the ring. Tell her how I feel about her, before it's too late.*

But what could he offer her? A continuing life of hardship on his lawman's meager salary? Maybe he should tell her about the mayor's pledge of a portion of the five-thousand-dollar reward.

"You're a lot more than a spinster schoolmarm," he managed to say.

The beautiful smile reappeared. "Thank you."

He took that as a good sign. Inhaling deeply, he readied himself to propose, his mouth dry, his hands soaking wet.

"April May," he said, leaving the remainder of the sentence dangling.

"Yes?"

Another deep breath . . . But before he could put together the words, he heard it: the unmistakable sound of a man on horseback drawing closer.

He turned his head.

The approaching rider bore a certain familiarity.

"Is that one of the outlaws?" April May asked after a sharp intake of breath. "The Bascom gang."

How the hell did she know about them?

But he knew there was no time to ask now. Instead, he got to his feet and told her to stay where she was. He walked over to the buckboard and reached under the seat where he'd stowed his gun belt. After picking it up and strapping it on, he undid the leather thong secured over the hammer of his Colt.

The man on horseback had gotten close enough for the vague familiarity to turn into certainty. It was Whitey, the same fellow who'd sneaked into town and taken Dayton to meet Bascom.

Coincidence, or had the outlaws been watching them the whole time?

Dayton strode forward, casting a quick glance to make sure April May was still over by the trees, and walked on an intersecting course to greet the outlaw.

Whitey pulled his horse to a stop about fifteen feet away and leaned forward in the saddle. Dayton was glad to see he kept both of his arms folded in front of himself on the pommel.

"Howdy, Sheriff," he said.

In the daylight, the boy looked even younger than Dayton had thought.

"Whitey," Dayton replied with a nod.

The young man grinned and tipped his hat toward April May. "Ma'am," he said.

Dayton didn't take his eyes off the man.

"What do you want?"

"Sorry to disturb your lunch," Whitey said. "But Dutch wanted me to ask you how them amnesty papers were coming."

"Should be here Monday, just like I told him."

The right side of Whitey's face twitched with an unspoken reply. "Much obliged, Sheriff. So, you're gonna be a-ringing them church bells Monday once they come?"

"That's our agreement," Dayton said.

Whitey smiled and nodded. "That's real swell. I'll be a-heading back to tell him so." His eyes shot toward April May, and then back to Dayton. "And I'm right sorry to be a-interrupting your courtin', sir."

My courting? Dayton thought. *Is there anybody who doesn't know my business?*

He gave a fractional nod of his head and kept his mouth shut.

Whitey tipped his hat to April May again, reined his horse around, and headed back toward the range of mountains.

Dayton remained standing where he was until the rider and horse were nothing more than a small black dot on the horizon. Then he turned and walked back over to her.

"Sorry about that intrusion," he said. "My job has a way of following me and rearing its ugly head now and again."

She laughed.

"You know, for a handsome lawman," she said, "you have a way with words. You remind me of Mark Twain."

Dayton didn't consider himself a well-read man, but he was familiar with Twain. A second later it dawned on him that she'd called him handsome as well.

"I'm a mite flattered," he said. "I read *Huckleberry Finn*, and liked it, but I ain't so sure about the handsome part."

"You are," she said. "Very. Take it from the spinster schoolmarm."

If he had his way, she wouldn't be a spinster much longer.

"April May," he repeated, trying to summon enough courage to complete his sentence.

Again an uncomfortable silence hung in the air between them.

"Yes?" she said, her eyes widening ever so slightly in expectation.

"There's something I been meaning to ask you myself . . ."

ᔕ

1913
Contention City Set
Thunderhead Motion Pictures Lot
Near San Diego, California

After the contentious and abrupt ending to the evening meal, Jim opted to go back to the hotel room that he shared with Larry to get what he felt would be some much-needed shut-eye. The day's journey and trepidations had exhausted him. Larry tried to convince him to go with Whitey and Bierce and him across the border to La Fronteriza.

"Whitey says he knows a place where the women are sweet," Larry said. "And cheap, too. They'll dance on top of the bar naked for you."

Jim was about to caution his friend about the dangers of frequenting such a place, not to mention the fact that Lobo and his boys were most likely lurking there as well, but Larry beat him to it.

"I know what you're a-thinking," he said. "That guy Lobo and his buddies might be around there. But I ain't worried. Whitey's got a gun, and Mr. Bierce does too."

For a moment Jim was worried that his friend was going to ask to borrow the Colt 1911, but Larry didn't ask. Jim was glad of that, not wanting to lose his prized possession in some Mexican whorehouse.

"And you seen Whitey shoot, too," Larry added. "They know better than to mess with him."

"Just remember to keep your pants where you can see them," Jim said. "And your wallet."

He gave Larry what little money he had, figuring he owed it to his friend for getting this job for them, and then some. His eyes swept over Larry's stiff leg, stretched out now at an oblique angle as they both sat on the soft bed.

I guess he deserves to get laid, Jim thought. *After all he's been through.*

"You sure you don't want to come with us?" Larry asked, pocketing the money Jim had given him.

"Positive. I'm pretty beat."

"Suit yourself." Larry grabbed hold of the bedpost and pulled himself erect. "I'll be back to tell you all about it."

"Do me a favor. If I'm sleeping, tell me in the morning."

After Larry left, Jim washed his face in the basin and tried to get some sleep, but that proved difficult. The tumultuous day, fraught with varied activities, made slumber an elusive commodity. He lit a candle and tried reading the magazine Bierce had given him with "The Damned Thing" inside. This proved to be a mistake. The story was vividly written and told the tale of a marauding monster, not discernible to the human eye due to its color being beyond the spectrum of visible light.

Jim was reminded of the monsters he'd seen in the Philippines—human monsters, capable of acts of gut-wrenching brutality. So gut-wrenching that they continued to haunt his dreams, just like the invisible creature in Bierce's story.

Another damned thing.

Finally, when he did doze off, he had visions of the Moros advancing toward him with their bodies tightly bound by those green vines, the veins in their arms standing out in bas-relief, their mouths framing feral teeth, and all of them repeating over and over again the rhythmic chant.

Tac-tac, tac-tac, tac-tac—Tagalog for Cut-cut, cut-cut, cut-cut.

Well into the wee hours of the morning he lay there, sweating and remembering, unable to close his eyes. When Larry finally stumbled into the room stinking of sweat, cheap perfume, and tequila, Jim pretended to be asleep. His friend fell into the other bed and after mumbling some off-key Mexican ballad, began snoring in a matter of minutes.

Jim wasn't sure when he finally drifted off as well, but he awoke with the sun, just as he had back in the Philippines. As usual, he was covered in perspiration with only a vague recollection of the night's bad dreams. It was too difficult to try and recall many details. They seldom made sense anyway, but always reinforced an overwhelming feeling of something dreadful about to happen. Larry was snoring and Jim figured he needed the rest. It was early and they weren't supposed to report to the set until eight.

After pouring a bit of water into the basin, Jim carefully ran his straight razor over his face and rubbed his fingers through his hair.

Presentable enough, he thought, although the network of red webbing in his eyes betrayed the fact that he'd had little sleep.

After getting dressed and visiting the lavatory down the hall, he headed down the stairs and began walking. The set was only a few blocks away and when he passed by the security guard at the entrance, the man smiled.

"Ah, the hero returns," the guard said. "Nobody's here yet, except the carpenters. They're putting up the set for filming today."

Jim heard some voices shouting, a few swear words, and the sound of heavy pounding. He waved to the guard and walked on through.

It would feel good to be doing something.

Going down the main street, he saw four men trying to drive some big wooden stakes into the ground. A roll of large white canvas lay off to one side.

One of the men swung the sledgehammer down on the wooden stake and the hammer's head slipped off, almost hitting the hands of the kneeling man who was holding the stake.

"Dammit, Pete, What the hell you doing?" The man jumped up. "Coulda took my arm off."

"Sorry," the man called Pete said. "Getting tired."

"Looks like you fellas could use a hand," Jim said.

A big guy who'd been pounding a stake on the opposite side of the street came marching over. He stopped and regarded Jim askance.

"Yeah," he said. "We sure could. But ain't you that fella that—"

Jim smirked. "Yeah. But I know my way around a sledgehammer, too."

The big guy's eyebrows rose.

"Well, grab that one from Pete there," he said. "And let's see if we can get these stakes pounded in and this damn tent erected."

Jim stripped off his shirt and hung it on a horse hitching rail along with his hat and his rucksack. He accepted the hammer and stepped over to the big stake. The man who'd jumped up now knelt, gripped the stake, and gave a quick nod, his expression showing some nervousness.

"Go ahead," the kneeling man said. "Can't be no worse than Pete there."

Pete spat on the ground and muttered something unintelligible.

Jim tapped the top of the stake with the flat portion of the sledgehammer a few times to get his bearings and then lifted it up above his head and brought it soundly down on the misshapen wooden top of the stake. He hit it square on the button and it sank into the earth a few inches.

The kneeling man grinned and nodded.

"You got a good eye," he said.

With a few more strokes, Jim had the stake firmly planted. Despite his lack of sleep through his restless night, the physical exertion had a salubrious effect on him.

"What's next?" he asked. A thin sheen of sweat covered his upper body.

"You ever get tired of doing motion picture work, partner," the big guy said, "you got a job working for me."

"That's good to know," Jim said.

The big man had pounded his stake into the ground as well and pointed to the next section. Working together, they had all the stakes fixed and the canvas unrolled. The five of them worked in unison to quickly erect the tent. Jim threw himself into the task. As they all stood in front of the structure admiring their work, Jim heard a voice behind them.

"That tent looks good."

Jim turned and saw the man named Tucker standing there holding a copy of the Contention City shootout book that Bierce had shown them last night. Tucker held it up to compare the photo therein to the new structure. "Now make sure that damn banner's in place."

"Yes, sir, Mr. Tucker," the big guy in charge said. "Come on, boys."

As they went over and started unfolding the banner, Jim noticed Tucker watching him as he busied himself with the task.

According to the photograph in the book, the banner was to be strung several yards away from the tent, suspended from the balconies of two buildings on the opposite sides of the street. As Jim helped to tug the rope holding the banner taut, he couldn't help but wonder what it must have been like back in the 1880s when the band of outlaws rode into town and the shooting and the dying started. Those thoughts blossomed into a lot of unpleasant memories and he abruptly found himself debating whether or not he really wanted to be a part of this make-believe carnage.

He'd already seen enough real bloodshed to last him a lifetime.

Yet he also recalled, as they'd labored securing the ropes, that it was the same street where yesterday he'd rushed on horseback to save Faith. And she'd smiled and kissed him. Holding her had been like getting to grasp a dream, and he wondered if she'd be coming around this morning. He hoped she would. If so, he'd have to clean himself up a bit. He could already smell himself.

Then he recalled the way that actor fella, Weeks, had put his arm around Faith's waist and squeezed her as they'd walked away. And she hadn't pulled away or anything. It suggested more than a casual familiarity. It suggested possession.

Not that Jim actually figured he had a chance with a girl of her likes, anyway.

He took in a deep breath and glanced around. A few more people were meandering past the main entrance gate, but Tucker seemed to have vanished. Busying himself in the work, Jim concentrated on the last few tasks that needed to be accomplished.

Off somewhere he heard the sharp tones of something ringing. It sounded like one of those old cattle bells.

"What's that?" he asked.

"That means the food tent's open," Pete said. "And I'm hungry."

"Hold your damn horses, Pete," the big man said. "We ain't finished here yet."

He was lashing the rope holding the bottom portion of the banner in place around the base of the support strut. It had taken them the better part of fifteen minutes to erect the wooden poles on opposite sides of the main street. The upper portion of the banner was secured to a metal eyelet screwed into the top of the pole. Across the street, the other end of the banner had already been secured in similar fashion. The big man tied the thin rope in a square knot and grunted that he was finished. Jim released his hold and the big man grinned, turning to look up at the banner.

A good three feet in width, *AMNESTY PROCLAIMATION* was neatly lettered along the strip of canvas in bold black letters. It didn't look quite right to Jim.

"Can we go eat now?" Pete asked.

"In a minute," the foreman said. "Let's pick up these tools and hammers and stow 'em over yonder."

After placing the equipment out of sight and off to the side, the big burly man turned toward Jim. "Appreciate your help." He held out his hand. "I wish I could pay you something for your work. You done good."

"No need," Jim said. "I'm already getting paid. Or at least I hope I will."

"You'd better, after all you done yesterday, saving Miss Stewart. I seen it. You sure can ride. You're a real-life hero."

"I'm no hero. Just happened to be there at the right time is all." Jim smiled and shook the man's hand. "Let's go wash up and get some breakfast."

"That, my friend, sounds like a very good idea indeed," a deep voice said. "I totally concur."

Jim turned and saw Ambrose Bierce standing there. The author looked a bit shopworn and Jim concluded that Bierce must have had a late night along with Larry and Whitey. His face had a haggard look to it, and several bloody nicks stood out on his recently shaven chin. But despite all that, he looked fairly dapper in his dark gray suit.

"Mr. Bierce, I didn't expect to see you here." Jim joined the other men at a nearby water barrel. When it was his turn, he scooped some water out with cupped hands and rinsed his face and then dashed a couple of handfuls under his arms. The olfactory evidence made painfully obvious his lack of overall effectiveness, and he reminded himself to see about finding a place to get a bath as soon as the opportunity arose. In the meantime, he'd have to try and keep downwind of Faith, but it wasn't like he was going to be able to sit next to her at breakfast anyway.

"I stopped by your room to rouse our companion, Mr. Rush," Bierce said, "and noticed you were conspicuously absent. The desk clerk advised me you'd gone out a while ago."

"Yeah," Jim said. "Couldn't sleep."

Bierce raised a questioning eyebrow. "Old ghosts?"

Jim nodded.

"I read your story, too," he said. " 'The Damned Thing.' "

"Oh? And what did you think of it?"

Jim smiled. "Well, I liked it, but I have to admit it did kind of contribute to my nightmares."

Bierce's head bobbled with fractional understanding and acknowledgment.

"Old ghosts have no colors and are often unseen." He pursed his lips. "It is one of my regrets that my story caused you some consternation."

"It's not your fault, Mr. Bierce. The memories are in my head for good."

Or bad, he thought.

Hoping to change the subject, to distance himself from the troubling memories, Jim said, "What you doing over here?"

Bierce sighed. "I was venturing over this way as part of my constitutional. I must say, that cattle bell call to breakfast is a welcome sound."

The other workers were hurrying toward the main entrance and the food tent. Jim retrieved his shirt and rucksack and then fanned himself dry with his hat as they walked. The morning sun felt good on his bare shoulders. It was a tepid companion compared to the sun's heat in the Philippines.

"You just missed Mr. Tucker," Jim said. "He was over here supervising us."

"Actually, I did see him," Bierce said. "As I was walking earlier. He stopped me and asked to borrow the Contention City book that Godfrey'd loaned me."

Jim recalled the sight of Tucker with the book, comparing the picture to the banner they'd strung across the street.

"You getting a pretty good handle on your article?" Jim asked.

Bierce shrugged and kept his voice low. "While I do feel some perfunctory obligation to pen something, I shall not be affixing my name to it."

"Why not? I mean, if you wrote it?"

Bierce took in a deep breath as his mouth drew tight.

"That, my young friend, is a long story. One that I shall leave for another time. Suffice it to say that I made a vow that I was finished transcribing the written word, for reasons I'll not mention." He glanced over his shoulder at the banner and chuckled. "They do know that they've spelled the word wrong, don't they?"

Jim looked up at the lettering and then it hit him.

"Proclamation," he said. "There's no *I*, is there?"

"There is not," Bierce said, "just as there is none in the word *team*. I suspect that fact went unnoticed as many a line continued to march over the edge of the cliff."

Jim wasn't sure what the author meant, but he let it go, and sought to change the subject.

"I'm glad Larry made it back in one piece," he said. "He was bound and determined to go with you and Whitey to La Fronteriza. I take it you all had a good time?"

"Actually . . ." Bierce's eyebrows rose in unison once again. "It proved quite enticing. And . . . informative as well."

"Informative?" Jim laughed. "Surely them Mexican maidens didn't have anything you hadn't seen before, did they?"

Bierce laughed as well.

"A good point," he said. "One could say that if you've seen one, you've seen them all, but as a connoisseur of the female form, I've come to appreciate the variances and exquisiteness of each and every one I'm blessed to have laid eyes on."

Jim grinned. "Artfully put. I was plenty worried, though. I take it you didn't run into that Lobo fella?"

"Not overtly. But I did catch sight of him while Whitey and Mr. Rush were still otherwise indisposed. Which brought about the informative portion of last night's little foray."

"So you saw Lobo?"

"I did. And his corpulent friend and ex-employee of the motion picture studio, Gordo." He paused and looked askance at Jim. "That monogram is most apt for that fellow. Do you know what it means in Spanish?"

Jim shook his head, intrigued now about where the author was going with all this.

"It means fat, but is often colloquially used to indicate large size or heaviness."

Jim recalled the physical altercation from the day before. The man was obese, certainly, but also obviously endowed with a toughness and considerable strength.

"So the big fella was with Lobo?" he asked.

"He was. They were ensconced around a table in the shadowy corner of the bar attached to the house of ill repute, *tres compeñaros*. Three companions engaged in deep and intense conversation."

"Three?"

The author's face twitched with an insightful relevance.

"Three indeed, there were," he said. "And it was the identity of this third man that piqued my interest and drew me away, temporarily of course, from devoting my attention to the comely *señoritas*, both of whom were trying to convince me of their particular elegance in the back room."

A vision of Bierce being put upon by two Mexican hookers was offsetting, but his obscure reference to the three *compeñaros* overrode Jim's curiosity about the *señoritas*.

"So who was it?" he asked.

Bierce turned his head slightly and cast a look directly into Jim's eyes. They were nearing the food tent now, perhaps twenty feet away, and already a line had formed. Teresa was serving the bigwigs seated in the VIP section.

"The man sitting over there, beside Agamemnon and across from Andromeda. None other than the jackal in a gray tweed double-breasted suit, our very own Mr. Tucker."

Tucker, Jim thought, and turned to look at him.

Why, if Tucker had made such a show of firing Gordo yesterday afternoon, would he take the trouble of meeting with him and Lobo that same night?

Something wasn't adding up.

As Jim was staring at the seated man, Tucker abruptly shifted in his chair and began glaring back toward him and Bierce.

Jim quickly looked away, but couldn't shake the uneasy feeling that he was still being watched. He rotated his head a little and sure enough, the pair of piercing, dark eyes was still fixed on him.

Or was the man looking at Bierce?

Or maybe . . . at both of them?

Chapter 10

1880
Main Street
Contention City, Arizona

Sheriff Lon Dayton watched as the group of men pulled on the ropes raising the long banner to a height of about twenty feet above the main street. They'd sunk two wooden poles into the ground on each side to allow the long strip of canvas to hang ceremoniously across the roadway. The banner was a good three feet in width.

AMNESTY PROCLAIMATION was neatly printed on it in bold black letters.

Martin Lipton, Dayton's rival for the hand of April May, stood off to the side. He looked up at the banner and the large tent just beyond it with a smile of satisfaction on his face.

Dayton sized the other man up with a newfound clarity. *He's a bit younger than me by five, maybe more, years,* he thought. *And pretty good looking, if you don't mind the soft, jowly sort.*

He recalled his own rather weathered reflection staring back at him from the mirror that morning, but took solace in the fact that his stomach was still flat and hard.

I got some wrinkles on me, he added mentally, *but I earned all of them through hard work. Man's work.*

Still, April May's words resounded inside his head from the other day when he'd asked her to marry him. *"That's very sweet of you, Lon. I care for you a great deal, but . . ."*

Oh, that "but . . ."

She'd told him she had a lot to consider and needed a bit of time before she could give him an answer. He'd pressed her for a deadline, a definite day when she would tell him, but she demurred.

"I . . . I can't right now. It's like my whole world's been suddenly turned upside down and shaken," she'd said. "I just need some time to think."

He'd left it at that, knowing she did have a lot to consider. And her choice of beaus. A lean, older September Gun, and a soft-bellied city slicker with a fat wallet in his pocket who could afford to buy her things. A lot of things.

It was no wonder she needed time to decide, but the clock was ticking. In another twenty-four hours or so, the Bascom gang would be riding in, if the amnesty papers arrived as promised.

Dayton already had one too many time limits to deal with. Maybe after this amnesty thing was done and he had that cash reward in his pocket, he could go courting with something more to offer than an aging lawman's monthly salary.

If he had that reward money . . .

Somehow, relying on the assurances of Hizzoner the mayor and men like Martin Lipton wasn't all that reassuring.

The sharp whistle of the approaching train interrupted his reverie.

It must have been approaching noon. Dayton saw Lipton reach into his vest pocket and remove a fine-looking gold watch. He flipped open the lid, checked the time, and smiled.

"Looks like the train's right on time, Sheriff," he said. "Shall we go meet it?"

Dayton said nothing, but nodded.

Time and tide, he thought. *Wait for no man.*

❧

1913
Food Tent
Thunderhead Motion Pictures Lot
Near San Diego, California

As Bierce and Jim entered the food tent, Jim caught a glimpse of Teresa and her father dispensing spoonfuls of scrambled eggs, biscuits, and a slice of bacon to each person in the line. Both wore white aprons, and her father had on a tall chef's hat. Richard Phipps and Donna stood beside them handing out the other items. The girl's dark eyes flashed toward Jim for a second, and seemed to brighten. Jim forced himself to smile. He was in anything but a receptive mood. On the way over, he'd seen Weeks and Faith about thirty yards ahead of him, the big actor's arm around her thin waist, his hand patting her hip as they walked. And as if that sign of ownership weren't enough, Faith's arm encircled the other man's waist as well, and she was all giggles and smiles. Jim wondered if they'd slept together.

But that's none of my business, he told himself.

Bierce seemed to have read his thoughts. "Ah, the green-eyed monster rears his head."

"Green-eyed monster?"

Bierce smiled. "An allusion to Shakespeare's play, *Othello*. And also a lesson one might learn from it. Have you ever read it?"

Jim shook his head.

"That's a pity," Bierce replied. "There is much to be learned from the Bard. That particular play recounts the downfall of a great warrior and man due to the green-eyed monster of jealousy."

Jim felt his face flush. The author's words made him angry at first, but then he realized there was a lot of truth in them. He blew out a long breath.

"I guess I'm kidding myself thinking she might've been interested in the likes of me," he said. "Looks like that actor fella's already staked his claim."

"A beautiful woman often has her choice of suitors. Best to feign disinterest and see if that stirs any emotion, even as she passes in the arms of another."

"Meaning?"

Bierce chuckled. "Listen, I'm the last person to give advice on dealing with the fairer sex. My wife of many years deceived and divorced me long ago."

"Sorry to hear that. Did she remarry?" Jim figured he'd phrased the question with delicacy, if Bierce's wife had left him for another.

The author sighed and shook his head.

"It was after our second son's death. She withered away, dying of grief," he said. "We lost both of our sons."

Jim was stunned. Words failed him, and he regretted inquiring.

"My oldest son, Day, took his own life after the woman he loved thrust herself into the arms of another," Bierce said. "It was shortly after my wife and I separated. Then twelve years ago, my second son, Leigh, died. Pneumonia, but his drinking had a lot to do with it. My wife never got over it. Died a few months after that." The author's face had taken on a weary cast. "My daughter blamed me. Hasn't spoken to me since."

"I'm real sorry to hear that," Jim said.

"No need," Bierce said. "It is, as they say, water under the bridge. But as I told you, I'm the last person to give advice about the fairer sex."

They walked the remaining steps in silence and entered the tent. Weeks and Faith bypassed the chow line and went to the VIP table where Creighton and Tucker already sat, talking and drinking coffee. Their plates were before them on the long table, which was covered by a fresh white tablecloth. Monroe and another heavyset man were across from them, and they were all in a somewhat animated conversation. They paused and acknowledged Faith and Weeks as they came to the table and sat.

"I want more eggs than that," a voice in the food line said.

Jim took his eyes away from the actress to see what was going on. It was Pete, the less than ambitious construction worker Jim had seen earlier. The man's tone was gruff and it made Teresa, who'd been dishing out the eggs, lean back.

"*Monsieur*," Teresa's father said. "My apologies, but we must be very circumspect wit de food. Once everyone has passed through the line, you may return and we will—"

"Listen, you fat little Frenchie son of a bitch," Pete said. "I'm sick of you and your little tart of a daughter skimping on handing out the food. I been workin' hard this morning. Damn hard, and I deserve more than just a spoonful of eggs. Now tell your little hot tamale here to give 'em to me."

Teresa's father's face hardened.

"I shall tank you not to speak to my daughter in such a manner, *monsieur*." His emphasis on the last word was rife with sarcasm.

Pete's lips twisted into a snarl. He reached across and grabbed Teresa's father's white apron.

Jim strode over to the belligerent man and placed his hand on his shoulder. "Best you calm down and release Mr. Delacroix right now."

Pete turned and surveyed Jim with a sour expression.

"Git yer hands offa me," he muttered.

Farther down the chow line, the big guy who was the leader of the construction gang stopped and turned. "Dammit, Pete. Knock that crap off, will ya?"

"You go to hell," Pete shouted back. He released the chef's apron and at the same time, slung his plate of food at Jim's face.

Jim ducked out of the way as he grabbed the other man's shirt with his left hand and delivered an overhand right to Pete's jaw. The punch caught the man flush on the chin and he dropped to his knees, his expression dazed. The big foreman was there in an instant, holding his plate of food and looking down at the now-supine figure. He shrugged, glanced at Jim, and grinned.

"Can't say he didn't have that one coming," he said. "If you can help me drag him out of the way, we can all get to eating breakfast. He'll be fired as soon as he wakes up."

Jim nodded as he brushed the scattering of eggs and bacon off his shirt and rucksack. His hand was already starting to ache a bit so he kept flexing his fingers.

"Go ahead, Jim," Bierce said. "I'll get a plate for you. Good punch, by the way."

Jim declined any help and dragged the now semiconscious Pete off to a far table and left him there. When he came back to the line Bierce handed him a plate that was stacked with a heaping pile of eggs, four biscuits, and three strips of bacon.

Jim glanced over at Teresa and her father. Delacroix smiled and tipped his extended index finger off his hat in a mock salute.

"*Wit* my *tanks*, and compliments," he said in his French accent.

Teresa was smiling broadly at Jim and he noticed again how pretty she was.

Glancing over at the VIP table, he saw Faith watching him, her eyes wide and the tip of her tongue darting over her lips. When their eyes locked, she smiled. It was a beautiful sight.

Creighton, Tucker, and the others were regarding him as well.

"Sir Galahad rides again," Bierce said. "May I suggest you partake in some nourishment before you're called upon to slay another dragon? A true knight's work is never done."

Jim flexed his hand again as he accepted the plate, aware that everyone's eyes, and especially Faith's, were upon him now.

What a start to my first official day, he thought. *But I might as well roll with the flow.*

ᔕᔦ

1880
Railroad Station
Contention City, Arizona

Seven men got off the train first, three of them carrying rifles. Dayton figured that from the looks of them they knew how to use them, too. They walked past him without a word, nodding to Lipton and going straight to Burnside, who'd also shown up at the station.

Lipton called out to an obese man in a business suit carrying a heavy-looking leather valise as he now descended the metal steps from the train. He wore a derby hat and had an enormous mustache that virtually eclipsed the upper portion of his mouth.

"Chester."

The obese man looked at Lipton and his lips formed a smile under the fringe of hair. He quickened his pace once he got onto the wooden planks of the platform.

"Martin," the man said. "Good to see you. Is everything all set?"

"It is," Lipton said. He started to say something else and then hesitated and looked back at Dayton. After blowing out a long breath, he added, "Chester, this is Sheriff Dayton. He's the one that set up the amnesty surrender with the Bascom gang. Sheriff, this is Chester Aimes."

Aimes's friendly expression changed for a fraction of a second, before returning.

"Glad to meet you." He set the big valise down and extended his open palm.

Dayton shook it.

"I take it you've got the amnesty papers in there?" Dayton asked, motioning toward the valise.

"Yes, yes, of course," Aimes said.

A harsh-sounding laugh drifted over from the group around Burnside. The eight men were still clustered together and one of them had removed a highly polished rifle from its leather encasement. The men were passing it back and forth. One of them made a sound mimicking a gunshot and Dayton heard something like, "A hundred yards . . . Never misses."

The hairs on the back of Dayton's neck rose up and he turned to Lipton. "Those are the Pinkertons you sent for, I take it?"

"Yes," Lipton said. "All fine men, I assure you. Professionals."

"Professional what?" Dayton asked. "They look like a bunch of gunmen."

"Well, they were hired on as protection for the railroads, if that's what you mean." Lipton shrugged. "Just as you were hired here to ensure law and order."

Dayton cast one more glance at the eight men. Mayor Webber and his entourage of Fred Dyer and William Bradford Cox, along with Herman, Cox's photographer, all hustling along toward the platform. Hizzoner waved and called out to Lipton.

"I want to make sure we're all on the same sheet of music," Dayton said. "I've set this whole thing up to be a peaceful event."

Lipton's head turned and the man regarded him with an expression of mock surprise. "Of course," he said after a few seconds more.

Dayton saw the mayor stop by Burnside and slap him on the back, pausing to introduce Cox. Dyer already seemed familiar with the group.

"Just so we're clear on that," Dayton said. The uneasy feeling was growing within him. "And I'm in charge."

"I fail to see your point, Sheriff," Lipton said, his manner bordering on officiousness now.

Dayton stared at him.

"My point is," he said. "I've already got an understanding with Bascom and his boys. And I've got my three deputies to assist. I don't need a bunch of professional gunmen waving rifles around and provoking things."

Lipton frowned. "I assure you, Sheriff, that's not the case."

"Oh no?"

"No, we're all in agreement on how this is to be handled. We just have to be prepared."

"Prepared for what?"

The governor's man shrugged. "Prepared for . . . every eventuality, should one arise."

Another gruff laugh emanated from the crowd around Burnside. Dayton saw the mayor waddling over toward him, Lipton, and the obese Aimes.

"You must be the man from Territorial Governor Frémont's office," Hizzoner said. "I'm glad to meet you. Mayor Clyde Webber."

The two men shook hands.

"Come on over here and I'll introduce you to my publicist," Webber said. "He's doing a book on Contention City and we'd like to get a few photographs to commemorate the event. Then I'll buy you a drink."

Aimes grinned and picked up the valise. Mayor Webber slapped an arm over the other man's shoulder as they waddled together down the platform and toward the eight Pinkertons, William Bradford Cox, and Herman, the photographer. Lipton turned to follow and Dayton found himself standing alone.

"Feel free to join us, Lon," Hizzoner called out over his shoulder.

Dayton stood where he was and watched them all fall into step together, no one looking back.

Birds of a feather, he thought, as the uneasiness continued to creep into his gut.

But in another twenty-four hours it would all be over.

Hopefully.

Right now, he had some church bells to ring to signal Dutch the papers had arrived as scheduled.

✑

1913
Contention City Set
Thunderhead Motion Pictures Lot
Near San Diego, California

The two wardrobe men fussed over Jim after he'd once again slipped into the same light blue shirt they'd given him yesterday.

"Now make sure you don't wrinkle it with that," one of them said, pointing to Jim's rucksack.

"*Eeeuw*," the other one said. "Is that thing *clean*? I'd hate to have some dirt rub off the strap and onto the shirt."

"I'll see that it don't," Jim said.

"*Puhleeze*," the other one said, making a show of pointing again at the rucksack and holding his nose shut.

"And you could do with a wash yourself, big boy," the other one said. "You smell like a lumberjack."

At least this damn shirt's been washed, Jim thought as he strode off toward the center of things, holding the rucksack in his hand.

The main street of the motion picture set was bustling with people. The cameramen seemed to be stationing themselves on platforms at various points along the way and all kinds of other actors were milling about with their horses. Both Henry and Whitey were busy checking saddles, and off to the side Arthur Weeks and Faith sat under a large umbrella drinking what appeared to be iced tea. Weeks was smoking a cigarette. Creighton was busy shouting orders to the lead cameraman, Howard Willis, as Tucker stood alongside smoking a cigarette and looking around. Jim caught a glimpse of Lobo and five of his vaqueros as they rode up on horseback. Lobo's face was covered with a couple day's growth of beard and he was smoking one of his sweet-smelling cigarettes. His eyes locked with Jim's and he smirked, but nodded in acknowledgment. Jim was surprised they were still around with all the problems they'd caused, but he guessed they were needed to fill things out.

As he passed, he noticed the Mexican lean over and point, saying something to his *compadre*. The other man's eyes went directly to the rucksack in Jim's hand.

Jim was suddenly cognizant that he'd need some way to secure his gun. The sight of the unctuous Lobo and company and their prying eyes made him leery of just leaving it off to the side unwatched. He made his way over to Henry and Whitey, who were saddling up a couple of horses that were tied to a hitching rail.

"Henry," Jim said. "You know any place around here where I could lock up my weapon?"

The black man finished adjusting the cinch and cocked his head to the side.

"I could put it in my footlocker at the stable," he said.

"That'd be swell," Jim said. "Can I give it to you to hold on to? I'm supposed to be doing some riding shortly."

Henry looked to Whitey, who nodded.

"Go ahead," Whitey said. "I'm just about finished here and will keep on checking them saddles."

Jim handed Henry the rucksack and the black man took it. After a few steps, Henry turned and glanced back at Whitey. "You sure you don't need me to stick here for a bit?"

Whitey gave his head a quick shake and patted the neck of the big stallion he'd been saddling. It was the same horse Jim had jumped on yesterday to ride after Faith and her errant mount. The horse snorted and Whitey continued to pat it.

"This here big fella's kind of camera shy," he said with a smile. "I seen you lay out that feller this morning at the food tent. You got a nice punch."

Jim shrugged.

"Wasn't nothing much," he said.

"Just the same," Whitey said. "We'll have to take you with us next time we go to La Fronteriza to see the ladies. Can always use a man with a good right hand."

Jim's right hand was still feeling a bit stiff and sore from delivering the punch earlier.

"All right," Howard Willis yelled as he stepped up on an adjacent camera platform. "We need everybody to clear away from this section here. We're going to do a quick take of Art mounting up."

"And Art," Creighton said, stepping onto the platform as well. "As soon as you get onto the horse, turn and smile into the camera. Then—where's my stuntman?" His head swiveled around until he saw Jim. "All right, Bishop, you're in costume. As soon as Art gets off the horse, you get on and make sure you keep your hat pulled down tight and your face away from the camera as you ride off. Got it?"

"Yes, sir," Jim said.

He watched as the personnel faded away from the outskirts of the immediate area.

"Art," Willis said. "Remember, it's the left side of the horse you get on."

Weeks replied with a dismissive wave of his hand and took one last long drag on his cigarette. He tossed it off to the side, expelling a plume of smoke as he strode purposefully toward the animal.

Whitey gave the horse one more pat and stepped away.

"I just want to get a few shots of Arthur in the saddle. Close-ups," Mr. Creighton repeated. "Then we'll film Jim from the back as he takes off and rides out of town."

"Do I really have to get on this damn critter?" Weeks said. He shot a quick glance at Jim. "What did you hire that stooge for?"

"We just need some close-ups," Creighton said with a forced smile. "Now let's get to it."

Both cameramen slipped on their black shawls.

Weeks heaved a sigh and stepped toward the horse. The big stallion shuffled.

"Approach him nice and easy," Whitey said. "I just got him calmed down and he can smell your sweat."

"Go to hell," Weeks said, reaching for the tied reins and then the pommel of the saddle. He shoved his foot into the stirrup. "I know what I'm doing. This is the left side, right, old man?"

As Weeks began to pull himself up, the whole saddle suddenly slid sideways and the actor fell onto his butt. Just about everybody was stunned, but Jim couldn't help a chuckle at the unexpected fall. Two equipment men rushed forward to help Weeks up. He brushed them away with angry arms and strode over toward Whitey. Without warning Weeks drew back his fist and smacked the old cowboy squarely on the jaw. Whitey, who was a couple of decades older than the actor and a hell of a lot smaller, crumpled into the dust.

"You damn old coot!" Weeks yelled. "You caused that on purpose, didn't you? You did something to that saddle."

Whitey rolled over and started to get on his hands and knees. Weeks stepped forward, drawing back his leg so he could deliver a kick to the older man's abdomen.

"Hey," Jim said, grabbing Weeks by the arm and pulling him back. "Leave him be."

The actor snarled and swung a looping roundhouse punch at Jim's head.

Jim blocked it with his left arm and moved back. Weeks advanced, his fists balled up, and swung with his right again.

Jim blocked it once more, and this time used both hands to shove the other man away. Backpedaling, he said, "That's two more punches than I'd give anybody else. You take one more step and I'll lay you out."

The pronouncement caused the actor to halt. He straightened up and thrust a finger in Creighton's direction. "Either these two sons of bitches get fired or I'm through here."

Creighton jumped down off the platform, his head bobbling in a conciliatory fashion.

"Art, calm down. There's no need for you to—"

"No," the actor said. "I'm through for today." He turned and thrust an extended finger toward Jim. "And you . . . You're lucky I don't finish this fight."

Jim felt like telling him to step on over, but knew if he did his employment, and quite possibly Larry's, would be over in an instant.

So he said nothing.

The actor blinked a few more times and then stormed off toward the main gate.

"Have someone give me a ride back to the hotel," he called out over his shoulder.

"Art," Creighton called out. "Wait. We've got filming to do. We're on a tight schedule."

The actor's arm rose and fell in a dismissive gesture.

Tucker glared at Jim and then put his hand on Creighton's shoulder. "I'll go talk to him, Frank," the waspish man said.

Creighton nodded.

Faith was still seated under the umbrella watching, the glass of brown liquid held gracefully in her hand. Her face had a hint of a smile.

Jim wondered what she was thinking as he went over and helped Whitey to his feet. It couldn't have been good, at least not as far as her costar was concerned. But Jim worried that she'd see him as a troublemaker.

The old cowboy dabbed at the stream of crimson flowing down his leathery chin.

"Damn fool," Whitey said between carefully measured breaths. "Don't even know when a horse has puffed himself up. He's a good one to play old back-shootin' Dayton, all right."

Jim looked at him quizzically. "Huh?"

Whitey took a few halting steps over to Creighton.

"It weren't my fault," Whitey said. "The damn fool tried to get on the horse too quick. Before I'd had a chance to adjust the cinch again. The horse was all puffed up after being saddled and when he relaxed a little the cinch was too dern loose."

Mr. Creighton looked at Jim, who nodded.

"Some of them horses are almost as temperamental as actors," he said.

Creighton took in a deep breath and then exhaled. "Hopefully, Don will calm him down. In the meantime, let's start filming the big shootout scene. We can't afford to lose time."

Everyone began hustling back to work.

"And let's finish this up today," Mr. Creighton shouted through the megaphone. "Remember, everybody's expected to be at the luncheon tomorrow at the train station in town. The real Sheriff Lon Dayton will be arriving on the noon train. The press will be there and I want a good turnout."

"You all right?" Jim asked Whitey.

"Hell yes," he replied.

"What did you mean about back-shooting Dayton?" Jim asked.

"Never mind," Whitey said. "Forget it, will ya?"

Jim nodded, but he wasn't about to forget anything.

Chapter 11

1880
Main Street
Contention City, Arizona

Dayton could feel the sweat dripping down from his underarms even as he and Lipton stood in the shade of the canvas tent. He fingered the knife. It was Bascom's knife. The same one that had been stuck in his door a week or so ago and that he'd given back to the outlaw at their midnight meeting. It had been once again jammed into the door of the sheriff's office last night along with another note:

> *DEER SHARIF DAYTON*
> *I HEARED THEM BELLS SO I GESS THE*
> *GUVINERS PAPRS ARE HERE. ME AND*
> *THE BOYS BE THERE TOMROW AT 10 FOR*
> *R AMNESTY.*
> *DUTCH*
> *PS—I WANT MY NIF BACK*
> *TOMORROW TO.*

The leather sheath that Dayton had given Bascom before had been dangling from the hilt. Another midnight visitor. He wondered if it had been the young man, Whitey. The youngster seemed most adept at sneaking around in town.

No matter, thought Dayton. In another hour or so, this whole thing would be over with. And he'd be hopefully collecting that reward money.

Hopefully.

He reinserted the blade into the sheath and stuck it into his gun belt. Dutch could have it back with Dayton's blessing. He saw the outlaw using the knife once again, for which he'd expressed a nostalgic fondness, as a symbol of trust between the two of them. Saying in the note that he wanted Dayton to return it was another way of expressing it.

It was all about trust.

And it was time to go collect his three deputies.

"Sure are a lot of townspeople turning out for this," Lipton said. His face was creased with concern.

"Well, once this tent was erected it was virtually impossible to keep this thing a secret," Dayton said. "Word spread around town like a wildfire."

"I just didn't think it would be this complicated. Hell, half the damn town's here."

"Well, the other half'll probably be showing up around ten. There'll be plenty of people to pose for Cox's pictures."

Lipton pursed his lips, and then forced what appeared to be either a smile or a grimace.

"Speaking of him," he said. "I'd better go find him. And the photographer, too."

"And I'm going to collect my deputies. I told them to be down at my office about now so I could swear them in, all official like."

"Good idea," Lipton said as he turned and walked briskly away.

Dayton watched the man leave and felt his uneasiness grow. He hadn't seen any trace of Burnside or the rest of the Pinkertons, which he hoped was a good sign.

The last thing we need is for those hotshots to be prancing around, armed to the teeth, he thought.

Then again, it was somewhat reassuring knowing that if he needed it, extra help was close by.

But that wasn't going to happen. He'd given his word to Dutch, and Bascom had given his in return. There would be no trouble.

Like he'd said, it was all about trust.

❧

1913
Contention City Set
Thunderhead Motion Pictures Lot
Near San Diego, California

The cameramen had filmed Lobo and his vaqueros riding down the main street simulating the deadly strike of the marauding outlaw gang. Jim had to give them credit for their horsemanship abilities as they artfully steered around the nervous prone extras who were supposed to represent the murdered townsfolk. Of course, they went slower than the real outlaws probably had, with lead cameraman Howard Willis's assurance that the whole filmed scene could be speeded up. After repeating this several times, it was time for the scene where Weeks and Faith were trapped in the middle of the roadway in front of the tent. They took close-ups of both of them simulating surprise and looking up. Then everything came to a halt and Creighton directed Weeks, whom Tucker had convinced to return to the set, to pick up Faith and run across the street to the boardwalk as the horses rode past them, and then set her down. After two repetitions, Weeks seemed to weaken and the last time dropped her abruptly down onto the hard surface of the boardwalk.

Faith's face wrinkled and she cried out in pain.

Weeks frowned.

The director called for a stoppage.

"Cut. Cut," he yelled, his voice amplified through the long megaphone. "Are you all right, Faith?"

"That wasn't exactly a pleasant landing." She glared at Weeks.

He canted his head to the side and rolled his eyes.

"Art, be more careful when you set her down," Creighton said. "And you're not moving smoothly. Can't you make it look more effortless?"

Faith was slowly getting to her feet. Weeks turned toward Creighton.

"Just how many times am I expected to do this? I am a bit tired." Weeks shot a scowl at Whitey and Jim. "Not to mention hurting my back in that stupid and unnecessary fall earlier."

Creighton lowered the megaphone and bowed his head. Willis came over and whispered something to him that perked the director's head up. He smiled.

"All right, Art, go ahead and take five. Somebody get the man something to drink." Creighton glanced around. "Bishop."

Jim stepped forward. "Yes, sir."

Creighton removed his dark glasses and his eyes narrowed to a squint as he looked Jim up and down. He turned to Willis, whose head bobbed in affirmation.

"All right," Creighton said. "You go take Art's place. Cameraman, go across the street and set up there. Film them from the back. And Faith, you keep looking over his shoulder and back at the camera as he carries you."

The actress smiled and nodded.

"And Bishop, make sure your hat stays on and don't look back at the camera," Creighton said. "Now get ready and don't move until I say, 'action.' Understand?"

"Yes, sir," Jim said. He walked over and picked Faith up, cradling her in his arms, cognizant that he smelled of sweat and wishing he'd been more thorough about washing up after helping the construction crew.

He was surprised at how light she was, but her body was firm under the heavy dress she wore. Thoughts of grabbing her off of the runaway horse that first day returned to him. She'd felt good then, too. Firm and nice, but in a soft, womanly sort of way.

"Oooh," she said into his ear as he held her in a cradled position. "You're so strong. I guess I don't have to worry about you dropping me, do I?"

Jim grinned and said he'd do his best not to.

She laughed, the sound once again reminding him of some kind of musical instrument—maybe one of those harps, or something. Her beautiful face being only inches away from his was exhilarating.

"Ready," Creighton's amplified voice said through the megaphone. "Set . . . Action."

Jim trotted across the street to the boardwalk on the other side and stopped.

"All right," Creighton said. "Cut. Now let's do it again from another angle."

Jim carried Faith back to the center of the street and turned so his back was toward the camera. He caught a glimpse of Arthur Weeks scowling at him.

Yeah, he thought. *Mr. Fancy Motion Picture Actor. I got your gal now, so eat your heart out.*

The sensation of Faith's body pressing against his was exhilarating and he hoped these retakes would take the rest of the afternoon.

If he could be so lucky.

"All right," Creighton said. "Action. Make that run, Bishop."

Jim took off and Faith tightened her grip around his neck and shoulders, burying the side of her face into his chest.

The real Sheriff Lon Dayton probably never had it this good.

ભ્ડ

1880
Main Street
Contention City, Arizona

The dozen or so riders appeared at the far end of the street, and word about their approach spread like a wildfire through the crowd of people standing along the boardwalk. Dayton had been a bit concerned about the number of townsfolk who had shown up for the event, but after the tent and the banner had been set up, he'd figured this would be the result, especially with Cox and the photographer around taking pictures. It was no wonder that everybody wanted to be present. Dayton just hoped it would all go as planned without anything upsetting the apple cart, so to speak.

He silently counted the number of riders.

Thirteen, he thought. A baker's dozen. And an unlucky number as well.

Turning his head slightly, Dayton looked over at his three deputies. The four of them stood in the center of the street under the banner and in front of the tent's wide opening. Twin lines of rope had been strung along each side of the boardwalk to keep people from crowding in front of the tent's entrance. Inside the canvas structure, seated at a long table near the back, were Mayor Webber, Martin Lipton, the railroad man Fred Dyer, and the potbellied Chester Aimes, who'd brought the amnesty papers from the territorial governor's office. The table had been moved from the courthouse to accommodate the seated dignitaries. William Bradford Cox was off to the side and closer to the front, along with the photographer, Herman.

"Mind if we get a photograph of you four, Sheriff?" Cox called out. "It'll make a dandy picture in the book."

Herman started to slip the black sheath over his head but Dayton replied in the negative.

"Wait until later," he said. "And Herman, don't be taking any photographs until I say it's all right, understand? The last thing we want is for that damn contraption of yours to go off and scare one of their horses."

Herman grunted that he understood.

Lipton came up to Cox and engaged him in a brief, but inaudible conversation, after which the would-be author and his photographer immediately slunk to the rear to the tent. Lipton continued forward and stood at a wooden lectern at the entranceway.

Both Elmer Abbey and Kevin Fitzgerald had Winchesters as well as Colt Peacemaker sidearms. Rich Swafford had a shotgun, a double-barreled Ithaca, that could most likely blow a man clear in two. He also had a Remington revolver stuck between his belt and his big gut. Dayton knew Big Rich had to have his belts specially made to fit his enormous girth, which prevented him from having a regular gun belt.

Hopefully, nobody here today will be needing a fast draw anyway, Dayton told himself.

It was all about trust.

"Looks like the gang's all here," he said. "Right on time. Stand ready."

"You think there'll be any trouble, Sheriff?" Abbey asked.

His voice had a slight tremor to it.

"Hopefully not," Dayton said, trying to sound reassuring. "Like I told you all, I met with Bascom a couple of days ago and he gave me his word there'd be none. Him and his boys just want to get their amnesty."

"You think Dutch was being honest with ya?" Fitzgerald asked.

So it was "Dutch" now, Dayton thought, sort of amused at how the tough, notorious outlaw was being referred to by his first name.

"He didn't give me any reason to think he wasn't," Dayton replied.

The riders were drawing closer now, perhaps forty yards off. Bascom was leading the way, his huge form looking almost ursine on top of the horse. Dayton fingered the hilt of the knife—Bascom's knife, looking forward to giving it back to the man once this amnesty ceremony had been concluded. He saw Whitey riding next to Bascom, his young face bearing a look of uncertainty. At least he'd have a chance at a new start.

A smattering of applause greeted the riders as they drew closer. Bascom, always the showman, removed his hat and held it at arm's length, smiling broadly at the throngs of people.

The outlaw as a folk hero, Dayton thought as the applause steadily got louder.

At first the crowd's adulation seemed out of place, but then, as Dayton considered it, he realized it wasn't so strange after all.

Bascom and his gang had directed their raids on the banks and the railroads, never stooping so low as to rob the sparse number of stagecoaches that still did an occasional route or hitting the small stores or farmhouses. It made perfect sense that the general public would see him in a more positive light than the rich men who sat behind fine mahogany desks and ran things while the rest of the folk sweated and struggled to scratch out a living. Dayton wondered how long it would be before Bascom and his boys found how hard living on the right side of the law might be.

But that wasn't his concern. All he had to do was get through this next half hour or so, and then go ask the mayor about that promised reward. After that, he would go find April May and ask her if she'd made up her mind.

The crowd was growing thicker along the boardwalks on each side as everyone began crowding in to get a better look. Dayton saw April May standing there smiling. She waved, and he grinned and started to wave back before Lipton strode past him and went to her.

Was she waving to him instead of me? Dayton wondered.

Lipton bent forward, as if to plant a kiss on her cheek, but she leaned back to deny his lips.

Thank God for that small favor, Dayton thought, suddenly feeling crushed that she'd apparently come at his rival's behest.

Maybe that reward wasn't going to matter so much anyway.

Lipton had hold of April May's hand now, trying to pull her toward the tent, but she resisted. For an instant her eyes met Dayton's, and then she pulled her hand away from Lipton's and shook her head. Lipton said something that Dayton couldn't make out in the escalating cacophony of the cheering crowd. April May answered him, and then Lipton cast a glance Dayton's way, frowned, and turned to hurry back inside the tent.

"Dutch, Dutch, Dutch," the crowd began chanting.

Frémont better hope that Bascom doesn't decide to run for governor if and when Arizona becomes a state, Dayton thought.

Burnside was standing near the open flap of the entrance, and he and Lipton shared some sort of conversation. The Pinkerton man's lips curled back in a tight grimace and he gestured toward the rear. Lipton glanced forward at Bascom and then hurriedly made his way toward the back to join the mayor and the other officials.

Suddenly, Dayton wasn't liking this at all.

Was it just precautionary, or was something up?

At the rear of the tent Lipton said something and the group of men melted into the shadows. Burnside, however, was still upfront, standing by the wooden lectern.

"Hey Dutch," someone in the crowd shouted. "Good to see ya!"

"Same here," Bascom said, his head lolling a bit to the side, his mouth stretched with a prodigious smile. He made a show of dismounting, as did the other riders with him.

"Welcome home, boys," someone else in the crowd yelled.

Bascom turned with an acknowledging wave toward the other side of the street. "It sure feels good to be among friends," he said.

The chanting roar continued: "Dutch, Dutch, Dutch . . ."

Just then someone burst through the solid line of humanity, ducked under the rope barrier, and began skipping toward the big outlaw's horse.

Dayton saw that it was Simple Sammy, prancing around in a circle.

"Sammy," he yelled. "Get back over here."

"I wanna take his horse," Sammy said, his face overcome with a guileless simper. "And them other fellers' too."

Bascom's horse veered to the side to avoid the scampering man, emitting a startled whinny.

Dayton was just about to yell again at the impetuous simpleton when the piercing noise of the first gunshot rang out.

☙

1913
Contention City Set
Thunderhead Motion Pictures Lot
Near San Diego, California

Standing off to the side now, Jim was still basking in the pleasant memories of having held Faith in his arms as he watched the final scenes being shot before him. Arthur Weeks stood in the center of the dusty street, a six-gun in each hand, blazing away at the group of riders clustered in front of him. Faith lay supine on the boardwalk, watching and mimicking terror at the unfolding gunplay.

Gunplay, Jim thought. *That dumb son of a bitch probably never fired a gun in anger in his life. He doesn't even know how to aim.*

Whitey, who was next to him, muttered his disapproval. "That son of a bitch couldn't hit the side of a barn with a peach pit if'n he was standing right next to it."

"Sure couldn't, no how," Henry said.

"I concur with that," added Bierce, who was also in the group.

Jim chuckled a bit. The actor obviously knew next to nothing about firearms.

Weeks took turns extending one arm after another with an almost careless, tossing gesture as the blanks pushed out bursts of white smoke from the end of the six-guns' barrels. One by one the outlaw riders tumbled from their saddles, their horses dancing away from the simulated gunshots. Jim had to admit that Lobo and his vaqueros were doing some fancy riding and falling.

Finally, after the last of the Dutch Bascom gang had met his fate and bitten the dirt, Creighton shouted through the megaphone for Faith to get up from the boardwalk and run to Weeks.

"We're still rolling," Creighton's amplified voice shouted. "Art, put your arm around her, then survey the scene with one of your piercing looks, then smile and give her a kiss. Then both of you freeze, cheek to cheek, and just keep staring forward with utter happiness. Ready . . . Action."

The beautiful actress rose from her prone position, surveyed the scene as she got to her feet, and then ran toward Weeks, who was still holding his two six-guns, wisps of smoke rising from each barrel. She threw herself at him and his arm encircled her waist, gun still in hand. Then he dropped both of his weapons and embraced her fully, initiating a long, languishing kiss.

Their faces seemed pressed together for the longest instance and Jim wondered how much passion was really involved.

"All right," Creighton said. "That's good. Now both of you press cheek to cheek and look out, like you're seeing a glorious sunrise."

The pair did as instructed.

"Howard," Creighton yelled, "have one of your back cameramen get a long shot of the whole scene."

"Got it, boss," Willis said.

Jim looked at the seemingly happy pair, standing triumphantly in front of the large open-air tent amidst a field of fallen bodies, and was reminded of the carnage of the Philippines . . . of Bud

Bagsak. Of the scattered bodies—the real dead on the red dirt and crusty black ash of that volcanic crater. Although the smell of burnt gunpowder was present here, lacking were the other gut-wrenching odors—the sweat, the vomit, the fear, the stench of death. The unpleasant visions danced through his mind's eye like unwelcome intruders. There was no way any fancy new motion picture camera could capture that.

He felt a hand on his shoulder and turned.

It was Bierce.

The author smiled.

"Lacking in a certain veracity, isn't it?" he said.

Jim wasn't exactly sure what that word meant, but he caught the author's meaning regardless and nodded.

"A bunch of hogwash," Whitey said after depositing a load of spittle into the dirt.

Creighton stood up on his platform and spoke into the megaphone once again.

"All right, it's a wrap," he said, his tone ebullient. "And today we've completed the vast majority of our filming, and we'll reach our goal of having finished the first four-reeler in motion picture history. Believe me, it's the beginning of something that's going to sweep the nation, and you all can say that you were a part of it."

A wave of applause swept through the people standing there. Jim applauded too, as well as Henry and Bierce. Whitey only stood there, head angled downward, appearing lost in his own thoughts.

"You all right, Whitey," Jim asked.

The old cowboy didn't answer.

Jim looked away from him and saw Tucker, who was standing several feet from them, glaring at them both.

Damn, Jim thought. *I hope Whitey doesn't get in trouble for not clapping.*

"Now," Creighton continued. "Let's get this street cleared and then call it a day. And I want everyone to remember that I expect a full turnout on set here at noon tomorrow when we welcome the real Sheriff Dayton. Word is he'll be bringing his daughter with him, so everyone be cleaned up and on your best behavior. We're having a gala lunch and the newspapers and photographers will all be there. This is the start of our publicity launch for *Code of the West*, the first four-reeler western in history. And I expect a hearty round of applause when he steps off that train. Remember, this man is a real live hero . . . a living legend, and I'm sure he'll be proud of us telling his story."

Jim wondered for a moment how close the motion picture was to what really happened that fateful day back thirty-some years ago. He recalled Arthur Weeks wielding a six-gun in each hand and shook his head.

"Makes a man wonder if folks are gonna believe that's what it was really like," Henry said with a trace of wistfulness in his voice.

"Undoubtedly," Bierce said, imbuing his tone with a healthy dose of skepticism. "Never underestimate the stupidity of the American public when it comes to romanticizing the past."

"I never seen such a bunch of horseshit in all my life," Whitey said, and spat again. He slapped Jim on the arm and motioned to Henry, who was behind him. "Come on. Help me get them horses rounded up, unsaddled, and wiped down. After we eat, I'll buy y'all a drink at the El Caliquño down in La Fronteriza."

"As an old cavalry man," Bierce said, "I think I'll give you gentlemen a hand. And I'll take you up on your invitation, as well."

"Suit yourself," Whitey said. "But time's a wastin'."

As the four of them moved forward Jim took another fleeting glance at Faith. She and Weeks were still standing side by side, gazing into each other's eyes. She reached up and caressed the actor's face, and then he leaned down and kissed her. She hadn't even looked Jim's way the entire time she'd been standing there.

She's back to not even knowing I exist, he thought. *But what did I expect?*

That drink in La Fronteriza was sounding pretty damn good to him right about now.

೪

1880
Main Street
Contention City, Arizona

Seconds after the sound of the gunshot faded, Simple Sammy did a pirouette in the middle of the street, displaying a jagged crimson gash in his throat. As his body twisted to the ground, a solitary hole in the back of his neck became visible.

He was shot from behind, Dayton thought, and looked toward the tent, but Bascom's horse surged forward and obscured his view. The happy cheers and chanting of "Dutch, Dutch, Dutch" had instantly transformed into screams of full-scale panic. People pushed and jostled on the boardwalk, running away from the tented enclosure like a stampede of frightened cattle. The cluster of thirteen horses began rearing up, snorting and squealing in terror and alarm. Dayton cast a quick look to see if April May was all right but couldn't see her, so he could only hope she'd managed to stay with the flow of the crowd. The entire scene began unfolding in a slower than normal motion, as if he were looking at a series of photographs in a book, one page turning at a time. Drawing his gun now, Dayton stepped forward and saw Burnside standing inside the front of the tent, his gun drawn and a trail of smoke rising from the end of the barrel.

There'd been only one shot, and that meant it had to have been Burnside who'd shot Sammy.

The dirty son of a bitch must have been trying to hit Bascom, Dayton thought. *He hit the boy instead.*

Dayton raised his weapon and yelled for Burnside to drop his, but the command was lost in the sea of noise.

He and Burnside locked eyes and the Pinkerton man extended his gun hand in Dayton's direction.

He's gonna shoot me now, Dayton thought, extending his Colt Peacemaker at his adversary.

Burnside's head jerked back, a small, round black hole suddenly visible between his eyes, his mouth lolling open to release a torrent of blood.

Bascom's arm was outstretched, smoke springing from the muzzle of his gun. The big outlaw turned, his mouth twisted in a feral snarl as behind him, the Pinkerton man crumbled to the ground.

Dayton saw the unmistakable expression of fury in Bascom's eyes. The gang leader leveled his gun toward the sheriff but before he could fire, his errant horse sidestepped, sending him sprawling as the animal plunged through the entranceway of the tent, trampling over the prone figure of Burnside on the ground. A fusillade of rounds rained down, and Dayton looked up. Four armed Pinkertons, two men with rifles on balconies on each side of the street, continued to fire, re-cock their weapons with levered efficiency, and fire again. Three of Bascom's men twisted and fell.

Bascom pointed his weapon upward and a blast of fire spewed from the barrel. One of the men on the balcony grabbed at his chest before toppling over the banister. The supine outlaw's arm swiveled and his gun spat two more times. The second man on the balcony did a stutter-step backward and collapsed. Whitey was holding his own gun at arm's length, fanning back the hammer. Peripherally, Dayton saw the two men on the opposite balcony drop over the edge, one of them striking the tent as he fell, ripping the canvas and collapsing one of the tall struts. Whitey's young face was set in a fierce contortion. He whirled, pointing his Colt Peacemaker directly at Dayton and fanning back the hammer once more.

Dayton held his breath, preparing for the impact of the rounds, but none came.

A split second later Whitey must have realized that his gun was empty as his face registered surprise.

Instead of shooting him, Dayton jumped forward and smashed the barrel of his six-gun against the young man's left temple. The youth twisted to the ground like a clothesline unraveling.

Another shot whizzed by Dayton's head. He saw the other three Pinkertons emerging from the interior of the tent, their guns blazing. Big Rich stepped forward and let loose with both barrels of the Ithaca. Two of the Pinkertons cried out and fell. The third aimed and fired. Big Rich took two halting steps toward them and then toppled over, face-first to the ground. Enraged, Dayton leveled his own gun at the remaining Pinkerton and pulled the trigger. The man stumbled forward a few steps, his gun tumbling out of loosening fingers, and collapsed.

"Rich," Dayton yelled, running over to the massive form of his fallen deputy.

With Fitzgerald's help, Dayton managed to roll Swafford's body over onto his side. The tiny gold-rimmed glasses on his face were bent, the lenses caked with dirt. Dayton ripped them away and saw the glazed, sightless eyes seeming to stare back at him.

"Is he dead?" Fitzgerald asked.

Dayton nodded.

"Oh, good Lord," Fitzgerald said, tears forming in his eyes.

A gunshot sounded behind Dayton and he felt the heat of a round sailing past him. Several feet away, Elmer Abbey grabbed at his chest, dropped his rifle, and fell back against the horizontal barrier of the hitching post, before going completely down.

Before Dayton could turn his head to look back, he heard the ominous four clicks of the hammer of a Colt revolver being cocked back to firing position.

"I told you, Dalton, if you crossed me, I'd kill ya."

It was Bascom's voice, gravelly and mean sounding.

Dayton assumed he had mere seconds to live, and no time to try and explain.

The hammer made a hollow clicking sound as it fell on a spent round in the cylinder.

Saved twice by an empty gun, he thought as he surged to his feet, turning to face Dutch Bascom, who dropped his weapon and was pulling another one from the front of his gun belt.

In an instant, Dayton knew there would be no reasoning with the big outlaw. That time had passed. It had been all about trust, and that trust had been destroyed. Only one thing mattered now—the drive to survive.

Still, Dayton yelled as loud as he could as he raised his gun. "Dutch, no! Don't do it."

Bascom's visage, frozen in a confluence of rage and hate, leered back at Dayton, the outlaw's gun hand thrusting forward with deadly intentions.

Knowing he couldn't wait a moment longer, Dayto
own weapon and saw the outlaw quiver with the convulsive reflex
of being shot. Tough bastard that he was, Bascom gritted his teeth
and continued to extend his gun. Dayton fired a second time,
this one causing a more severe spasm as Bascom fell forward.

Dayton stepped over and kicked the gun from Bascom's slack
fingers. He knelt by the dying man, not knowing what to say.

Bascom's words were somewhat garbled, but Dayton could
make them out.

"Gimme back my knife, you son of a bitch."

With that, the outlaw legend's eyes froze, taking on the
sightlessness of the dead.

Slowly, Dayton rose from his kneeling position and surveyed
the bloodshed. So many bodies . . .

Seeing no further threats, he jammed his Colt back into its
holster and turned toward the boardwalk. Elmer Abbey was in a
sitting position now, holding his blood-soaked left hand over his
right side.

"Kevin," Dayton said, "Go help Elmer over to the doc's."

Dayton's eyes searched the rest of the boardwalk area.

No sign of her.

Please, God, he prayed. *Let her be all right.*

"Dayton," someone shouted.

He turned and saw Mayor Webber waddling down the center
aisle of the partially collapsed tent. Behind him were Lipton,
Dyer, and the governor's man.

"You've really made a mess of things," the mayor continued.

Before Dayton could respond, the whooshing blast of flash
powder echoed. Dayton saw Herman emerge from under the
black hood and grin. Cox was right beside him, exhibiting what
appeared to be an expression of outright glee.

"This is going to make one *hell* of a chapter," he muttered. "Herman, quick. Take another one."

Dayton was just about to say something when the mayor's voice intruded once again.

"You've ruined everything with your bungling," Mayor Webber yelled. "Look at this mess."

"Now, now, Clyde," Lipton said. "Things could have been a lot worse. And I'm sure Billy Bradford can write this up so we all look like the heroes we are. Right, Cox?"

Cox emitted a giddy laugh and nodded vigorously.

"Like hell," Webber spat back. He turned to face Dayton again and shook his finger in the sheriff's face. "You listen here. I appointed you sheriff, and I can *unappoint* you just as easily."

"Here," Dayton said, gritting his teeth to keep from belting the little fat son of a bitch. He reached up and pulled the sheriff's star from his shirt, ripping the material as he did so, and threw the star into the dust at the mayor's feet.

Webber was silent as he looked down.

Lipton muttered something about Dayton reconsidering and added that a substantial part of the reward was still his.

"Lon," a feminine voice shouted, suddenly blocking out all the rest of the sounds.

Dayton turned and saw the dirt-stained and disheveled form of April May Donovan running toward him. A moment later she was in his arms and he was holding and kissing her and nothing else mattered.

Nothing else.

Chapter 12

1913
Contention City Set
Thunderhead Motion Pictures Lot
Near San Diego, California

Jim felt more than just a trifle bit hungover as he made his way through the many Thunderhead employees mingling around the big food tent. He scanned the area for Larry and Bierce. Larry had left him in their hotel room earlier, telling him to keep sleeping it off, but to make sure he made it to the food tent by noon. Although he didn't have a watch, Jim figured it was close to the noon hour now. At least that's what the maid at the hotel had told him when she woke him up. Bedraggled and wishing he'd had time to wash the underarms of his shirt, Jim had hurried over to the motion picture lot.

The night before, Jim, Larry, Bierce, Henry, and Whitey had all hit the bar on the southern side of the border and he'd ended up having way more tequila than he'd intended. Now he was feeling it.

It had been a strange evening. Whitey had started off telling the three of them that he was going to drink them all under the table, but then he'd strangely vanished for a time. Bierce had gone off to look for him, and returned shortly before Whitey reappeared.

"I found him. He's off conversing with the redoubtable Mr. Tucker," Bierce reported to Jim and Henry.

"I wonder what *he* wants?" Jim asked.

He had a simmering dislike for the waspish assistant director, but really couldn't say why. Maybe it was due to Tucker not wanting to hire him and Larry when they first arrived. Or maybe it was because Bierce had seen Tucker talking to Lobo and that big Mexican who got fired.

"Mr. Tucker keeps a pretty tight rein on everything," Henry replied. "Plus, he got that big whoop-de-do tomorrow with the real Sheriff Dayton coming to town."

Jim's alcohol-dazed mind reviewed the "shootout" of earlier that day. How ridiculous it had seemed, and yet, it was all true. It actually had happened. Probably not the way it had been depicted that afternoon, but it was history. He found himself wondering what the real Sheriff Lon Dayton would be like.

And then he remembered Whitey's comment: Back-shooting Dayton.

Strange that the old cowboy would choose to malign a man he didn't even know. But wasn't he doing that same thing to the movie actor, Weeks?

But it didn't really matter.

Weeks could bed down the girl Jim dreamed about, and probably was at this very moment, and there was nothing to do or say about it.

It didn't really matter.

Nothing mattered except another drink of tequila.

Even the image of the rat-faced Tucker, with his beady little eyes and frequent stares, didn't bother him anymore.

Nothing bothered him.

Anyway, he thought, feeling charitable as the alcohol did the slow burn down to his stomach. *It's the man's job to keep things on track and I shouldn't really hold that against him.*

Still, there was something indefinable about his dislike of the fellow. And of Weeks, too.

When Whitey returned, he seemed deep in thought and uncharacteristically subdued. In fact, he barely touched any alcohol.

But Jim more than made up for the old cowboy's abstinence.

After an hour or two of Jim's unsuccessful attempt to drown his disappointment at seeing Faith and Weeks strolling off into the sunset together, the actor's arm encircling her waist with a casualness that suggested more than a friendly familiarity and drifting downward to squeeze her posterior, the others convinced him to go back to the hotel. He'd awoken with a jarring headache and parched throat. Another reminder that he should have obeyed his previous pledge not to engage in smoking or drinking.

I made a damn fool of myself, he thought as he pushed through the crowd now, feeling way worse for the wear of the previous evening's activities.

Then he saw Bierce standing off to one side conversing with Godfrey Monroe, the scriptwriter. Jim made his way over to them.

"Howdy," Jim said.

Bierce smiled. "Ah, I trust you got some sleep? Feeling better after your night of imbibing?"

"Not hardly." Jim forced a smile. "Guess I made a pretty big fool of myself, huh?"

Bierce reached up and patted him on the shoulder. " 'Life's a poor player who struts and frets his hour upon the stage,' " the author said, " 'and then is heard no more.' Thankfully."

"Where's the rest of our gang?" Jim asked.

"If you mean Whitey and Henry, they're off tending to the horses. Your friend Larry got roped into helping his sister and brother-in-law with the food preparation. And the heroic and iconic Sheriff Lon Dayton is with Mr. Creighton, who's about to deliver another of his thrilling speeches."

Jim glanced over at the crowd of men standing by the VIP table about twenty-five feet away. Creighton was wearing his customary tweed jacket and necktie. Tucker was next to him, his dark eyes darting about. He and Jim caught sight of each other, held the lock, and then Tucker looked away. Lon Dayton was a tall man with a lantern jaw, broad shouldered and hard looking. He was wearing a low-cut white Stetson and had on a gray business suit and one of those string ties. Even at this distance Jim could see the network of wrinkles on the man's leathery face, which was almost as darkly tanned as a Mexican's or Indian's. Jim wondered how old Dayton might be.

The Contention City shootout was in eighteen-eighty, he thought. *Thirty-three years ago. If he was in his prime back then, he'd be pushing sixty or maybe even seventy by now.*

"You look as though you could use a cup of coffee," Bierce said, nudging Jim toward the serving tables. Jim's head bobbled around as they walked and he took another look at the VIP section. Creighton was standing off to the side now, speaking to a group of what appeared to be reporters who were all scribbling stuff down in their paper notebooks. A couple of them had small, portable cameras. Sheriff Dayton was off to the motion picture director's left and Arthur Weeks was next to him, dressed in his cowboy outfit, complete with the silver sheriff's star pinned on his shirt. Even at his advanced age, Dayton looked like he could still handle himself in a fight. He exuded toughness, which made the softness of Weeks even more apparent. Two men with cameras stood off to the other side.

Jim continued to survey the area near the VIP table. "You seen Faith around?" he asked Bierce.

"She and Sheriff Dayton's daughter, a very comely lass by the way, went back to the hotel to, ahem, freshen up." Bierce turned to Teresa, who was standing behind the serving table. "My dear, could we trouble you for two cups of coffee?"

Jim turned and noticed she was smiling at him. He gave her a quick nod in acknowledgment and her smile disappeared.

"Sure," she said, picking up one of the large coffeepots and pouring the dark liquid into two standing cups. After setting the pot back down, she asked if they needed any cream or sugar.

"Nothing of the sort for him," Bierce said, gesturing toward Jim. "He's sweet enough. But this bitter old man will need a cube of sugar or two, if you don't mind."

Teresa's smile appeared again as she used a small fork to pick up two sugar cubes, dropped them in the author's open palm, and then handed him the steaming cup. Bierce tilted his hand over the cup and deposited the cubes. After swirling it a few times, he took a careful sip and emitted a loud, satisfied exhalation.

"Perfect, *mi señorita guapa*," he said.

Teresa blushed, apparently at the compliment. She picked up the other cup with both hands and extended her arms toward Jim so the handle of the cup was facing him.

He reached out and took it, then sipped. The hot coffee scalded his tongue and he grunted.

"Are you all right?" Teresa asked. Her smile had disappeared again. "Larry said you all went down to La Fronteriza last night, drinking."

Jim's tongue was still sore, but he took another sip, feeling the heat as the liquid worked its way down to his stomach. He emitted another gasping breath.

"Yeah," he managed to say. "I shoulda known better than to mess with all that tequila."

"Is that all you messed with?" Teresa asked, her tone almost accusatory.

Her words surprised him and he wondered why in the hell she'd asked him that. And her damn tone was almost accusatory. He raised both eyebrows and shrugged self-effacingly.

"I suspect it was," he said. "But I'd have to ask Mr. Bierce here. Did I do anything last night that I shouldn't have?"

Bierce drank some more from his cup, and then licked his mustache on both sides.

Laughing, he squinted at Jim and then Teresa.

"Our Sir Galahad here remained pure at heart," Bierce said. "Bowing only to the Devil's nectar and leaving all the ladies of the evening wishing for that interlude that never came."

The girl was staring at Jim now and she blinked twice, her eyelids fluttering quickly. She turned away and said over her shoulder, "Here, I'm not supposed to serve any food yet, but I'll sneak you both a couple of biscuits. Just don't let Mr. Creighton see."

She wrapped the bronzed disks in a cloth napkin and set the bundle next to one of the massive serving pots.

"*Cherie*," her father said, moving toward the three of them. "What are you doing? You know we are not supposed to start serving yet."

She replied to him in French and the two exchanged more words.

Bierce grabbed Jim's arm and tugged him away.

"It's best we bid a hasty retreat," he said, releasing Jim's arm just long enough to grab the folded napkin. "You need to get something in your stomach."

Jim agreed with that. The hot coffee felt like it was burning a hole in his innards. He surreptitiously accepted one of the biscuits from its cloth prison and took a bite. It tasted delicious, even without any butter.

"Teresa was sure acting strange," Jim said. "I wonder what's got her britches all in a bundle?"

He shoved the rest of the biscuit into his mouth and chewed.

"You don't know?" Bierce said.

Jim waited until he'd finished masticating and then ran his tongue over his teeth.

"Quite simply put," the author said, "she's got a crush on you."

"A crush? On me?"

Bierce bit off some of his own biscuit, chewed, and then washed it down with more of the coffee.

"Most assuredly," he said. "And why not? You're big, strong, and heroic. What girl could resist?"

Jim snorted, then drank from his cup.

"Faith sure doesn't know I exist. Even after me saving her that day and carting her around yesterday. She's still letting that sorry son of a bitch Weeks roam his hands all over her."

Bierce sighed and shook his head. "Sometimes it is wise to remember that jealousy is being unduly concerned about the preservation of that which can be lost only if not worth keeping."

"You saying I'm jealous of him?"

Bierce smiled and clapped Jim on the shoulder.

"What I'm saying is, don't fret over a fading carnation and miss noticing the beauty of a blooming desert rose."

Jim was about to ask him what the hell he meant when he caught sight of Henry's rapid approach. The black man's head moved from side to side like a pivot on a stick as he surveyed the crowd. There was a bloody welt on his left temple.

"Henry," Jim called out. "What's the matter?"

The former buffalo soldier's face and neck were slick with sweat, the blood glistening amongst the perspiration. "You seen Whitey?" he asked.

"No, I haven't." Something was definitely wrong. "Why?"

Henry glanced around again, saying nothing.

"How'd you get that?" Jim asked, pointing to the welt.

The tip of Henry's tongue traced over his lips. "Whitey."

"Whitey did that?" Jim asked.

Henry nodded. "After we finished beddin' down the horses, he went to his foot locker and grabbed his gun belt, strapped it on. Then he grabbed this bottle and commenced to drinking."

Jim thought it was a bit early for alcohol, but then recalled that Whitey hadn't drunk much at all the previous evening in La Fronteriza.

"Maybe he's trying to make up for last night," he said.

Henry shook his head, his expression worried.

"It ain't that at all," he said. "I asked him what the hell he was doing, getting drunk with this big affair coming up, but he just kept right on doing it."

Henry paused and checked the room again.

"I tried to take the bottle away from him and he went and clipped me upside the head with one of them old Colts. It dropped me to my knees. I was trying to get up when he cocked back the hammer and told me to stay down."

"What the hell?" Jim looked at Bierce, who seemed equally befuddled.

"He was drinkin' a lot of liquid courage," Henry said. "Started mumblin' something about Sheriff Dayton and courage and honor and paying old debts." Henry stopped and took in two quick breaths. "I'm a-feared he's fixin' to do something bad. Real bad."

Back-shooting Dayton . . . The words Whitey had said the day before danced through Jim's memory.

"We got to find him," Henry said.

Jim and Bierce set their cups down and started glancing around. There was no sign of Whitey.

"Ambrose," Creighton called out, motioning for the author to come over to the table. "Bishop, you too."

Jim and Bierce looked at each other and then got up and headed over. Once there, Creighton placed his hand on Bierce's shoulder.

"This is Ambrose Bierce," he said, "the celebrated author. He's doing a write-up for the newspapers on *Code of the West*, our upcoming new motion picture. Ambrose, this is Sheriff Lon Dayton, the hero of the Contention City shootout."

"My late wife was a schoolmarm," Dayton said. "She loved your stories."

Bierce smiled. "I'm very flattered to hear that."

The two of them shook hands.

"And this," Creighton continued, "is the young man I was telling you about. Jim Bishop. He also acted as you in the motion picture."

Weeks spat out a derisive snort.

"I'd hardly call what he did acting," he said. "It was merely one dumb animal on top of another." He smiled and turned to Dayton like they were sharing a joke. "He merely did a few of the riding scenes."

Jim felt like giving him a smack. He was about to say something when he felt Bierce grip his upper arm.

"Well, actually," Creighton said. "He did a lot more than that. He saved the day like a real live hero, rescuing our starlet from a wild horse. And he's a war hero, too. Just came back from fighting in the Philippines."

"Is that a fact?" Dayton said, extending his open palm once more. "Welcome home, son."

"Well," Jim said. "Most of it's factual, Sheriff, but I'm no more of a hero than any other soldier was."

"Modesty is one of his virtues," Bierce said.

"Pleased to meet you, Bishop." Dayton turned his head toward the director. "But it's not 'Sheriff' anymore. I'm not a lawman now. Haven't been for quite a while."

A harsh, bellicose voice interceded: "Dayton! You son of a bitch. I been lookin' fer you."

The words were slurred.

A hush fell over the crowd as Whitey stumbled into the front section of the tent, a Colt Peacemaker in each hand. His mouth was twisted down at each end and his eyes held a crazed look.

The old lawman's head rotated slightly and he and Whitey locked eyes.

"You addressing me, friend?" Dayton said.

Whitey leveled one of his pistols, the right-hand one, at Dayton and snarled, "Don't you be callin' me that, you scum-suckin' back-shooter."

Creighton stepped forward, his face ceased with angry wrinkles. "Hedlund, what the hell do you think you're doing? Put down that gun. You can't talk to Sheriff Dayton that way."

The mention of the name seemed to pique the sheriff's interest. He focused his gaze on the belligerent old cowboy.

"Shut yer mouth, boss man," Whitey shot back. "And step away. This is between me and him."

Creighton started to say something else, but Dayton put a hand on the director's shoulder and gently pushed him back. Jim wanted to run forward and put a stop to this but he'd left his forty-five locked in Whitey's foot locker the night before.

"Been a long time, Whitey," Dayton said. "A long time. How you been?"

"How've I been?" Whitey emitted a snorting sound. "How the hell you think I been? I was in prison for twenty-five years. Twenty-five years."

Dayton was silent for several seconds, and then said, "I'm sorry to hear that."

Whitey spat onto the ground.

"Not as sorry as you're a-gonna be." He looked at the gun in his left hand, scowled, and threw it on the ground in front of Dayton. "Pick it up."

Dayton's gaze never left the other man's face.

"Why would I want to do that?" he asked.

Whitey expelled three breaths before answering.

"'Cause if'n you don't, I'll shoot you where you stand."

Creighton stepped forward again, waving his arms. "This is ridiculous. Someone send for the sheriff."

Whitey turned slightly and aimed his gun at the motion picture director. "Stay outta this. It's between me and him."

"What are you—" Creighton started to say.

"Shut up!" Whitey screamed, his voice sounding almost brittle. "I been waitin' thirty-three years for this. It's a debt that's gotta be paid. In blood. Either his, or mine."

"It doesn't have to be this way, Whitey," Dayton said, extending his hand to move Creighton farther away. "Believe me, I have a lot of regrets about the way things turned out."

Whitey shook his head vehemently. "No, no, no . . . You ain't talkin' your way outta this. Now pick up that gun. I'll give you a fair chance to stick it in your belt and draw. A lot fairer than you give me and Dutch."

Dayton shook his head.

This seemed to infuriate Whitey all the more. His voice was almost a shriek when he yelled, "I said, pick it up."

All was silent for several more seconds, and then the stillness was broken by the uneven sounds of staggering footsteps—footsteps that were accompanied by the hoarse, grating exhalations of labored breathing. Godfrey Monroe, all disheveled and bloody, rounded a corner and kept stumbling forward, his delicate glasses broken and hanging down along his jaw, dangling from one ear.

"Howard's dead," he muttered.

Creighton turned and stared at him. "Godfrey? What the hell are you talking about?"

"They killed him." Godfrey took a few more staggering steps and then his hands dipped downward and he settled onto the ground, lying on his side.

All eyes were on the injured man. Whitey turned his head briefly to look at him as well. Dayton moved forward in a flash and grabbed the gun from Whitey's hand. The old cowboy tried to hit the lawman with his left fist, but Dayton slipped the blow and sent a quick punch into Whitey's gut. The old cowboy sagged to his knees, his head hanging down. The ex-lawman pointed the Colt revolver at him.

"Don't move, Whitey," Dayton said.

Whitey heaved out a forced breath and looked up at him. "Go ahead. Shoot me. That's what you wanted to do all along, ain't it?"

Dayton stood staring down at him. He slowly took a step back, bent, and retrieved the weapon that Whitey had thrown on the ground.

"If that's what I wanted to do," Dayton said, "I would've done it thirty-three years ago."

Whitey's heavy breathing, almost a pant, continued.

It took a moment before Jim realized the man was crying.

After feeling assured that Whitey was subdued, Jim ran to the fallen Godfrey, knelt, and cradled him in his arms. "Get me some water and one of them napkins."

Bierce quickly moved toward the serving table. Teresa met him with a bowl of water and the napkin.

"They took them," Godfrey gasped, barely able to get the words out. "And all the film, too."

"Took who?" Creighton said. "And what did you say about the film?"

"It's gone." Godfrey's ragged lips left a bloody layer over his teeth. "All four reels of film. And they took Miss Faith and Sheriff Dayton's daughter, too."

"My daughter?" Dayton said. His gaze went back to Whitey. "You son of a bitch. If they've hurt her, I swear I'll kill you this time."

Whitey shook his head. "I don't know about that part. Honest. I don't hold with hurting no women."

Dayton continued to stare at him for a moment and then turned back toward Godfrey.

"Who took my daughter and the other woman?"

Godfrey managed to swallow, his breathing still ragged. "It was Lobo and his boys. And Gordo was with 'em."

"Gordo?" Creighton turned to Tucker. "I thought I told you to fire that son of a bitch."

The waspish man's tongue darted over his lips as his eyes shifted back and forth.

"I did," he said.

Jim and Bierce exchanged a glance.

Dayton strode over to the injured man. "Did they say why they took my daughter?"

Godfrey winced as Jim delicately wiped some of the blood away from a gash on the man's torn left cheek.

"I think they said something about holding them for ransom. They were talking mostly in Spanish, but I heard Lobo say to Miss Faith that she'd fetch a fine price where they were going."

A fine price, Jim thought. *That sounds like they're heading to Mexico.*

"Where are they now?" Dayton asked. His voice was calm, but demanding.

Two panting breaths followed by a coughing spasm prevented Godfrey from immediately answering. Then he managed to reply. "Don't know. They had horses . . . Rode off."

"Where?" Dayton said. "And how long ago?"

Godfrey's eyes rolled back in his head and he blacked out, his breathing faint.

"Better send for a doctor," Jim said.

"He's going into shock," Bierce said. "Somebody get a blanket."

"Yes, yes." Creighton's brow was furrowed now. "Phipps, take the truck into town and bring back the doctor and the sheriff. Move."

Phipps was already taking off his apron and running toward the vehicle.

"I'll go with him," Tucker said quickly and started to walk away.

Jim glanced after him and then to Bierce, who was shaking his head. The author reached inside his coat, pulled out a nickel-plated revolver, and pointed it at Tucker.

"Not so fast, buster," Bierce said. "Stay where you are."

Tucker's mouth curled downward. "What the hell?"

"You're going to have to answer a few questions first," Bierce said. "About you and Lobo and Gordo." He shot a quick glance at Whitey, who was still on his knees. "And about what you said to that man there last night in La Fronteriza."

Tucker grimaced.

Damn right, Jim thought. *Maybe now we'll get some straight answers.*

∾

It didn't take long for the truth to come out.

Bierce stuck the barrel of his pistol under Tucker's jaw and asked him what he'd said to Whitey the previous night in La Fronteriza.

Creighton tried to intercede, but Bierce told him to be quiet and back off.

At first the waspish man refused to admit anything. That was when Whitey spoke up from his position on the ground.

"You're right, Ambrose," he said. "You did see me and him talkin' last night. The truth be told, he hired me months ago to come here and cause trouble. Had some Pinkerton detective track me down. Offered me some decent money. Said all I had to do was wait until Sheriff Dayton arrived and make a ruckus when he told me to." He blew out a breath. "Fool that I was, I seen it as a chance I'd been waitin' for to finally get my revenge."

"Revenge?" Jim said.

Whitey gave a slight nod. "I was part of the original Bascom gang. Survived the shootout and they put me in prison for twenty-five years."

Jim looked to Dayton, who stood there in silence for a moment, and then said, "Something you didn't deserve."

"You," Whitey said. "You were the one that set us up. Killed Dutch and the rest of the boys . . . Sent me away to—"

"Know this," Dayton said, his voice calm, but forceful. "It was the Pinkertons that started shooting that day. They'd assured me that the amnesty was going through. I was just as much in the dark about what they had planned as you were."

Whitey's lips twitched. "Liar. You betrayed us . . . Betrayed me. You gave your word."

"And I kept it," Dayton said. "I lived with my regrets about that day for the past thirty-three years. I resigned as sheriff and never looked back." He paused and took a breath, still staring down at Whitey. "One of my regrets is that I should have stayed and helped you."

"Helped me?" Whitey said.

The eyes of the two men locked. Neither said anything more.

Bierce stepped forward. "The historical account in the book indicates that the lone surviving member of the Bascom gang was taken into custody, transported to Phoenix, and subsequently sent to the penitentiary. It makes no mention of Sheriff Dayton. Only that he resigned."

As Whitey continued to stare up at the ex-lawman, his mouth gaped open slightly. Slowly, his eyes moved from Dayton's face to the ground, as if some realization had suddenly overtaken him.

"But about last night," Bierce continued. "What were you and Tucker talking about?"

Whitey's head lowered. "Last night he come and found me in La Fronteriza. We'd already planned to meet up there. He said the time had come and I was to come here today and accuse Sheriff Dayton of being a back-shooter." His nostrils flared. "I had to drink myself into doin' it. Bringing my guns, wantin' to shoot it out with ya, that was my own fool notion. It's just that the hate I felt was the only thing that kept me goin' for all them years." He paused and took in a few more breaths. "I don't think I coulda went through with it no how. I'm just as glad it turned out this way. I know I'm a-gonna go back to prison now, but . . ." He briefly stopped talking, his breathing audible and ragged. "It's what I deserve. But believe me, I never knowed nothing about them women being taken." He looked up at Dayton. "Please, Sheriff. You gotta believe me about that."

Dayton continued to stare down at the forlorn figure, and then he nodded.

"But that damn son of a bitch was in on the whole thing." Whitey pointed at Tucker. "Told me Lobo was gonna steal the film while we was here. And that's all."

Tucker bowed his head and seemed to be staring at the ground.

Creighton lurched forward and grabbed Tucker by the lapels of his tweed jacket. "You son of a bitch," the director yelled. "You lousy bastard . . . Why?" His fingers gripped Tucker's thin face.

Jim pulled Creighton back.

"That ain't gonna do no good, sir," he said.

"I still have to know." Creighton turned back to Tucker. "Why, Don? Why?"

The waspish man's eyes traced downward.

"Go ahead," Whitey said. "Tell 'em. Or I will."

Tucker took a deep breath.

"It was Klayman," he said. "He made me do it."

"Klayman? What the hell . . ."

"He's fanatical about buying Thunderhead." Tucker's face was slick with sweat now. "And I owe him a lot of money."

"Money?" Creighton said, his lips curling back over his teeth.

Tucker exhaled loudly. "Ten thousand dollars. My gambling debts. Klayman bought up my notes. He owns me. Said I'd be debt free if I helped him."

Creighton turned away in disgust.

Godfrey started to come around a few minutes later and filled in the rest of it.

"Me and Howard had all the film reels loaded into the trunk at the hotel," the bedraggled scriptwriter said. "We were talking with Faith and Sheriff Dayton's daughter, explaining about the process used with the cameras and all." He swallowed hard and closed his eyes. "Then all of a sudden Lobo comes pushing his way through the door along with a bunch of his boys. I noticed right away that big fat one who was fired was with 'em. Howard did too. He asked what the hell they thought they were doing, and Lobo just grinned and pulled his gun. Like he was some kind of mad dog."

Godfrey paused to take a couple of breaths.

"Lobo made us open the trunk and he saw the reels. They were speaking mostly in Spanish so I couldn't understand them. They said something about *el patrón*."

Jim glanced over at Bierce, who said, "The boss."

"Yeah," Godfrey continued. "He said some more and two of his men picked up the trunk and started to carry it out of the room. Howard tried to stop them and that Gordo fella hit him real hard across the head, and he went down. Then they hit me, too. The women started screaming and Lobo told them to shut up. When they didn't . . ." He paused and blinked several times. Tears rolled down his cheeks. "He slapped Faith hard. Your daughter too, Sheriff. Tied us all up."

Dayton's face tightened into a grimace.

"Well, sir," Godfrey said, "we did all we could to try and stop 'em, me and Howard, but they hustled us all out the back stairs and outside. They'd already loaded the trunk into a wagon, and then Lobo said something more and his boys picked up Faith and your daughter, sir, and put them in the wagon too. They was just about to ride off when Howard started yelling real loud. Lobo said something else I couldn't understand, and Gordo took out a knife and stabbed Howard three times in the stomach and let him drop. They just left him lying there by the back stairs."

He brought his right hand up and covered his eyes. Head still down, he kept talking.

"I thought they were gonna kill me too. I . . . I . . . I felt like crawling into a hole somewhere. Instead they beat me some more and then put me in the wagon. Both of the women were crying. I guess I was, too. We went for what seemed like about fifteen or twenty minutes and then we stopped. Gordo come around and lifted me outta the wagon and threw me down onto the dirt. Lobo was on his horse but he rode right up to me. He was smoking one of his funny-smelling cigarettes and he told me to go find Mr. Creighton and tell him if he wanted the motion picture reels back, as well as the two women, he'd better be prepared to pay for them."

He took in a few more deep breaths.

"Pay for them?" Creighton said. "Did he say how?"

Godfrey shook his head. "Then they rode off. After I got my hands untied and figured out where I was, I run all the way over here."

"What direction did they go?" Dayton asked.

"South," Godfrey said. "Towards the border."

Dayton's expression was grim.

Phipps arrived in the truck and four other men got out. One of them carried a black valise and Jim figured that one was the doctor. The other three all wore badges. The doctor went immediately to Godfrey and began examining him. A dumpy, overweight man dressed in a white shirt and dusty brown pants sauntered over and introduced himself as Sheriff Rand Jenkins. The collar of his shirt was open and the ends a bit frayed. The star on his chest was tarnished.

Dayton gave him a quick summation of the whole situation.

Sheriff Jenkins listened and then motioned for his deputies to take both Whitey and Tucker into custody. Whitey stood up, looking dejected.

I guess it's back to prison for him, Jim thought.

But he had more pressing matters to think about, namely Faith and Dayton's daughter in the hands of those reprobates.

"How soon can you get a posse together?" Dayton asked the sheriff.

Jenkins licked his lips, his mouth working.

"Well, that depends," he said. "If they did go down to Mexico like you said, I ain't got no jurisdiction down south of the border. We're gonna have to get hold of the Mexican authorities."

"And how long will that take?" Dayton asked. "They've got my daughter and another woman."

"I realize that you're concerned," Jenkins said. "But there are procedures that have to be followed."

"Procedures," Jim said. "Those sons of bitches took two American women hostage and you're worried about jurisdiction and procedures?"

"Now listen here, young fella," Jenkins said, his voice taking on a tone of authority. "I'm the duly elected sheriff of this county and I have procedur—rules I have to follow. I'll thank you to not tell me how to do my job."

Jim was so angry he thought about hitting the man, but knew that would do no good. Faith and the other woman, Dayton's daughter, needed him right now and he had to be able to respond. He turned to Henry. "How many horses you got in the stable?"

Henry considered the question. "Enough of 'em."

"One for me?" Jim asked.

"How about three?" Henry smiled. "One for you, one for me, and one for him." He pointed toward Dayton, who nodded.

"And one for this old soldier, too," Bierce said. "I would hope."

Dayton started to speak but Bierce raised his hand, palm outward in a silencing gesture.

Dayton nodded again, this time in obvious thanks.

"You ain't going down there without me," Larry said, ambling forward on his stiff leg. "I can't ride so good, but me and Richard'll be in the truck."

Jim clapped him on the shoulder.

"And you'll need someone who can speak Spanish," Teresa said, stepping from behind the serving table and taking off her apron. "No offense, Mr. Bierce, but your Spanish isn't very good. I'll go along in the truck, too."

The author raised his arm in a two-finger salute.

Teresa's father grabbed her arm and the two let loose with a spirited exchange of French.

"Aw, hell," Jim muttered.

Bierce leaned close to him. "She does have a point about my Spanish. And it would be fortuitous to have a native speaker, especially a woman, with us. The locals would probably tell her things they wouldn't tell a bunch of gringos."

Jim considered this, but still had his doubts. "It don't look like her father's gonna let her go."

"Never underestimate a determined female," Bierce said. "And besides, she seems to have presented her father with what the French call a *fait accompli*."

Jim didn't know exactly what that meant, but watched as Teresa stopped conversing and walked purposefully from the other side of the serving table.

Her father had tears in his eyes. He removed his chef's hat and threw it into the dirt, muttering something that Jim took to be a swear word.

"I'll do my best not to let nothing happen to her, Mr. Delacroix, sir," Jim said.

The chef's gaze went from his daughter, to Jim, to the ground, and then back to Jim again.

"*Monsieur*, I beg of you," he said. "Please, watch over her."

"I will, sir. You have my word."

After that assurance Delacroix closed his eyes and placed his hands in a steeple-like gesture.

"Like I told ya, Sheriff Dayton," Whitey said. "I didn't know nothing about them taking your daughter. If you want another gun, I'd be mighty proud to ride with ya as well."

Dayton stared at the man. Whitey's eyes drifted downward, fixating on the ground.

"It'd give me a chance, maybe, to set things right," he said.

Dayton gazed at him for a few moments longer, and then reached up and smacked the old cowboy on the shoulder.

"You got a horse for Whitey?" he asked.

Henry nodded. "Sure do, Sheriff."

"Hey, you listen here," Jenkins said. "He ain't the sheriff. I am. And you're not going nowhere except to jail." He motioned for his deputy to put the hand irons on Whitey and Tucker. "Hook 'em up. Both of 'em."

"Not him." Dayton indicated Whitey. "He's coming with us. And so is that one."

He pointed at Tucker.

Jenkins appeared befuddled. "But you said the old fella threatened you with a gun."

"I'm not swearing out a complaint against him," Dayton said.

Whitey's eyes brightened and the trace of a smile graced his lips.

"But . . ." Jenkins was stammering now as he canted his head toward Tucker. "This one admitted being part of the scheme, didn't he? He's my prisoner in a homicide investigation."

"I'll bring him back to you," Dayton said. "If I can. But first he's going to take me where they're holding my daughter." The expression on his face was stern. "Don't try to stop me."

Jenkins shook his head. "But I've got a murder to deal with."

"We'll bring back the men responsible," Dayton said, "if we can. But right now I'd be obliged if you would lend me the use of some hand irons and a couple of guns."

Sheriff Jenkins's jaw dropped a bit as he breathed through his mouth.

"Sheriff," Dayton said. "This is my daughter we're talking about. And Miss Stewart, too."

"Not to mention my film reels," Creighton said. He stepped forward and tapped his index finger on Jim's chest. "Bishop, if you bring those reels back to me, I'll pay you a hundred—no, wait . . . five hundred dollars. And the safe return of Miss Stewart, as well."

Five hundred dollars, Jim thought. *Is that what the lives of two women are worth now?*

He didn't say anything to Creighton, but turned to Weeks, who'd been silent the whole time.

"We could use another hand," Jim said. "I know you ain't much for horses, but you could ride in the truck."

The actor's reply was a low, derisive utterance. "Don't be ridiculous."

"Ridiculous?" Jim said. "They got Faith and Sheriff Dayton's daughter down there, and it's up to us to get them back."

Weeks tilted his head to the side, his eyebrows rising. "I'm not going to be a party to any type of vigilantism. This is a job for the law."

"The law ain't gonna do nothing," Jim said, shooting a glance toward Jenkins. "Now are you in, or what?"

Weeks stared back at him and then shouted, "You're all a bunch of fools. I only hope you realize the folly of your actions before it's too late."

Jim felt like belting him one, but didn't.

That won't accomplish anything, he thought. *But it sure would be nice to set him on his ass, once and for all.*

"You yellow bastard," Whitey said. He spat on the actor's shoes. "Some hero."

Weeks's mouth puckered and he reached out, grabbing Whitey by the hair and pulling hard.

"You damn old coot," he shouted. "I'm going to—"

"Let him go," Jim said.

Weeks spat at him.

Jim stepped forward and pivoted as he slammed his right hand into the actor's gut. Weeks let out a harsh gasp, released Whitey, and sank to his knees, holding his abdomen.

"I owed you that one from before," Jim said.

Whitey let out a howl of joy.

"That was a good one, Jim," he said. "I'll bet he crapped his drawers. If'n I was thirty years younger I'da done it myself."

Weeks was still on his knees, his breaths coming in quick gasps.

Steering the old cowboy away from the kneeling man, Jim turned to Henry and Dalton.

"Let's get rolling," he said.

෴

Just across the U.S./Mexican Border
La Fronteriza, Mexico

Jim took his forty-five and his extra magazine out of the rucksack, checked to see that the safety was on, and stuck the Colt into his beltline. He stuffed the magazine in his back pants pocket. The weapon felt heavy and uncomfortable against his hip, but it also gave him the feeling of assurance.

The small border town looked different in the midafternoon sunlight than it had the previous night when it was all periodic lighted bonfires along the street and drunken men stumbling about between the rows of wooden shacks and adobe buildings. Even *El Caliquño*, the bar and whorehouse they'd frequented the night before, appeared to be in a state of tranquility, although several of the *señoritas* Jim remembered seeing were walking around carrying freshly washed laundry. Leaving Dayton, Larry, Henry, Whitey, and Richard with the horses and the truck, which had the handcuffed Tucker in the rear bed, several buildings away, Jim, Bierce, and Teresa approached the house of ill repute.

It was an elongated adobe building with a thatched roof. Jim remembered that the main room housed the crude bar and there was another entranceway inside that he guessed led to the various rooms where the *prostitutas* plied their trade. As they pushed through the hanging curtain of beads that was the front door of the establishment, the air within was redolent of spices, booze, and body odor. A couple of the exiting women saw Bierce and smiled broadly.

"*Mira. Es el viejo de la noche pasado*," one of them said, leaning over to whisper in her friend's ear.

"*El viejo guapo*, *por favor*," Bierce said with a broad grin.

The two women giggled excessively and continued out through the entranceway, the swinging beads making a clacking sound.

"They seem to know you well here," Teresa said, casting a knowing look toward Bierce.

"Did I neglect to tell you about my evil twin brother?" the author said, the wicked smile still on his face.

The expansive room had numerous tables covered with threadbare cloths. The chairs were pushed into the center of the room and two old, bent-over men worked at sweeping the wooden floor with a couple of shabby brooms.

Teresa stopped and held up her open palm. "Do either of you have any money I can offer the proprietor? Once I find out who he is, that is."

Bierce reached into his pocket, extracted his wallet, and removed two bills from a thick bundle. He handed them surreptitiously to her. "If memory serves me correctly, this should suffice. And the proprietor is not a he. It's a she, and she's that *mujer grande* standing behind the bar."

Jim looked over and saw the big, heavyset woman he recalled from the night before staring at them with an aroused curiosity. Her face had the same hard look to it.

"Hold onto the rest of it," Teresa said, closing her hand around the bills, "and put your wallet back in your pocket. Make sure to pull your coat back so they know you have a gun."

Bierce did as instructed.

Teresa went over to the big woman and they began conversing.

"In case you've forgotten," Bierce said, "the termagant's name is *Señora* Varges. Last night she kept your glass filled with tequila while extolling the virtues and lascivious talents of her array of fine *coquetas* in the back room."

"*Coquetas?*" Jim said.

Bierce smiled. "Better you don't know. Just be glad we kept you on the straight and narrow path of virtue."

The woman was glancing and pointing at them now, saying something Jim couldn't understand. He did see her take the bills from Teresa and jam them in the cleft between the massive breasts visible behind her low-cut blouse.

Teresa said something more and came back to them. "She says Lobo and his group came by here about an hour and a half ago. They were all on horseback, along with a wagon with two *americanas* in it, who appeared to be very scared, but all right." She paused and took in a breath, her gaze moving down to the floor. "She asked him if the women were for sale, and he said they were, but for much more than she could afford."

This hit Jim like a gut punch. It was hard to fathom the lack of regard for human beings, but then again, back in Bierce's earlier days, and not that long ago, a war had been fought to end that practice in their own country.

"Lobo bought *cervezas*—beers—for his men. He did allow the women in the wagon to get out and use the outhouse, and to drink a little water, but then he put them back in the wagon."

At least he seems to be treating them all right, Jim thought. *So far.* "Did he say where they were going?"

Teresa shook her head. "He didn't, but something else happened. About an hour later, maybe thirty minutes before we got here, another set of gringos came by."

"Another set?" Jim asked.

Teresa nodded. "Yes. She said they were driving a big, black car. One of them was a small man who looked like a frog, and the other one was a giant."

Jim and Bierce exchanged glances.

"That sounds like our friend Klayman and his immense bodyguard," Bierce said.

"That's what I thought too," Teresa said.

"Well, if they were here about thirty minutes ago," Jim said, "we've got a chance to catch them."

Bierce pulled out his gold watch and flipped open the lid.

"It's quarter of four," he said. "Does she have any idea where they might be now?"

"I was getting to that," Teresa said. "The frog man asked directions to *la Hacienda del Castillos.*"

"What's that?" Jim asked.

"It's a big estate owned by a rich family named Castillo," Teresa said. "The main house is enormous and the surrounding land is divided up into smaller units—*estancias* or *rancheros*. It was taken over by the *Mexicalis*, the revolutionaries, a couple of years ago."

"I thought the *federales* had taken it back," Bierce said.

"They did," Teresa said. "Two years ago, but the rumor is they were recently attacked and wiped out again by the *Mexicalis*. It's anybody's guess who's in control there now."

"From what I've heard," Bierce said, "those places are changing hands more often than a game of five card stud."

"Well," Jim said, "whoever it is, they got to be in cahoots with Lobo and Klayman."

His mind raced with the new possibility that his ragtag posse would now be facing significant opposition.

"Not a good prospect for an easy rescue," Bierce said, obviously thinking the same thing.

Jim took in a deep breath. He'd faced significant odds before and knew the battle wasn't over until . . .

He left that thought unfinished. There was no use in speculating without all the facts.

"Come on," he said, turning and starting for the exit. "We better go brief Sheriff Dayton and get moving."

As they headed back outside, the crack of what sounded like a gunshot made Jim crouch and pull out his forty-five. Two small boys holding matches and firecrackers stood wide-eyed as they saw the big pistol.

Jim shoved the gun back in his belt as he straightened up and grinned.

"Teresa," he said. "Tell those little fellas I'd like to buy their fireworks." He still had a supply of Mexican pesos in his pocket from the night before and pulled out the bills.

Both boys grinned as Teresa spoke to them. One of them ran to the side of the building and came back with a wooden box overflowing with all sorts of fireworks. Jim looked at it and handed over the pesos.

Maybe a diversion of some sort can even the odds a bit, he thought.

ℭℨ

Mountain Road
On the Outskirts of La Hacienda del Castillo

The truck was covered with a patina of gray dust, which stirred up in a three-foot cloud over the surface of the macadamized roadway. Jim called a halt on the winding mountain road just as they rounded the curve that allowed them to look down upon the Hacienda del Castillo, which was perhaps a mile or so away in a flat basin. At this distance, the hacienda looked like one of those distant feudal castles described in a novel he'd read on board ship from the Philippines. He hadn't been prepared for just how expansive the layout was. Dayton was right beside him and emitted a low whistle. Bierce rode up and handed Jim a long, tubular retractable telescope.

"Perhaps this will help," the author said.

Jim thanked him and held the device to his right eye, closing the left.

He could see the road they were on wound down the rest of the mountain, through a long patch of flat land populated by cactus and stunted mesquite trees, leading up to a pair of tall, white stone pillars—obelisks with round, decorative stones on top that formed an entrance gate. The pillars bracketed a four-foot stone wall that seemed to go on for miles, surrounding and isolating the estate from the bleak landscape on the other side. It looked more decorative than defensive. A lone man in a big sombrero, with a rifle in one hand and a bottle in the other, leaned against one of the pillars to shade himself from the setting sun.

Jim watched the man's movements as he brought the bottle to his lips and tilted his head back. *A less-than-diligent sentry*, he thought. But an armed sentry all the same.

On the other side of the wall, the estate contained what appeared to be a miniature village replete with several houses, wells, and small patches of growing vegetables, and livestock confined in small pens. Numerous good-sized trees populated the area. Fruit trees, Jim surmised, imported and planted in the sandy earth to provide rewarding sustenance to the populace. There was also a smattering of smaller stone buildings in the massive field area leading up to what could only be described as a mansion. The multistoried, tan-colored house had a red stucco roof that covered several interlocking lower sections. At one end of the house an elevated bell tower that must have gone up close to a hundred feet or more was perched atop the large mansion like a watchful eye.

The high ground.

A good place for a sniper to be stationed.

He focused the telescope on the bell tower. A huge bell hung in the center of a square confine, but there was no sign of any human presence.

That wasn't so for the rest of the compound. He could see men and women and a scattering of children running about. It looked to be a servants' village leading up to the main house.

Off to the eastern side, a stitching of railroad tracks ran parallel to the long wall. He could see several breaks in the barrier, and one major one that allowed a branch of the steel tracks to go inside the hacienda grounds. A large cistern with a waterspout sat next to the tracks.

Probably for exporting the produce from the fields, he thought, as he looked to the lines of greenery off to the western area of the estate.

His eye settled on something else: a stack of dead bodies that had to number close to thirty. Almost all of them were clad

in the tan uniforms of the Mexican *federales*. He remembered
Teresa saying that they'd recently been ousted by the *Mexicalis*,
the guerrilla army of revolutionaries following Pancho Villa and
his group. The bodies didn't appear to have reached the bloating
stage yet, which meant their demise had been fairly recent. If the
rebels had taken down the telegraph lines, word of the *federales'*
defeat might not yet have been widespread. But the madam at
the border-town whorehouse knew of it. That meant the news
must be traveling. It also meant the possibility of getting caught
in an army retaliatory attack was in the cards, not that they didn't
already have a significant time factor.

The spyglass came to rest on something else—something
familiar: a fancy automobile, the sleek, black Cadillac limousine.

At least we're in the right place, Jim thought.

"I see Klayman's vehicle there on the east side of the house,"
he said, lowering the looking glass and handing it to Dayton.
"Take a look."

The former lawman raised the telescope to his eye and
surveyed the area.

"Looks like we got our work cut out for us. They could be
anywhere down there, but my guess is they'd be holding the
hostages in the main house. That'll still be like looking for a
needle in a haystack."

"First thing we gotta do is figure out a way to get in there,"
Jim said.

Dayton grunted an agreement.

"Armed sentry at the front gate," he said. "Though it looks
like he's imbibing a little. Still armed with a Winchester and a
sidearm. And even if we could somehow take him out without
the noise of a shot, we'd still have to get across that hundred yards
or so of terrain. Any suggestions, Jim? You're the war hero."

Jim was somewhat stunned that the famous Sheriff Lon Dayton was asking him about tactics, but when he thought about it more, it made sense. Dayton may have been a western legend, but he'd been out of the game for a long while, and knew that Jim had come directly from some heavy fighting in the Philippines. Plus, the man was emotionally involved due to his daughter being held captive.

"I was figuring on a diversion," Jim said, "but now I don't see how we could do it."

"If I may make a suggestion," Bierce said, reaching for his telescope. "Fortune favors the bold."

"Meaning what?" Jim asked.

"The sentry at the front gate appears to be a bit of a souse. Most unreliable." Bierce paused and took in a long breath. "He's a key weakness. I'd suggest we let Teresa approach him, looking fetching, while two of us slink along the outer edge of the wall. Once her beauty has distracted him, we jump and subdue the man, and one of us takes his place as sentry. Then the other one and Teresa stroll inside the compound toward the house. Stealing the man's sombrero should afford a modicum of anonymity."

"What about the rest of us?" Dayton asked.

"The second group can work its way along the far wall and enter through that break," Bierce said. "It doesn't appear that there are any guards there."

It made good sense to Jim and he said so. He knew the others were looking to him as the leader. But he also felt uneasy about taking Teresa into the compound, especially after promising her father no harm would come to her.

But what other choice did they have?

He made up his mind as the three of them rejoined the rest of the motley group and explained the plan.

"All right," he said, "here's the breakdown. Teresa will approach the sentry at the gate while me and Henry sneak along the wall. See if you can stay in front of him so his back is toward our approach."

The girl nodded, her expression placid. Jim admired her pluck.

"We take out the sentry, silently if we can," he continued, "and then Henry, you take his place. You're too noticeable to go walking inside the area, so it'll be me and Teresa doing that. Sheriff Dayton and Mr. Bierce will go up along the eastern wall to that break and then angle inside toward the house. Use as much cover as you can, and we'll meet up at the house right by Klayman's automobile. The rest of you stay with the truck. Richard, we need you to move the vehicle over to the main gate in case we come hightailing it out of the house and need to get moving fast. Larry and Whitey, stay with Richard and the truck as rear echelon. And keep tabs on the horses. You also got to guard Tucker."

"Seems we can tie the horses on a tether line to the truck," Whitey said. "That would free up another man to get inside. Help searchin'."

Jim had silently considered this option, but didn't know how Dayton would feel taking along the man who'd challenged him earlier.

Dayton's gaze met Jim's and he nodded.

"Whitey makes a good point," Dayton said. "We may have to spread out to search for June and Miss Stewart."

Taking in a deep breath, Jim reviewed all the alternatives as his eyes sought Whitey's. The old cowboy held a steady gaze.

"You sure about this?" Jim asked Dayton.

"I am," the ex-lawman said. "It's all a matter of trust."

Whitey blinked a few times, his lips pulling taut, and whispered, "Thanks, Sheriff."

❦

Taking out the sentry at the gate proved to be fairly easy. Teresa's exaggerated, swaying hips and accompanying lascivious saunter piqued the man's interest from the onset. As he straightened up and staggered toward her, it was obvious he was highly inebriated. Henry jumped up and spun the man around, delivering a quick series of punches that rendered him unconscious.

"Should we kill him?" Henry asked.

Jim thought about it. It would have made sense to do so in Bud Bagsak, but this wasn't the Philippines and this wasn't their war.

"Let's tie him up and gag him," Jim said. "We can stash him over there."

"I'll do it," Henry said. "Y'all go ahead."

He took off Jim's hat and slipped on the unconscious guard's sombrero.

"Best you look the part," he said with a grin.

Jim grinned back.

"See you in a bit, Buffalo Soldier," he said.

He and Teresa began ambling through the gate. She put her arm around him and told him to do the same.

"Like you said," she whispered, "we have to look the part. Hopefully, they'll think we're *campesinos*. So keep your head down."

The walk through the village went without incident. Anytime anyone regarded them, Jim ducked his head and pretended to nuzzle her neck. The wide brim of the sombrero shielded both their faces. As they passed the stack of dead *federales*, the odor was pungent and he felt her body stiffen against his. Death was all around. The promise he'd made to her father loomed large in his memory and he regretted letting her come along at all. He hoped they would be able to make it through this.

It was dusk now and in the fading sunlight Jim figured their chances of not being recognized were even better. He was feeling more confident until he saw a group of three men heading toward them.

"Aw, hell," he whispered.

"Let's go off this way," Teresa said, angling him to the right.

One of the three pointed at them and yelled out something in Spanish.

"Say, *estoy bien*," Teresa whispered to him.

Jim intentionally slurred his words and repeated the phrase.

The man shot back something else and Teresa whispered another quick response to him.

"*Chingate*," Jim said with the same slurred affectation.

The three men laughed and continued on their way.

"What did I say?" Jim asked.

"You don't want to know," she said.

They were at the corner of the big house now and Klayman's fancy automobile was only about thirty feet away. Something moved in the shadows off to their right.

Jim came to a stop and then saw Dayton, Bierce, and Whitey.

Jim and Teresa kept walking until they were around the corner and then flattened themselves against the building. The others joined them.

"Any problems?" Jim asked.

"Smooth as a baby's bottom," Whitey said. He held one of his Colt Peacemakers in his hand.

"Remember," Jim said. "No shooting unless it's absolutely necessary. One shot will bring the whole place down on us."

Whitey grunted an affirmation.

They went under an overhang to a door with a glass window. Jim tried the door and found it locked.

"Here," Dayton said, stepping forward. "Let me."

He removed a knife with a fancy handle from a sheath on his belt. The blade looked worn but sharp. Wedging it between the door and the jamb, he twisted the knife and the door popped loose.

Jim pulled the door open a bit more and glanced inside. The immediate area was empty, but the sounds of laughter, off-key singing, and some guitar music wafted in from a distant room. A portly maid wearing a black dress with a white apron strode by them and stopped suddenly, gasping.

Jim thought about reaching out and grabbing her, trying to cover her mouth with his hand, but Teresa spoke out. "*Estamos con el gringos rico,*" she said. "*¿Dónde está?*"

The woman eyed her with suspicion, and then seemed to relax, saying something as she pointed to the nearby stairway.

"*Gracias,*" Teresa said and motioned for them to follow her up the stairs. The heavyset maid continued down the hall.

"Damn," Jim said. "I hope to hell she doesn't alert everybody."

"I don't think so," Teresa said. "I told her we were with the rich gringo and she seemed to believe it."

"Let's hope she does," Dayton muttered. His face was drawn now.

"This ain't right," a voice said in English from the landing above. "It just ain't right. You promised me."

The voice had a ring of familiarity to it. Jim placed it almost immediately. Maynard, Klayman's huge bodyguard. He motioned for everyone to slip underneath the staircase.

"Relax, will ya." The words were squeaky sounding and Jim recognized this voice too: Klayman. "When we get the hell out of here I'll buy you two whores in La Fronteriza. Just get those reels into the tire trunk."

The sounds of their descent down the staircase continued.

"But you promised," Maynard said again. "You said I could have her."

"Look," Klayman said. "If Lobo wants to get some ransom money, let him keep the bitches. Like I said, I'll buy you—"

"I don't want no smelly whores," Maynard said, his voice rising. "I want that Faith bitch. And you promised."

The giant seemed to have a one-track mind.

Jim debated what to do as the staircase creaked with their weight.

"Just put the reels in the limo and we'll be gone," Klayman said. They stopped at the bottom of the stairs, and the little man opened the door.

Suddenly a loud boom sounded. Jim peered around the corner and saw that the giant had dropped a heavy black trunk in the doorway.

"You put 'em in there, dammit," the big man said. "I'm going up and get her. I'm taking her."

"Wait," Klayman said, his tone verging on panic now. "We can't do that. If Lobo finds out, he's not gonna like it."

"So what?"

"He'll kill us."

"Not if I kill him first." Maynard turned and headed back to the stairway. "Stay here. I'm going up to get her. Sneak her out. I'll put her in the limo too."

Klayman's pleading apparently fell on deaf ears as Maynard trudged up the stairs.

Jim gave it a minute, letting Maynard's footsteps recede. Klayman was grunting and pulling the trunk outside as Jim stepped forward into the yard and pointed his forty-five at him.

"Where are the women at?" Jim said.

Klayman jumped back, startled, his eyes as wide as saucers.

"You—how'd you get here?"

The others emerged from the house and joined them. Jim kept the pistol aimed at the little man's face and told him to shut the hell up. "Where are they?" he asked again.

"Upstairs," Klayman said. "Lobo's got 'em locked in a room. But if he catches Maynard, he'll kill us all."

"Sounds like they're fightin' among themselves," Whitey said.

"*La révolution dévore ses enfants*," Bierce said. "The revolution always devours its children."

"My daughter—she there too?" Dayton said, his voice leaving no doubt that he meant business.

The little man nodded.

Jim knew the clock was ticking.

Fortune favors the bold, he thought.

"Whitey," he said. "You and Mr. Bierce put him in the trunk of the automobile along with his precious reels and wait for us."

The old cowboy nodded.

Jim turned to Dayton. "Let's go."

The ex-lawman pulled out the .38 Smith & Wesson the sheriff had given him. The weapon looked inadequate to Jim, thinking back to the tough little Moros who kept advancing after being shot with rifles and forty-fives. He couldn't imagine trying to stop a monster like Maynard.

But they only needed the giant to lead them to the captives.

He and Dayton ran back into the building and upstairs. At the top, an archway opened into a long hall. The opulence stunned him. The red carpeting was plush and the walls were covered with bluish-purple wallpaper. A series of white wooden doors lined the corridor, flanked by a series of dangling ivory arabesques hovering over an extended, three-foot-high white banister. About thirty feet down the passage, the enormous form of Maynard was positioned inside a half-open doorway. Faith's blond hair was visible at the bottom of the doorjamb, slipping out onto the carpeting at Maynard's foot. Beyond him a group of four or five Mexicans were rushing up what appeared to be a main staircase, guns in hand and yelling in Spanish. Jim recognized the two in the lead: Lobo and Gordo.

One of their guns spat lead, the sound reverberating, and it was followed by several more shots. Maynard's body jerked slightly and he lumbered all the way out into the hall, his arm extended, the pistol in his huge hand spitting fire and lead.

More shots echoed in the hallway . . .

Dayton raised his six-gun and fired once, twice, three times.

Two of the approaching Mexicans fell.

Down the hall, flame burst out of Lobo's gun, a long-barreled revolver, and Jim felt something whiz by him. Maynard crouched momentarily, but then continued his stumbling walk forward.

His gun barked two more times and then stopped spewing fire.

Another of the Mexicans collapsed.

Lobo fired again and then danced away, apparently out of ammo. Maynard was almost on top of him. The giant tossed down his gun and, massive hands outstretched, grabbed Gordo by the throat. The heavyset Mexican was a big man as well, but looked like a recalcitrant schoolboy now, his boots dangling as Maynard lifted him completely off the floor. Lobo, who was reloading his weapon, paused long enough to slip behind

Maynard and bring the barrel of his gun down hard on the giant's neck. The big man maintained his grip on Gordo, but turned and Jim saw Maynard's enormous chest was a bloody mess. Lobo struck him again. Both Maynard and Gordo lurched sideways, their large bodies striking the ornate banister and then toppling over the edge and out of sight.

Bierce was right, Jim thought as he flattened himself against the wall and brought up his pistol, aiming it at the Mexican. *The revolution always devours its children.*

Lobo grinned and then whirled, his arm outstretched, his gun pointing in Jim's direction.

"*Hola, héroe,*" he said, a smile twisting his lips. "*Sabía que vendrías.*"

The barrel of his revolver erupted in flame. Jim instinctively ducked just as he felt the bullet tear through his shirt along the left side. A wave of pain washed over him a split second later. He squeezed the trigger of his forty-five and the slide jumped back, expelling the empty shell casing. Lobo grunted as his gun spat fire again, but this time Jim felt nothing. He jerked back on the trigger twice more, spitting out two more casings. Another bullet clipped Jim's sombrero, almost creasing his scalp. Taking in a deep breath, still feeling the sting along his rib cage, Jim lined up the M-shape of the rear sights with the single bar of the front.

Words echoed in his mind as he squeezed the trigger: *Keep them damn sights flat across the top.*

The muzzle of the forty-five rose upward and fell back as Jim felt the distinctive punch of the expended round in his right hand and wrist. The shell casing floated out from the ejection port and tumbled end over end, with a seemingly retarded grace, toward the floor.

Lobo's smile was fierce and the black hole of his revolver muzzle suddenly looked as large as a bucket. Then, suddenly, the edges of his mouth drooped and his eyes rolled up into his head. He toppled forward, the big revolver slipping through his slackening fingers. Both he and the gun landed on the floor with twin thuds.

Voices called from down below.

"You hit?" Dayton asked.

"I think so."

Jim pulled at his shirt. The material was soaked with blood, and he felt a stinging pain, but not a deep penetrative one.

"Looks like a graze," Dayton said, perusing the wound. "You're lucky."

"Let's hope that luck holds out," Jim said.

He and Dayton ran down the hall, stopping at the door where Faith was struggling to get to her feet. Beyond her a pretty young woman with shoulder-length brown hair was standing in the middle of the room, her face ashen.

"June, honey," Dayton yelled. "Come on. Let's get out of here."

Jim grabbed Faith and pushed her forward into the hall, stopping to let Dayton and his daughter go past him. Down the way, more Mexicans were running up the long staircase from the main room below.

Assuring himself that Dayton and the two women were almost to the archway at the end of the passage, Jim turned back. He raised his forty-five and fired three spaced shots at the group coming up the stairs.

The ascending men stopped and flattened out.

If we can only get Klayman to drive us out of here, Jim thought, *we just might make it.*

He'd reached the end of the hallway now. Dayton and the two women were trundling down the staircase. Jim descended a few steps, crouched and pointed his pistol down the hallway again, and fired in the direction of the far staircase.

The slide on the Colt was locked back and he pressed the magazine release button. As the spent mag fell from the gun's grip, he slammed in his remaining magazine and used his thumb to press the slide release. The slide lurched forward, chambering a round. Stopping to pick up the empty magazine, Jim reflected how imprudent his action was, but he figured he'd never get another one.

He ran down the stairs and burst through the doorway into what was now evening darkness. Dayton was pushing Faith and his daughter into the rear seat area of Klayman's automobile. Teresa was next to them and Whitey was crouching over the front seat, his gun outstretched toward the door of the hacienda. The ex-lawman whirled, gun in hand, and then saw Jim.

"Come on," he yelled, his words sounding like they were coming through a long tunnel. "Get in."

"Where's Klayman?" Jim asked.

"I packed him in the trunk," Whitey said.

"But we'll need him to drive us out of here," Jim said, and then saw Bierce sitting behind the steering wheel, motioning at him. "Won't we?"

"I think I'll be able to serve as the vehicle operator," the author said. "I've driven one before in San Francisco."

Jim rushed forward and jumped onto the running board on the side of the vehicle as it lurched forward.

"Oh, Jim," Teresa yelled. "You're bleeding."

Jim reached over and pushed Faith lower.

"Stay down," he said. "We ain't out of the woods yet."

The big auto zoomed over the dirt road, and a few of the wandering *campesinos* jumped out of the way. As the vehicle got to the macadamized section of the roadway, it increased its speed. They covered the expanse quickly, coming to a stop at the twin pillars.

Henry appeared from around one pillar, lowered his rifle, and then stood at port arms.

"Saw you coming," he said. "We good?"

"Not quite yet," Jim replied, satisfied that his hearing had mostly returned to normal. "Get the horses." He looked around and saw the truck angled off to the side of the roadway with Larry and Richard standing next to it.

Jim ran to them. "Get in that thing and get moving," he said. "But first . . ."

He reached in the rear bed and pulled out the box of fireworks.

This might do the trick, he thought, but he wanted something more to hedge his bet.

"Richard, you pack that extra gasoline?" he asked.

"Yeah," Phipps said. "That one there."

Jim grabbed the big five gallon metal can and lifted it out.

"Sheriff Dayton," Jim said, "I could use your knife."

"Take it," Dayton said, and handed it to him, hilt first.

"Go!" he yelled at the two vehicles. "Me and Henry will take the horses and catch up."

Henry appeared, pulling the five animals on the tether line.

Jim stripped his horse off of it and handed the reins to Henry. "Mount up," he said. "And hold my horse for me."

Henry's white teeth flashed in a wide grin.

Jim turned and ran to the gate juncture. He set the box of fireworks down in the center of the opening and arranged the collection of bottle rockets so they faced toward the hacienda. He pulled the cap off the gasoline container and poured some of the liquid onto the box. Then he cut a long strip of cloth from his shirt and dipped the end into the gas. After stuffing the rest of the cloth into the top opening on the gas can, he patted his pockets for a match.

Nothing.

Jim swore but then Henry rode up next to him, towing all the horses. The black man leaned over and handed him a box of matches.

"Lookin' for some of these?"

Jim grinned and grabbed the box.

"Move the horses away," he said, slipping the knife into the top of his boot. "I don't want them to get spooked by the flames."

As Henry moved off, Jim flicked the match's primer with his thumbnail, igniting the head with a sudden orange-red flame. A quick glance toward the hacienda told him nothing. There was no way of knowing if the remaining group of vaqueros was coming after them or not.

Well, if they do, he thought as he lowered the flaming match to the tip of the gasoline-soaked strip of cloth, *they'll have a little reception waiting for them.*

Hopefully, it would give them second thoughts about any pursuit.

He had his foot in the stirrup and was swinging his right leg over the saddle as the gasoline ignited with an audible whooshing sound. The fireworks exploded, sending the rockets streaking into the air toward the hacienda, accompanied by blasts of gunpowder, sounding like a plethora of gunshots. The horse took off, carrying Jim swiftly in Henry's wake.

Far above them, a swirl of dark clouds momentarily obscured the brightness of the full moon, but then cleared away. The ambient light should be enough for them to make their way along the low mountain road and get back by morning, Jim figured.

Glancing back as they rounded the turn leaving the plateau and heading up the hill, Jim saw that the fire at the main gate was still burning. There was no sign of anybody following.

Epilogue

Several long hours later, the ragtag posse passed through the sleeping border town and crossed back into California. The sunlight of a new day was cresting the mountains and shining bright on the crude wooden structures of the motion picture set. Jim was struck by how primitive and fraudulent they looked. Even the big tent, now partially collapsed, looked pathetic. The banner that he'd helped erect a few days before sagged lugubriously. Henry and Whitey and Bierce took the weary horses toward the stable. Whitey paused and came walking back. He stopped in front of the remaining group and spoke to Dayton.

"I know now you saved me from gettin' shot back then in Contention City," he said. His gaze moved to the ground, and then back to the ex-lawman's eyes. "I spent all them years hatin' you, and now I realize I wasn't worth your spit."

Dayton lifted his arm and patted the old cowboy's shoulder.

"Things didn't work out the way I'd intended back then," he said. "I wish it would've been different."

Whitey sighed. "Yeah, me too, but we both rode the trail we were given."

He extended his open palm toward Dayton, who shook it.

"I'm gonna help Henry wipe down and feed these horses and then catch myself the first train outta here." Whitey grinned. "Before that damn sheriff comes back and changes his mind about lettin' me go." With that, he turned and lead his horse back toward the stables.

Some thirty minutes later Phipps showed up in the truck with Creighton, the sheriff, and several uniformed deputies.

The grin was wide on the motion picture man's face as he surveyed the scene. He pointed to Jim's blood-soaked shirt. "You need a doctor?" he asked.

Jim shrugged. "I'll go see one in a bit. Once we get all this settled."

Creighton clucked his tongue as his head jerked with an admiring nod. "You're one helluva man."

The sheriff moved up and nodded as well. "This here fella, Phipps, filled us in on everything when he was driving us over. You all done good, and the less I know about it, the better. Where are my prisoners?"

Jim jerked his thumb toward the car. Tucker and Klayman were seated on the running board.

"Let's go, you two," the sheriff said in an authoritarian voice.

"Listen," Klayman said. "I can explain."

"I'm sure you can." The sheriff's voice still commanded authority. He motioned for his accompanying officers to take the prisoners. Jim felt nothing for the two of them, but assumed Tucker would come out on the short end. Klayman, Jim figured, would have enough money to buy his way out of trouble.

Beaming, the motion picture director had two of his crew carry the black trunk containing the film reels away. Then he turned to Jim.

"Bishop," Creighton said, "you deserve this. Every cent. And there's a hefty bonus in it, too." He handed over an envelope that appeared stuffed with currency.

Jim took it and nodded thanks.

"And you stick around," the director said. "All of you. You've all got jobs here at Thunderhead. For the duration."

"That's mighty generous of you, sir," Jim said.

Creighton clapped him on the shoulder. "Why, after saving my starlet and the film reels, you've earned my eternal gratitude. You've got pluck. Stick around long enough, boy, and I'll make you a star."

He extended his hand and Jim shook it.

Larry was next to him, and Creighton shook his hand too. Faith came by next, her starlet curls all but straightened out now. In the bright sunlight Jim could see the dark roots on the part in her hair. Without a word she threw her arms around him and kissed him on the mouth. After a long embrace, she broke away and smiled. Despite her rather depleted appearance, she still looked exceptionally beautiful.

"You're making a habit of saving my life," she said, her fingers tracing over his chest. "I hope we can make a motion picture together."

Jim shrugged.

She leaned up and kissed him again and held onto his hand.

"Come by my room when you're finished here," she said. "I'll get cleaned up a little, and we'll . . . talk."

Jim replied with a smile as she moved away, their fingers lingering together for a moment, insinuating a promise of things to come.

We'll talk, Jim thought, and chuckled.

Larry clapped him on the shoulder. "Looks like you're gonna get what you wanted," Larry said. "You lucky fella."

As Jim turned, he saw Teresa standing about ten feet away with Dayton and his daughter. Teresa's father was also there, smiling broadly. He glanced at Jim and nodded.

Dayton and his daughter said something to both of them and then came over to Jim.

He reached in his belt, extracted the ex-lawman's knife, and handed it to him, hilt first.

Dayton shook his head and handed Jim the knife's sheath.

"It's called the Bascom Special. Belonged to Dutch himself. You keep it," he said. "You earned it."

"Well, thanks, Sheriff," Jim said.

Dayton shook his head again. "Not sheriff. Just a proud and grateful father."

They shook hands. June Dayton gave Jim a hug and they walked away.

Teresa was still watching.

Jim motioned for her and she walked over.

"Looks like Miss Stewart's planning on giving you a special thanks for rescuing her," she said. "Not that you don't deserve it."

Jim smirked. "How'd you like to do me a favor?"

"A favor?" she said.

Jim handed her the envelope.

She looked at him questioningly.

"Count the money in this," Jim said. "And then divide it up amongst everybody, you, Mr. Bierce, Henry, Richard, Larry . . . And give my portion to your father toward him starting his restaurant."

Teresa's eyebrows rose. "Are you sure?"

"Yep. And then see if you can run over to the horse stable and give Whitey his share before he leaves. But I don't think there'll be any trains going out for an hour or two."

"Are you sure you want to give away all your reward?"

"There's only one reward I want," he said.

She compressed her lips for a moment. "Faith?"

"No." He reached out and gently touched her cheek. "You."

She gazed up at him, then wound her arms around his neck and kissed him long and hard. When they separated, Jim saw Mr. Delacroix standing about ten feet away squinting at him.

Oh swell, Jim thought. *I hope he didn't bring his cleaver.*

Bierce came walking over, the reins of a fresh horse in his hands. "This fine animal is payment enough for me," the author said.

Jim hadn't even heard him arrive. "A horse?" he said. "You got to be kidding."

Bierce shook his head. " 'A horse, a horse,' " he said. " 'My kingdom for a horse.' " He held up a large envelope. "This contains what I term the final reflections and true story of the Contention City shootout of 1880 and the adventure we've been through today. It's my reflections on this entire affair, though without a title."

Jim reached for the envelope, but the author hesitated and drew it back. Removing a pencil from his pocket, he examined the point and frowned.

"Give me that knife," he said.

Jim handed him the Bascom Special. Bierce used it to sharpen the point, then handed the knife back. He drew some papers from the envelope, scrawled some words across the top of the first page, and smiled.

"There," he said. "It's title-less no longer." He handed the papers to Jim, who glanced down at the newly written words: *Where Legends Lie.*

"What do you think?" Bierce asked.

A grin touched Jim's lips.

"Sounds appropriate, but I was sort of hoping for 'The Damned Thing, Part Two.' "

Bierce emitted a harsh-sounding laugh and shook his head.

"My boy, with a flair for phrases such as that, you should definitely consider doing some writing yourself."

"Maybe I will," Jim said.

"Indeed." Bierce reached into the inner pocket of his black jacket, withdrew another envelope, and handed it to Jim. "Here. I'd be indebted to you if you would mail this for me. It's to my niece, advising her of my current destination. She's the only member of my family who speaks to me now."

Jim tucked the envelope into his pocket. "Certainly. But your story here. You forgot to sign your name on it."

"That was intentional," Bierce said. "I didn't sign my name because before I met you on the train, I'd sworn a blood oath that I'd never write anything again. But, as you know, oaths have a way of getting stretched and broken. So . . ." he gestured toward the pages in Jim's hand. "I wanted you to have the last written work of Ambrose 'Bitter' Bierce. The last *unsigned* work."

He leaned back with a stern expression of resolve and took in a deep breath.

"But why don't you want to put your name to it?" Jim asked. "I don't understand. You're such a good writer."

The author sat silent for a moment, and then his mouth twisted into a lopsided grin. "Because I think it's the most melodramatic piece of wretched prose I've ever written. No one would ever believe what happened here today, so no one would ever take the story seriously. And I don't write fantasy. Or melodrama."

"But it's true, ain't it?" Larry asked.

"Indeed," Bierce said. "It is. And another sad reminder that truth is often more platitudinous than fiction." He canted his bushy gray head, wrinkling the right side of his face in what looked like contemplation. "In fact, that might make a good title after all."

"What's that?" Jim asked.

"The Farcical Reminder of Truth," Bierce said. "Better yet, write that on the top of the first page for me, will you? And don't forget to mail my epistle to my niece."

"I'll do that, sir." Jim smiled. "Where you going now?"

"Since I've still got a pocket full of money and a trusty steed, I'm bound for El Paso, hopefully to meet *Generalissimo* Pancho Villa there and my pursuit of destiny's embrace."

"You talking about the Mexican Revolution?" Jim said. "There's a lot of trouble brewing down there."

"Indeed there is."

"But it sounds kind of dangerous, Mr. Bierce."

"At my age getting out of bed is dangerous," Bierce said, the space between his bushy eyebrows furrowing. "Do you know how many times a man my age has to get up during the night to urinate?"

Then his expression softened into a smile. "Besides, I never wanted to die in bed. Or from a fall down the cellar stairs. No, I'd rather be lined up against a cement wall facing a firing squad." He drew in a substantial breath, coughed twice, and then shrugged. "And who knows. I probably will be. This trip will be euthanasia for me."

"Youth in Asia?" Jim said. "We're nowhere near any of them, are we?"

Bierce's laugh was bitter, but genuine sounding. "It's one word. Look it up. That was one of the words I missed putting in *The Devil's Dictionary*. I wish I could send you a copy, but I've now divested myself of all of my written elocutions."

He moved to his horse and fitted his left foot into the stirrup. As he pulled himself up into the saddle, he gazed down at Jim. "I think it's time you put those old ghosts behind you, boy. Live for the here and now. One can't change the past, nor should one. So live your life and take care of that pretty *señorita*. I'm glad to see that you weren't so enamored by a decorous carnation that you'd miss the true beauty of a precious desert rose." His gaze returned to Teresa. "Don't ever lose her."

Jim put his arm around Teresa and grinned up at the author. "I don't intend to, sir. Good luck, Mr. Bierce."

"And one more matter," Bierce said. His fingers dipped into his vest pocket and withdrew the gold timepiece. After staring at it for a few seconds, he leaned down in the saddle and handed it to Jim.

"Mr. Bierce, your watch."

The author shook his head. "Not any longer. It's *your* watch now."

"Mine? You're giving it to me?"

Bierce grinned. "As a testament that I am no longer a slave to time's witness."

"Mr. Bierce . . ." Jim felt overwhelmed. "I don't know what to say. I—"

"Well, if you do, remember to choose your words carefully," Bierce retorted. "But it's doubtful that we'll ever meet again."

Jim held the watch, looked at it, and then peered up again at Mr. Bierce. "Godspeed," he said.

"Excellent advice, my boy. Excellent advice. And with that, I bid you farewell." He doffed his hat, swinging his arm in a sweeping arch, and tugged on the reins. The horse's head wheeled toward its hindquarters.

Damn, Jim thought, *he looks so majestic.*

"Hey," he yelled, pointing. "El Paso's the other way."

Bierce smirked. "I know that. This trusty steed and myself are going to take the next train east."

Jim laughed. "I should've known."

"Good luck, Mr. Bierce," Larry called out.

"It's Ambrose, remember? 'Mr. Bierce' left this place a long time ago." His head lolled back in laughter. "Goodbye, and good luck to all of you, especially yonder young knight and his fair maiden." He pointed at Larry. "And his faithful squire."

Larry looked perplexed. "Squire?"

Bierce laughed. "Another apt, but obsolete word left out of *The Devil's Dictionary*."

"*Vaya con Dios*," Teresa said. "I will never forget you."

"Indeed. Sage advice," Bierce replied, his expression serious once more. "Go with God."

He pulled the horse's reins turning the beast's head yet again, and kicked the heels of his boots into the animal's sides. With that he was off, waving his gray hat as he rode away.

"Damn, he sure is something," Jim said as he watched the lone figure on the galloping steed gradually fade into oblivion like a character in one of the author's stories. "We won't see the likes of him again for a long time."

"You think he'll be coming back?" Larry asked.

The gold watch shimmered in the afternoon sun. Jim gripped it tighter and thought about the author's last words. After a moment, he shook his head.

"Don't think he intends to. I think he's right where he wants to be."

"In the middle of some damn revolution?"

"In destiny's embrace," Jim said.

He felt Teresa's arm tighten around his waist.

"And how about you?" she said. "Are you where you want to be?"

"I sure am," he said, giving her a gentle squeeze. "What do you say we mosey on over to the food tent and see if your father will fix us breakfast?"

Teresa glanced up at him, a radiant smile tracing her lips.

"I'm sure we can convince him," she said.

About the Author

Michael A. Black is the award-winning author of 50 books, most of which are in the mystery and thriller genres. He also has written in the sci-fi, western, horror, and sports genres. A retired police officer from the Chicago area, he has done everything from patrol to investigating homicides to conducting numerous SWAT operations. Black was awarded the Cook County Medal of Merit in 2010. He is also the author of over 100 short stories and articles, and wrote two novels with television star Richard Belzer (*Law & Order SVU*). He wrote 11 novels under the name Don Pendleton in the Executioner series, and his Executioner novel, *Fatal Prescription*, won the Best Original Novel Scribe Award in 2018. He has written numerous westerns under both his own name (*Legends of the West: A Deputy Bass Reeves Novel*) and as A.W. Hart *(Killer's Ghost, Killer's Gamble, Killer's Requiem, and Border Blood)*. He is exceptionally proud of his latest western, *Where Legends Lie*, which he considers his finest work to date.